Secrets of a [illegible]

Rosie Walker is a novelist who lives in Edinburgh with her husband Kevin and their dog Bella. 'Secrets of a Serial Killer' is her debut novel, "an edge-of-your-seat serial killer thriller that you won't be able to put down".

Rosie has a Masters in Creative Writing from the University of Edinburgh and an undergraduate degree in Psychology from Lancaster University.

@ciderwithrosie
@rosiewalkerauthor
Author website

Secrets of a Serial Killer

Rosie Walker

One More Chapter an imprint of
HarperCollins*Publishers*
The News Building
1 London Bridge Street
London SE1 9GF

www.harpercollins.co.uk

HarperCollins *Publishers*
1st Floor, Watermarque Building, Ringsend Road
Dublin 4, Ireland

This paperback edition 2020

First published in Great Britain in ebook format by
HarperCollins*Publishers* 2020

A catalogue record for this book
is available from the British Library

EB ISBN: 9780008399962
PB ISBN: 9780008399979
EA ISBN: 9780008440244

Set in Birka by Palimpsest Book Production Ltd, Falkirk Stirlingshire

Printed and bound in Great Britain by
CPI Group (UK) Ltd, Croydon CR0 4YY

To my grandparents:
Ted and Joan Phenix
Harry and Phyllis Walker

Map

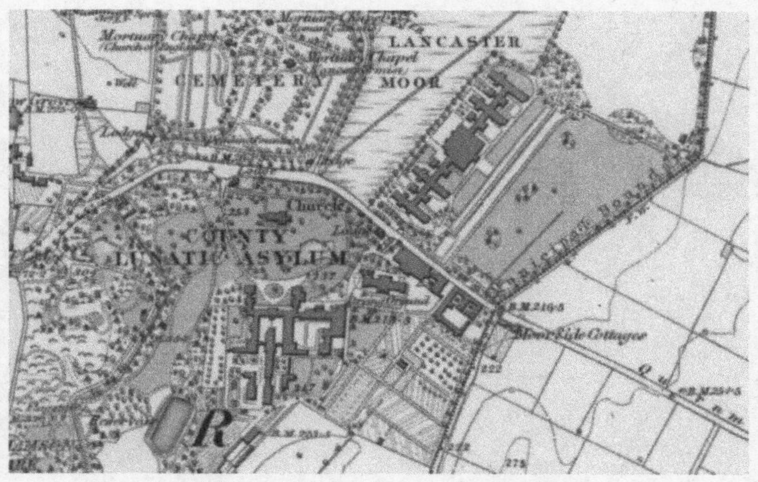

Detail from the 6-inch OS map, surveyed 1891.
Reproduced with the permission of the National Library of Scotland

Letter from the Leonard McVitie Archive,
John Rylands Library
Date: 1959–1985

Lancaster Lune Hospital
Lancaster, Lancashire
LA1 3JR
23 November 1984

Dear X,

I have watched the life leave the eyes of so many that I easily identify the signs as my own body begins to shut down. I know I will soon die, so I write to inform you that it is your turn to take up the mantle.

Work your charm; they will like you. You wear it well; they won't sense who you are underneath. They can't understand that you're not interested in their thoughts, their feelings, their love. You're interested in their fight, their attempts to flee, the smell of fear oozing from their skin.

I know that fear has always been your favourite, especially when you are the cause. Fear is vigilance. It's universal to all animals, but only humans can override it and pretend it's irrational. Only humans would experience fear, push it away and instead share a conversation with the predator; accept an invitation, smile and flirt and hope for more than they deserve. You were born for this life.

My teachings are complete, and your personal range of emotions is small yet efficient: joy, neutrality, or pure rage. All other emotions you choose to project are the result of careful study, manufactured for the benefit of your audience. The slight drop of your eyebrows to demonstrate disappointment. The narrowing of your eyes to indicate disgust. The barely detectable dip of your head to suggest disapproval. You have mastered it all.

You have been my best student. I trust that you will protect and enhance my legacy.

Yours sincerely,

Leonard McVitie

DAY ONE

Helen

Helen leans her elbows on the railings and gazes up at the Gothic turrets of the derelict hospital as the sun begins to rise. A light mist hovers just above the ground, highlighting the dew on the grass.

Some window panes are broken, probably by stone-throwing vandals before the security company began twenty-four-hour patrols. She's been taking regular walks around the grounds for the past couple of months, getting a feel for the building in all seasons and weathers.

She scans each window, searching for movement inside. As a child she was fixated on the supernatural, but now that she's in her fifties, the history of such places is far more fascinating than spirits and ghouls. She shakes her head, smiling at her overactive imagination.

The wind picks up, rustling through the trees above her head and needling her skin through her woolly jumper. She shivers.

Why did the architects build their 'lunatics' such an ornate prison? It is a magnificent structure; she loves the flying buttresses, like the legs of a spider about to scuttle away. The dirty red sandstone seems more suited to a reclusive prince living on a stormy cliff-top in a Victorian novel than for the so-called 'feeble-minded' of nineteenth-century Lancashire. This massive building was once known as 'The Annexe', an extension of the original County Lunatic Asylum constructed in the 1880s to house the masses of mental patients shipped to the county from all across the north of England.

Once looming over barren moorland and visible for miles, it's now almost hidden from the city, concealed within the trees. She loves the way that nature takes over a building once mankind abandons it: shoots sprouting from rooftops and ivy pushing apart the brickwork. It feels life-affirming that the natural world will still continue after we're gone.

It's a shame they can't just leave it as it is: retain the ivy and the moss and the spindly saplings that grow from the gutters. But, sadly, people want to make money, and part of Helen's job is to help carve up this beautiful old building.

Alfie pulls hard on his lead, his tongue hanging from his mouth as he struggles against the collar. She bends down.

'Alright, but don't run off,' she says as she releases the clip.

As expected, the dog immediately disappears into the nearest clump of bushes, flushing a squawking pheasant into the air and away. She hears him burst out from the other side of the undergrowth and jogs ahead to keep him in sight. He is running away, and fast. Helen shouts and whistles as she sees him push through a gap in the fence and run towards the building.

'Alfie! No! Bad dog!' she calls, but he ignores her and continues running until he is out of sight. She knows he won't run far; he just gets excited. But the building is derelict and riddled with asbestos.

Helen groans.

She follows at a jog, squeezing through the gap in the fence and pushing across the overgrown lawn in front of the hospital, thistles tugging at her jeans.

It's thrilling to get closer to the building, with a genuine reason if anyone challenges her. So far in this phase of work she's only seen dusty floor plans, concept sketches and asbestos reports during dull scoping meetings and budget discussions.

She slows for a moment to take in the imposing façade up close, initials carved above each tracery window and ornate parapets along the roof. The six-storey water tower looms over the main entrance, where a stone staircase rises up to wooden double-doors. The basement floor is half-submerged, with letterbox windows at knee-level.

She remembers the floor plan she pored over last week: there's a double-height entrance hall behind those doors, with a sweeping staircase in the centre, and long corridors branching off to the east and west wings: the wards and seclusion cells. East for female patients, west for male. The hospital was designed to house the infirm in small rooms, crammed to maximum capacity and maximum practicality.

She passes the main entrance, where the doors are secured with a chunky padlock and chain. 'Alfie?' she shouts, but he still doesn't return.

She passes through a stone archway into a horseshoe-shaped courtyard, which must have been the loading dock with access to the kitchens, laundry and store rooms. A door stands open in the far corner where the main hall branches into the west wing, a dark hole gaping in the stone wall.

She feels a shiver of anticipation. Alfie must have gone inside. She has to go after him.

It is at least fifteen years since she was last inside the Lune Hospital, completing an inspection before the hospital closed. She remembers the eerie quiet on the upper floors, punctuated with sudden shrieks and howls. Hunched figures rocking incessantly in chairs, back and forth, staring into space. And, Helen remembers with a shudder, one female patient who followed Helen for the duration of her visit, bare feet shuffling ten feet behind, black eyes glinting at Helen through her straggly hair as she hissed insults under her breath.

Now, Helen ducks through the open door, holding her arms in front of her face to break the cobwebs, which cling to her hands. The air in the corridor smells damp, and she covers her nose and mouth with her scarf. It's so quiet.

She pulls her phone from her pocket and switches on the torch, shining it around to peer through the dark hall. She marvels at the changes time has wrought on the empty building. Mould covers the ceiling, and the wallpaper has peeled from the walls to reveal old layers in many colours: deep red, a bit of yellow, and, underneath it all, a light sky-blue.

Her footsteps crackle in the quiet. Every flat surface is coated in dirt and tiny shards of broken glass.

She reaches the main entrance hall and gazes up at the huge Imperial staircase in its centre. The first flight rises to a half landing, where the staircase divides into two symmetrical flights which curl around to the first floor. There's a wooden barrier across the landing, with a crudely-painted sign hammered into the wood: 'DANGER: WEAK FLOORS. ASBESTOS!'

Chipped white paint edges the treads of the stairs, with bare wood running up the centre where a carpet used to be. Strips of torn wallpaper litter the ground, and each bare expanse of wall has been a canvas for amateur graffiti artists.

A door is tucked away in the corner of the entrance hall, almost out of sight. It stands slightly open: the door to the basements. Helen would love to pop down quickly and get a look at the layout down there, assess if they could tweak the plans to bring in more natural light.

A sudden skittering of glass shatters the silence. She gasps and drops her phone to the floor.

Alfie bounds around the corner, his tail wagging, his claws clattering on the bare floorboards. 'Alfie! You scared me,' she says, laughing with relief. Helen bends and ruffles his dusty fur. 'Where've you been?'

He shakes, and dust plumes from his shaggy coat. He peers up at her through the black and white fur that almost hides his eyes. He looks a bit like an English Sheepdog from this angle, but he's much sleeker under all that fur.

She picks up her phone, brushes it against her jeans to get rid of the muck from the floor.

The dog drops something at her feet and bows to ask her to play, gazing at her with his big brown eyes. His legs are dark with grime that she's sure he will rub all over the kitchen walls when they get home.

She takes a step forward, reaching out to Alfie's toy. 'Come on then, let me have it.' She stops. 'What *have* you got, Alfie?'

On the floorboards between Alfie's paws is not the usual stick or muddy ball. He's got a small shoe; a ballet flat like all the teenage girls wear now. It's electric blue under the mud caked to its surface. She picks it up, examining it. Not mud, but darker, like tar or something. Alfie looks up at her, expectant.

'No, it's not a toy.' A gust of wind rushes through the empty windowpanes and Helen shudders. 'Come on, let's get out.'

She drops the shoe back on the ground, and Alfie scrambles to pick it up again, thinking it's a game. She turns to leave, takes one step.

'You shouldn't be in here.' A voice from behind her.

Helen freezes, dragging air in through her teeth and deep into her lungs. Her heart pounds as she turns towards the voice.

A man stands in the shadows, leaning against a graffiti-covered wall. In the murky light, Helen can only see his silhouette and a faint impression of his face. White teeth stand out against the darkness. He's smiling at her.

She flattens her hand to her chest, willing her heart to slow. 'You made me jump!'

Before the man can say anything else, Alfie rushes at him, barking and snarling, hackles raised and muscles tense.

Helen reaches down, grabbing her dog's collar. 'Sorry. He's not normally like this,' she says. 'Shhh, Alfie, it's alright.' She strokes him but he ignores her, all senses trained on the stranger.

The man steps forward into the light. Alfie stops barking but remains with his nose thrust forward, emitting a low warning growl.

'Sorry about that,' says Helen. 'We were just on our way out.'

'Not a problem.' Now that the morning light has touched him, she can see his features easier. She's seen him before, but they've never spoken; he's one of the security guards that patrol the grounds. They've nodded to each other in passing on a few exterior site visits with the NHS Planning Team. His head is closely shaved, and he's got a short black goatee. His nose is bent, probably an old break. His piercing green eyes reflect the light shining in through the panes above the front door.

'Do you know you're trespassing?' His voice is smooth and low. He takes a step forward again.

'I'm the architect on the redevelopment.' Alfie backs behind Helen's legs, his warm fur pressing against her calf. 'Getting the property ready to sell.'

'I see. It's early in the day to start work.' The man smiles at Alfie, but Alfie's growling increases in volume again. The man looks up at Helen, still smiling. 'And this must be your architectural assistant?'

She reaches down and strokes Alfie, trying to reassure him everything's okay. She glances around to assess the nearest way out. There's something unnerving about chatting with a stranger inside this building, out of sight from anyone. Even if he's just doing his job.

'Yes, I'm walking my dog. I thought I'd get a quick look at the building from the grounds, but then Alfie ran inside. I wasn't intending to trespass.' She feels a kernel of frustration now. Why should she defend herself to this guy just because he's wearing a 'Security' badge? She's a grown woman with full professional right to be here, and she's spent her whole life doing exactly as she should. She shouldn't have to explain herself.

The man's expression shifts; he smiles and steps forward. There's a small dimple in his left cheek when he smiles. 'I'm Alexander, a security guard here. I do the night shift for Diamond Security.' His handshake is firm, his skin soft and dry. 'You shouldn't be in here, it's not safe. Especially for dogs.' He reaches towards Alfie as if to stroke him, but Alfie shrinks away. The man frowns, as if disappointed.

'I had to come in to find him,' she says again.

'Let me see you out,' says the security guard. 'The floors aren't secure in places. Some rotten floorboards and joists. Don't want anyone getting hurt.'

Reaching down, she clips the lead onto Alfie's collar, patting his head in reassurance. He hasn't moved from behind her legs and the vibration of his neck under her fingers tells her he is still quietly growling. She scratches him behind his ear.

Outside, Helen can see the man better. His shoulders and arms look solid, like he lifts weights. She feels small walking alongside his large frame; her head barely reaches his shoulder.

'I heard they're still waiting for planning permission to carve it up into flats,' he says. His tone is chatty and relaxed now they're out of the building.

The air is cold against her cheeks and hands. She shoves her fists into her pockets, Alfie's lead looped around her wrist. 'Actually, things are starting to move forward. Pretty soon you might see some big changes happening around here.' She smiles at him.

'Sounds exciting,' he says. His tone is casual, but he doesn't return her grin. 'Sorry, I'm sure you can understand it's a bit unsettling for our team. Our jobs depend on this old place being empty, patrolling the grounds, you know.' He waves a hand at the building, with its broken windows and weeds sprouting from the brickwork.

'Don't worry though; I'm sure they'll still need a security team for a long time yet,' she says. Helen supposes his job might be threatened once the redevelopment begins.

They walk across the grounds towards the driveway, where grass pokes up through cracks in the tarmac. He glances at her occasionally, and then over his shoulder back to the hospital.

'Well, at least they're not knocking it down,' he says. 'It's an important building.'

'Yeah, that really would be a tragedy. So many people love this place; it's a bit of the town's history. The whole county's history, really.' She looks back. Bushes grow along the front of the hospital at either side of the entrance. The grounds were once a huge open space where patients got fresh air and exercise, but after years of neglect the whole area is tangled with brush and thistles. 'It's great to be involved in its future and imagine what could be done with it.'

'Oh yeah?' the man asks. 'To me it's the building's past which is more interesting.'

'The architecture, you mean?'

He shakes his head. 'No. The old mental hospital. There's still some old wheelchairs and beds kicking around the corridors, things they just left behind when they locked it up. There's an old ECT machine down in the basement.'

Helen's mouth drops open. 'I thought they stopped doing

that.' In Helen's mind, electro-convulsive therapy belongs with trepanning and lobotomies in the category of 'barbaric treatments from centuries ago'. Perhaps ECT isn't so far in the distant past after all.

He shrugs. 'The machine looks pretty old, probably hasn't been used since the sixties. Interesting to see, while you're on patrols.'

'What does it look like?'

'Just a box with buttons and dials, and two metal things.' He points at his temples with a grin, demonstrating where the electrodes would go. 'It's part of history but that stuff will all get chucked away soon, I guess. Modernisation and sanitisation.'

She nods and smiles over at him. 'It'll never be lost though. There's some interesting videos on YouTube, nurses talking about working at the hospital before it closed. A typical day in the life kind of thing.' She remembers the petty arguments at her office in recent weeks about flat sizes and light. 'You're right that they'll strip a lot of the old features out. Still, it'll make beautiful flats. Even better would be a school, or a fantastic hotel, like what Urban Splash did with the Midland in Morecambe.'

He continues as if she hasn't spoken. 'There were some interesting patients locked up in here too. Clever people who just didn't fit society's mould.'

They reach the narrow drive, which slopes downhill through the trees and out of sight. She expects him to leave her and return to his office, but he continues to walk beside her.

Alexander looks at his watch. 'We don't get many people

up here at this time of the morning. This shift is usually very quiet.' He looks right into her eyes, and Helen wants to hold his gaze but has to look away. He pushes his hands into the pockets of his black fleece. 'Don't go inside the building again without an appointment. It's not safe.'

Helen nods and glances back up the drive at the building. Through the trees she can just see the slate roof, tinted gold with the autumn sun. They have reached the end of the driveway and the main road into the town.

'Nice to meet you,' he says.

A red car slows and turns into the drive, the driver's face obscured by the peak of a black baseball cap pulled low over his eyes. The car rolls past and up the driveway towards the hospital; the driver raises a hand in greeting. Helen nods, and the guard waves back.

'That's Paul, come to start the day shift,' Alexander explains. The red car has pulled up outside the old gatehouse. The driver gets out, gathering a bag from the passenger seat. 'He's worked here since he left school. Knows the whole place inside out.'

Helen and Alexander watch as Paul enters the office, leaving the door open. He crouches at a mini fridge, unloading his lunch and getting ready for the start of his shift.

'How many in your team?' she asks, wondering how many guys will lose their jobs when the building sells.

'There's another full-timer called Bruce. Bit of a creep.' His grin and quick shrug indicate this might be an in-joke at Bruce's expense. 'Then some contractors come in for holidays and sick cover. It's pretty solitary work, a bit like being a lorry driver I suspect.'

'It was nice to meet you, Alexander.' Helen smiles and walks away with Alfie towards the road. 'Enjoy the rest of your day.' She turns back before she rounds the bend in the lane, taking a last glance at the building.

Alexander stands at the end of the drive watching Helen leave, his hand raised in a motionless wave. At this distance, his face seems finely sculpted, almost beautiful.

Zoe

Dane grumbles and turns over in bed, pulling Zoe into his arms. He kisses the back of her head, mumbling 'Morning Zo' into her hair.

She smiles. 'I've been awake for ages.'

'Mhmmm,' Dane replies, clearly still half asleep.

Zoe reaches for her phone, pulling out the charging cable. Abbie's added loads of Instagram posts overnight, mainly filtered selfies and elaborate poses taken in her bathroom mirror. She looks amazing in all of them, of course, and Zoe raises an eyebrow at Abbie's attention-seeking hashtags: #doilookfat and #balletdancer. The comments are unbearable.

A Facebook message pops up from Max, Abbie's boyfriend. As Zoe clicks the notification, Dane rests his chin on her shoulder, peering at her phone. He smells of shampoo, and a faint tang of the outdoors. 'What's Max saying?'

Zoe skims the message. 'Nothing really.' She locks her phone and puts it on the bedside table, next to her old Simpsons alarm clock.

She feels Dane's muscles tense.

'Aw, you jealous?' She giggles. They've only been together

four months, so another boy messaging her overnight must make him nervous. She turns over to look at his face. Light filters through her thin curtains, illuminating two tiny frown lines etched on his otherwise smooth forehead. A faint dimple on his left cheek tells her he's not too worried about Max's text. 'It's only Max. You'll meet him tonight, in the pub with Abbie. He's really sweet, crazy in love with Abbie, and obsessed with serial killers. And comics. And trespassing in derelict buildings.' She shakes her head. 'Not my thing at all.'

His dimple deepens as a grin spreads across his face. 'Sounds like we'll have a lot to talk about.'

She nods, and points at her phone. 'He sent me another message about weird murder stuff. Freaks me out a bit, but it's classic 2am Max.'

Dane rubs his face with both hands, then digs his fingers into the corners of his eyes. He shrugs. 'You could ask him to stop.'

'I'll definitely tell him tonight. He's an insomniac, stays up all night creeping around weird sites. Dark web stuff sometimes, true crime and murder blogs, that sort of thing.'

'Sounds pretty normal to me.' Dane sits up, leaning his bare shoulders against the headboard. He lifts his knees and pulls the quilt up to his chest. 'The dark web's harmless really. Not much going on.'

Zoe gapes at him. 'You've been on the dark web?' Even though she's creeped out by Max's obsession with true crime, she feels a thrill of excitement thinking about this network of people whose interests are so illegal that they have to make their own illicit underworld to pursue them. 'What's it like?'

He shrugs again. 'Dunno really. There's a lot of stuff that's pretty similar to the normal web. And a lot of people who like to think they're doing something illegal, but they aren't really. To be honest, I've seen worse things on the normal internet.'

'Places to buy drugs and stuff?'

'All sorts. Lots of data, like people selling stolen logins and credit card details. That's what we were there for, me and my friend Niall. You can buy a pre-paid Netflix account for a tenner.'

Zoe's transfixed. She doesn't want to visit the dark web, ever, but she also somehow wants to know everything about it. 'What about the murder stuff that Max finds?'

Dane's mischievous grin disappears. 'We didn't see any of that sick stuff. We weren't looking for it. But, I mean, it's probably there. Everyone's into that kind of thing these days. Murder podcasts and DIY detective stuff.'

'I just think it's creepy. Melanie – Dad's wife – she's really into it all too. Keeps trying to get me to listen to some podcast about a teenage girl that got murdered. I just don't want to know.'

'Fair enough. I think it's all quite interesting, serial killers, but only when they've been caught. What's interesting about a mystery where you never find out the answer?'

'Max sent an article he's written for a creepy website, *Urban Dark Reporter*. Not on the dark web though.'

Dane smiles. 'Oh, I've heard of that site. It's pretty good.'

Zoe's surprised. Dane seems a lot cooler than Max, so she thought he'd just laugh. 'What is it?' she asks, picking up her phone again and clicking the link.

'It's like cool local weird news; they write articles about mysteries, hoaxes, conspiracies and some urbex stuff too. I've heard that most of the contributors are anonymous – they don't even know who each other are. Even though they're all from around Lancashire.'

'That does sound cool.'

'Yeah, but the comments section is always full of really dark stuff. Those kind of subjects really bring out the weirdos.'

Zoe shudders and hands him her phone. 'I think I'll give that one a miss, then.'

He glances at the headline and pulls her to his side. 'Read with me, this one's not too bad.'

Lancaster's Predator Professor: Investigating Leonard McVitie

By Urban Dark Reporter

New details reveal insight into the mind of our city's twisted genius, who ended his days in Lancaster County Lunatic Asylum.

Leonard McVitie was born in 1923 and lived a life of identity theft and serial murder until his incarceration in Lancaster County Lunatic Asylum at age thirty-six.

Until his capture in 1959, McVitie exploited his unique ability to impersonate and assimilate his identity into that of others, who often were accused and convicted of the crimes McVitie himself had committed. It is estimated that he was directly responsible for the incorrect incarceration of at least seven men who were found guilty of McVitie's crimes, while the criminal walked free to select up to 48 suspected victims.

McVitie is now famous for his meticulous approach and the detailed planning of his crimes. He carefully selected a 'false suspect', often a similar height and build to McVitie himself. He would then observe them for months, entering their homes and stealing small personal items he could plant at a crime scene or in a victim's home to connect the 'false suspect' to a killing. He would even disguise himself as the false suspect and introduce himself to people, blending his life into theirs until the two people were virtually indistinguishable. It seems he particularly enjoyed selecting people who worked 'behind-the-scenes': porters, caretakers, and cleaners – people with low levels of job responsibility who also hold the master keys.

Some of McVitie's false suspects include:

- Colin Redpath, aged twenty-five in 1948 at the time of his guilty verdict: Thought to be one of McVitie's first framings, Redpath was a porter at Cambridge University where McVitie studied. After observing Redpath's movements for over a term, McVitie began introducing himself to students as Redpath and even managed to take on some of Redpath's portering tasks without detection. By the time the body of Maureen Blast (eighteen) was found in a University porter's lodge, McVitie was long gone to another life, and Redpath was hanged.

- Phillip McNeil, aged twenty-five in 1952 at the time of guilty verdict: McNeil was a cleaner at Royal High School, Edinburgh, arrested for the murder of four teenage girls (ages fifteen to seventeen) whose bodies were found on Calton Hill on the morning of 1st May 1951.

After his eventual arrest and imprisonment in the lunatic asylum (later renamed Lancaster Lune Hospital, after the River Lune which flows through the centre of the city), McVitie turned his attentions to study and correspondence. He gained a reputation for his sharp intellect, often contributing to local presses in a similar manner to W.C. Minor's contributions to the *Oxford English Dictionary.* He died in the asylum in 1985.

Manchester's John Rylands Library holds the archives of his correspondence, donated after the Hospital closed in 2010. The archives have now been fully catalogued and are available for registered readers to view by appointment.

Comments:

rogersmith52: Check your facts. I think you'll find that McVitie was born in 1924, not 1923 as you wrote. I do hope this site gets more careful with accuracy if you're going to write about historical killers. Please email me if you have any questions; I have a very extensive knowledge of such people.

Phoneguy: I'm intrigued by this approach, with an added twist: why not frame the victim themselves? Make it look like a suicide, or slowly erase all evidence that they ever existed – by the time you're done, there's no victim left for the police to find. No victim, no crime. Job done.

When they've finished reading, Zoe stands up and picks up some crumpled clothes from the heap on her bedroom floor. She pulls an old t-shirt over her head and smiles at Dane, who's grinning at her from the bed. 'Can't believe that weirdo lived so close to here after he was caught. If he was still alive and stuck in there—' She points in the direction of the old asylum, just half a mile down the road. '—I'd be terrified he would escape and break into my house or something.'

Dane nods and runs a hand through his sleep-tousled hair. 'What an interesting guy though. I've never heard of a serial killer stealing people's identities before, and getting away with it for so long.'

She loves seeing him from a distance like this, five or six feet away. They're usually sat next to each other or lying down together, and that close up you can only see individual features: a nose, the eyes, teeth. But from this distance she can see the whole of him, head to toe in detail, and he's so striking. He looks a bit like Heath Ledger in *10 Things I Hate About You*: he's got the same wild curly hair and cheeky smile.

'You said Max is into urban exploring stuff. You ever been tempted? My Dad's got an old Canon we could take and get some sick photographs inside some of the old buildings around here.' He pulls back the quilt to reveal his legs, and swings his feet to the floor.

'Wait a second,' she says. He looks up at her, puzzled. 'I just want to look at you for a minute.'

He grins. 'Perve.'

She stares at his legs with their dusting of dark hair, tanned up to the thigh where he wore shorts to work all summer. 'Have you ever considered getting a statue commissioned?'

Dane looks confused.

She laughs. 'You know, a naked one like Michelangelo's David.' She keeps giggling and crosses the room to wrap her arms around him. She's standing next to him as he sits on the bed; she pulls his head to her chest and kisses the top of his curly hair. 'You're smoking hot, is all I'm saying.'

He raises his face to hers and kisses her on the lips. 'Come back to bed then?'

She looks in his eyes, and for a moment she's tempted. She could so easily slip back beneath the covers and into Dane's arms. It'd be so nice to feel the remains of his touch against her skin during her morning college classes.

This could be the day they go all the way. She's been waiting for the right time, and everything's going so great between them. He almost said 'I love you' last night. He stopped himself at the last minute and changed it to 'I like you so much.' She smiles thinking about it, how nice it feels to have that expectation, and know it's going to happen soon.

She's about to remove her t-shirt, but then she hears the front door open and close.

'No luck, Mr D. Mum's back from her walk.'

Dane doesn't argue. He never does; he lets her set the pace and just goes with the flow. Not like guys her own age, who're always push push push.

He stands up and pulls on his trousers. He searches around the room for his shirt, finally finding it under the bed. He pauses with it halfway over his head, arms lifted up. 'Zoe?'

'Mmm?' she looks up from her phone where she's typing a reply to Max. 'Your Mum doesn't know I stayed over, does she?'

Zoe gives him her best wide-eyed, innocent face. 'Oh, I'm sure it'll be fine,' she lies, and picks up her hairbrush. Her phone buzzes.

Dane glances at the screen. 'Max again.'

She groans and sets her hairbrush down. 'What does this one say?'

Dane opens her phone and reads Max's message aloud: 'Please, Zo: I think I've found something big. Talk tonight?'

Helen

'Zoe? You home?' A dull thud indicates that her daughter is in her room.

Helen steps into the hall, dropping her keys into the basket on the table. She toes off her muddy shoes by the door.

Alfie runs past her, straight into the kitchen to lap at his water bowl. She pauses, listening to the house. There's no sound except for Alfie's collar clinking against the bowl.

Five minutes later, Zoe pads into the kitchen, rubbing her eyes, hair sticking out in all directions. Zoe's a beautiful girl, brown hair down to her waist and blue eyes, with a mouth that turns up at the corners. A mole on her left cheek reminds Helen of the beauty spots that Hollywood silent film starlets would draw onto their faces to look more sophisticated.

'What are you up to? Don't you have class?'

'Hey Mum,' she mumbles, sitting down at the pine table. 'Got a free period first thing. Not been up long. I see Alfie enjoyed his walk.' She looks down at the dog's muddy paws.

Helen flicks on the kettle. She pulls a couple of teabags from the cupboard, and waves one in Zoe's direction. Zoe shakes her head.

'I thought you start at eight on Tuesdays,' says Helen. 'Are you skipping class again?'

Zoe grunts, non-committal, and gets up from the table. She opens the fridge and stares inside, the light illuminating her cheekbones.

'We've talked about this so much – now is not the time for messing around.'

Zoe raises her hands like someone with a gun aimed at them. 'No, Mum. Chill. I'm not a skiver.'

'Don't tell me to chill.'

Zoe shrugs. 'Where did you and Alfie go for a walk?'

'Up at the old Lune Hospital—'

'That asylum gives me the creeps. Proper,' she says through a yawn. 'I can't believe you walk up there on your own.'

'I like it up there. There's a comforting feel to the place, not scary.'

'I'd be scared that some crazy person would come running at me, straitjacket flapping behind him ...'

'Not very politically correct, Zo.'

Zoe sniggers, unrepentant. She grabs a yoghurt and closes the fridge.

'Anyway, some of the patients in there weren't even mentally ill by today's standards. Annoying wives, epileptics, promiscuous daughters of disapproving families, even just people being a bit eccentric ... Oh! And new mothers with postnatal depression.'

Zoe's eyes are wide. 'What?'

'Yep. I've been reading about it lately, since this new project started. Some really interesting cases up at the Lune.' Helen watches as Zoe peels open the yoghurt and spoons it into her mouth. 'And I bumped into one of the guards this morning. Appeared completely out of nowhere. Alfie wouldn't stop growling at him.'

'Ha! Good old Alfie, cramping your style.'

'Well, I don't know about that. But we talked about the building, it's history. He's worried about his job once the work starts, I think.'

Zoe slowly licks the last traces from her spoon, thinking. 'Was he good-looking?'

Helen puckers her lips sideways, pretending to think about it. 'I suppose he was quite handsome.' She ignores Zoe's raised eyebrows. 'But—'

'You should ask him out for a drink.' Zoe grins, her eyes twinkling with mischief. She goes through phases like this, when she fixates on matchmaking Helen with a guy. But Helen suspects Zoe would change her tune if Helen did meet someone; both Helen and Zoe like their cosy twosome. The times when it had looked like someone was taking an interest in Helen, Zoe took an immediate dislike to them. Maybe that's why Dane makes Helen so uncomfortable – his relationship with Zoe threatens to disrupt the last few years of just-the-two-of-us. Or maybe it's something else, something about Dane himself; even at this stage of life, Helen still has to remind herself not to disregard her instincts.

'No way. I'm not asking him out for a drink.' Helen's perfectly happy on her own. 'Plus he was closer to your age than mine.'

'I really don't get it: you're lonely, you're bored, and you've got nothing to think about except me and what I'm doing—'

'Hey.' Helen's voice is quiet.

Zoe doesn't seem to notice her Mum's cautioning tone. 'Seriously, though, it'd be great if you got a boyfriend. You'd be less stressy about me and what I'm doing all the time, for one thing.'

Helen opens her mouth to argue. 'Not everyone wants a—'

'Hi, Mrs Summerton.'

Helen jumps at the male voice in her house. Dane is, as usual, lurking – this time in the darkened corridor outside the kitchen. He sidles into the room, bringing with him the smell of patchouli, sweat and wood.

'Dane. Didn't know you were here.' She opens the fridge and peers inside. She can't look at him while she feels invaded like this. A virtual stranger in her house first thing in the morning is not comfortable. She grabs the milk from the fridge door and turns back to the room, trying to arrange a welcoming smile on her face.

He smiles sheepishly and looks at his hands. 'Yeah, I was just upstairs.'

Even from across the room, Helen can see the dirt on his hands, ingrained in all the creases and under his nails. He's a carpenter specialising in turning huge fallen tree trunks into beautiful coffee tables, stools and other furniture. According to Zoe, they met when Dane was invited to Zoe's college to speak about 'alternative career paths' – vocational careers which don't involve going to university. Helen suspects that Zoe met Dane long before that day at her college, and kept his existence secret for a couple of months because she was afraid to tell Helen about their seven-year age gap.

'You stayed over last night?' She doesn't want to think about what they were doing in Zoe's room before Helen came home.

He leans against the door frame, taking up a lot of space with his six foot four-inch height and wide shoulders. He tucks his hands behind his back, looking strangely military.

'Dane, I'm afraid you can't stick around this morning. Zoe's got to get to college.'

Zoe opens her mouth in protest. She seems happiest when Dane hangs around at their house, taking up too much space in their living room, eating all their food, his giant shoes cluttering their front porch.

'I'll see you tonight, though, babe?' Zoe says to Dane.

Helen cuts her off. 'Zoe has plans to go over to her Dad's house tonight.' She turns to Zoe, who is midway through rolling her eyes again. 'Remember?'

Zoe scowls, and Dane just looks confused. Zoe's clearly forgotten that plan. Zoe looks over at Dane and shrugs. Dane shrugs back, looking even more gormless than usual.

'Plus, don't you have coursework?' Helen doesn't know what it is about Dane's presence that puts her in this snarky, naggy mood. Something about him turns her into a shrew. Perhaps she's trying to make up for the negative influence he's clearly having on Zoe's college work.

Zoe groans. 'I don't have coursework today, Mum.'

'Revision then. Or reading. I'm sure there is something you're supposed to be doing which will prevent you from failing your A Levels. Plus, your Dad will want to catch up with you.'

Zoe groans and turns to Dane. 'I'm sorry about this,' she says, as if Helen is the teenager and Zoe is the adult embarrassed by Helen's behaviour. 'Wanna go back up to my room?'

Helen grits her teeth.

'I think I should head off,' says Dane.

Helen flashes him a thin smile. Maybe he's not that bad after all if he can pick up on *some* social cues.

'Got work, you know,' he mumbles.

They wander down the hall to the front door; Helen hears them whispering while Dane prepares to leave. There are whispers about a pub, but Helen chooses not to hear whatever it is. There's a limit to how much hovering and nagging she can do for one morning.

After a few minutes, the door shuts and Zoe stomps down the hall back into the kitchen, where Helen has poured herself a cup of tea in preparation for the upcoming argument.

'Why do you have to be like this? I'm actually embarrassed,' Zoe says, folding her arms and looking remarkably similar to a photograph Helen remembers taking when Zoe was about three years old, mid-tantrum because she could no longer fit her feet into a favourite pair of red shoes.

Helen takes a sip from her mug, delaying the start of the argument for an extra five seconds. 'This is the most—'

'Important year of my life,' interrupts Zoe. 'I know that. You tell me that all the time. Dad does too. But I still need a *life.* I'm allowed a social life and a boyfriend, for God's sake.'

'Remember last term? You skipped so many History classes

that they wrote a letter home. And you got a D on your Spanish exam. You need to pull your socks up if—'

'What a stupid phrase, pull my socks up.'

'My choice of phrase is not relevant here.'

'*You* got a D in one of your A levels. AND you were dating Dad at the time. You're such a hypocrite and you think you can somehow fix it all by nagging at me. You won't fix it, Mum – you won't fix YOUR bad decisions by obsessing about my life.'

'That's enough.' Helen taps her hand on the worktop. They've had this argument so many times, and it'll just go in circles. There's no point. Helen remembers being that age: no clue about consequences, no idea that danger might sprout from your decisions like a dandelion through gravel. 'This has nothing to do with my life or my past choices and everything to do with your future.'

During the argument, Zoe has been edging closer and closer to the door, ready to implement her usual tactic in the end stages of a disagreement: drop the last word like a bomb and then stalk out of the room, stomping upstairs and slamming her bedroom door.

'My choices are fine. Go on a date or something. It's not my fault you don't have a life of your own.' Her last word is shouted, and sure enough, she then storms out of the kitchen.

Helen tries to chuckle. She remembers similar arguments with her own parents at the same age, but she can't help feeling stung by Zoe's final parting shot.

Helen is proud of who she has become, although now Zoe is the same age that Helen was when she met Tony, a new panic has set in. She doesn't want to see history repeat itself, and there's something in the self-assured sparkle in Dane's eye that reminds her of Tony and his cheeky charm, which may have seduced more women than she knew of while they were still married.

She switches on the television and flicks to BBC News, as the coverage flashes to a photograph of a young girl wearing a graduation robe, flanked by two proud parents. Even though the volume is low, the grave expressions on the newsreaders' faces tell Helen that this girl's future is not bright, promising or full of potential. There are bigger dangers out there lurking for carefree teenaged girls: much, much worse than a boyfriend with a roving eye.

Helen shivers and takes another sip of tea. As she drinks, something catches her eye in the middle of the corridor just outside the kitchen. A dark shadow, the size and shape of a rat. Her muscles clench with dread. Please, not rats.

She slowly lowers her mug to the countertop, staring at the ominous shape on the floor. It doesn't move. If it's a rat, it's already dead.

She crosses the kitchen slowly and sighs with relief as she moves closer. Not a rat. She bends down to pick it up. It's a blue ballet flat, stained with mud. The one Alfie found at the hospital; that silly dog must have brought it home. She turns the shoe, examining it from all sides. Something about it doesn't look right. Under the orange-tinged hall light, the shoe's stain is metallic and brown, like rusted metal.

Thomas

Thomas pushes down on the handle and nudges the kitchen door inch by inch, wincing at the creaks and clicks. He steps into the still-darkened room.

Light sifts through the blue curtains, staining everything as if the room is underwater. The air smells musty with a faint reminder of dinner: southern fried chicken and baked beans.

He pulls open the curtains to let in the morning light. It is a combined kitchen-and-living room with high ceilings and windows that rattle when trucks drive by. He considers opening a window, but the traffic noise might wake Mum in the next room. She needs as much sleep as possible when she works long hours at the paper and does research late into the night.

He pulls the Coco Pops from the cupboard, the orange juice from the fridge, and is reaching for a bowl when Mum walks in. She is dressed for work in a smart skirt and jacket, her long brown hair tied in a low ponytail and an ID badge clipped to her pocket.

'You look pretty, Mum,' says Thomas.

She looks at him from under slightly swollen eyelids.

'Thanks, baby. I don't feel pretty; I feel knackered. You're dressed for school already? You're a good boy.' Mum stares at him, frowning. 'Where are your glasses?'

He reaches up to the cupboard where they keep the tumblers for juice.

'Thomas?'

'I maybe left them at school.' That could be true, he thinks to himself, hoping they are safely in his desk in Room 5B.

Mum doesn't say anything else.

She pours two bowls of cereal, Coco Pops for Thomas, muesli for herself. Mum's muesli looks to Thomas like the food they give to Ronald, the big fat hamster in 6D.

Thomas settles down on the sofa and reaches for the remote to see what good programmes are on.

'Did you remember Maggie's staying over for the next few days? I hope you cleaned your room last night.'

Thomas groans. 'Why does she have to sleep in my room?'

'Because we don't have a spare room.'

He frowns. 'But it's *my* room.'

'And Maggie's part of your family, and family shares things.'

Thomas folds his arms.

'You used to love it when Maggie stayed over.'

'Yeah, but that was before.'

'Before what?'

'Don't know.'

Before Dad disappeared and Mum got sad and busy and was always at work. And before Thomas began to spend more time outside, exploring nearby woods and paths because it gets him out of the house that smells different now Dad's gone.

The only part of the house he likes now is his own bedroom, and he doesn't want to share it with Maggie. Maggie has her own dad and her own bedroom on the other side of town. And he doesn't want to share Mum with Maggie either.

'Why does she have to stay here anyway?'

She looks cross. 'Because my sister has no idea that other people have lives and thinks I can just drop everything for her whenever she wants to swan off on a last-minute holiday. You'd think she'd have some consideration, what with everything that's been going on.'

'What about Duncan and Sandy? Where are they going to stay?' He hopes they can stay, too. They're much more fun than Maggie and they want to do daring stuff like rope swings, climbing over walls and staying up late.

'Julie says they're old enough to take care of themselves.'

'But not old enough to take care of Maggie?'

'Kinda makes sense,' she says with a shrug. 'I wouldn't want those two boys looking after anyone either. They're wild.'

Thomas frowns. 'Why can't Auntie Julie take Maggie with her on the holiday?'

Mum drops her spoon in her bowl with a clatter and looks at him, her eyes fierce. Her frown lines deepen and her lips get thin. She doesn't look as pretty anymore. 'Listen, I'm the mum here and I'm saying you have to let Maggie sleep in your room with you and be nice to her. You used to be best friends.'

'She's bossy. And she never stops talking. She's really annoying.'

'So what?'

'She always wants to play stupid pretend games.'

'Pretend games are normal, TomTom. You're ten.'

'Pretend games are for little kids. And I'm eleven, not ten.' He looks down at his cereal, where the milk has turned chocolate-brown and the pieces of Coco Pops are bleached a strange grey colour. 'Eurgh. Fine,' says Thomas. 'But she doesn't get to use the iPad.'

He does like Maggie really; he just doesn't want her in his room touching his stuff. She's nosy and she fiddles with everything.

'Weren't you two doing a school project together? Maybe you could work on that tonight.'

Thomas nods. The teachers always put them together for pair work because they're cousins. It's annoying sometimes, like when they've had a fight (like the time Maggie broke Thomas's massive Lego Star Wars project that he made with Dad. It took weeks to build and Maggie broke it when she picked it up and pretended it could fly like the real Death Star).

But other times it's quite fun being partners. Maggie is clever and has good ideas, so they get high marks.

'We did some of the project, but we've got to finish the ending. It's a ghost story in an old farmhouse and there's an old smugglers tunnel like in the Famous Five. It's got pictures we got from the internet and everything.'

'Honestly, it's all ghost stories and secret passageways with you and Maggie.' She stands up, yawning. 'I need to go to work. Feels like I've hardly been home five minutes.' She ruffles Thomas's hair. 'Short shift today. I'll pick up you and Maggie after school.'

He pushes his spoon into the chocolatey milk in his bowl,

letting the liquid seep onto the spoon and not allowing any of the Coco Pops to breach the dam of the spoon's sides.

'Look at me,' she says, bending down to lift his chin with her hand. Two faint frown lines between her eyebrows make her look even more tired than usual. 'You're a big boy, nearly all grown up and able to do anything you like, but I still need your help. Sometimes I need your help with chores in the house, and other times I need your help by making things easier for me, like not making a fuss when Maggie's coming over. You're the man of the house for now, alright?'

'Alright,' he says in a quiet voice. He wants Dad to be the man of the house, though, so he can be the kid of the house again, even though eleven feels much more grown up than ten. And Mum could be the Mum of the house instead of trying to do everything and not having any time to relax or play silly games together.

'I wish it wasn't just me, but I'm doing my best to be the best mum in the world.'

He nods. He does want to help. He's just so cross with everything and sometimes he's cross with her. Sometimes he thinks it's her fault Dad left. Maybe if she was different Dad would still be here. Maybe if *he* was different Dad would still be here.

She smiles at him. 'Now it's your cue to tell me I *am* the best mum in the world, silly billy.'

He smiles. 'You are the best mum in the world. Really truly.'

Mum kisses him goodbye, a big sloppy kiss on his forehead, which makes a loud noise and causes him to giggle. Mum's really funny sometimes, when she's in a good mood.

He hears the front door open and close and then his mother walks briskly past the window, turning to wave at him like every morning. Thomas finishes his cereal and takes both bowls to the sink, rinsing them under the tap and then laying them out to dry on the draining board.

Then he goes into his bedroom and hides the iPad under his pillow, so Maggie doesn't use it.

It was the last thing Dad gave him before he disappeared.

Helen

Huge thumps down the stairs herald Zoe's re-entry into the room, the air around her crackling with chaos.

'Thought you were running late ten minutes ago?' Now she's had a few minutes of quiet, she's ready to tease Zoe and be friends again.

Zoe groans. 'Yeah, yeah. If I didn't have to get the stinking bus, I'd have loads more time. It's full of wankers, by the way.'

Helen chuckles. 'Did you find your folder?'

'Yes, but not the homework. Mr K is literally going to shit on me.'

'I don't think you mean that literally.' Helen suppresses a smile. 'And watch your language, Zoe.'

'Whatever,' Zoe mumbles, grabbing an apple from the fruit bowl and shouldering her backpack. 'Don't suppose you could give me a lift?'

'Sorry. Got a conference call in ten minutes.' Helen grimaces.

Zoe pulls a face right back. 'Sounds boring.'

'Probably will be quite boring, yep. Building regulations, council regulations, and historical considerations and blah blah ...'

Zoe pretends to fall asleep, making enormous and exaggerated snoring noises as she pulls open the front door. 'Have fun with that, Mum! Laters.'

Helen gathers up her breakfast dishes and stacks them in the dishwasher. 'Looks like it's just me and you for the day now, Alfie.'

In his bed in the corner of the kitchen, Alfie thumps his tail in acknowledgement, his head resting on his paws. He's always a little glum when someone leaves the house. When Tony left, Helen worried about Alfie more than Zoe – he wouldn't get out of his bed for three days except for wees in the garden. That suited Helen at the time, however, because she couldn't get out of bed very easily either.

Helen pours herself another tea and carries it to the desk in the living room. Piled high with papers and tucked into a corner surrounded by bookshelves, this desk is exactly what teenaged Helen would have imagined as the ideal workspace. The only difference from her youthful imaginings is that instead of drawing elaborate children's book illustrations, she drafts architectural concepts for the NHS's Property Services, getting outline planning permission for the sale and eventual redevelopment of former care homes. It's Helen's job to visualise the transformation of large crumbling buildings into perfect little units for upwardly mobile young professionals, so that big property companies will buy them and inject much-needed cash into NHS coffers.

Secretly, Helen thinks the kind of apartments she designs on projects like these are soulless and identical, like a dozen prefabs stacked on top of each other. And the insides of these beautiful buildings are often gutted, with only the outer walls remaining to fulfil a local council's minimum preservation requirements for maintaining the historical features. There's no real desire for anything with aesthetic merit; just box ticking to avoid getting sued. Still, at least these buildings no longer get demolished under the guise of 'progress', like in previous decades. Helen shudders to think of it; such waste.

In Helen's ideal world, the Lune Hospital would be made into a museum, exposing and showcasing the evolution of mental health treatment and its brutal history. They could start on the ground floor with the unethical freak shows of the Bedlam era, where the nobility used to pay to gawp at the poor souls. Then move up the floors ascending through lobotomies, ECT and padded cells to modernisation and the present day, which is hopefully much more civilised. Unfortunately, Helen is an architect, not a museum curator.

She dials into the conference call and waits on the line, listening to the tinny music piping in her ear before the next attendee dials in. She opens Firefox and clicks to the news, trying to find that news story from the TV earlier – she'd only caught the last few seconds before the next story began, but something about the faces in the picture looked familiar.

Alfie shuffles into the room and flops down in the corner to watch her from his paws.

'Hey doggie,' she says, glancing over to smile at his furry face. 'Have you come to join me on this deathly dull conference call?'

'TREVOR has entered the call!' a computer voice announces.

'Morning Trevor,' says Helen brightly, hoping he didn't hear her. She minimises the browser window and clicks through to the conference call agenda. 'How are you today?'

Trevor is the NHS's Historic Buildings Regulations Officer, seconded from Lancaster City Council, appointed to respond to every one of Helen's designs with a mealy-mouthed whine of 'I'm afraid the regulations won't allow you to do that.'

They make small talk until Pam hops on the call thirty seconds later, followed by Craig. Pam and Craig both work for the property development firm which might buy the Lune Hospital; they are driving the redevelopment into 'luxury living spaces for professionals'. They want it to look great, but to spend no money achieving that.

Helen sits in the middle of all of them, feeling like the only voice of reason and the ambassador for good design, fighting off bad decisions with her drafting board and carpenter's square.

Today's call is particularly frustrating because it's about the basements: big storage chambers connected by breeze block-lined service tunnels with concrete floors. Pam and Craig want to cram as many 'apartments and townhouses' into the Lune site as possible, and that includes extending development into the basements.

Helen finds a gap in the chatter and tries to break into the call. 'I just think that these flats—'

'*Luxury living spaces*,' interrupts Pam. 'We need to use the right words, Helen, so we keep in mind that we're not building anything less than luxury. *Flats* is just so ... brutalist.'

Helen runs her hands through her hair and grits her teeth. Just a few more weeks and this project will be over, planning permission granted and all the contracts signed. 'We need to incorporate larger windows. If we're extending into the basements, they need light so they aren't depressing caves of misery. It's dark down there with the current windows; they're like letterboxes.'

'It would compromise the façade of the lower levels,' whines Trevor. Helen can hear him shuffling his papers on the other end of the phone.

'If we can't put windows in, we shouldn't extend the living spaces into the basement,' says Helen. 'They should be storage only.' She lowers her forehead to the desk and clunks it gently against the wood a couple of times, taking deep breaths. There should be a Project Manager to handle these tedious conference calls and just relay any decisions back to Helen, but sadly Maxine went on maternity leave a couple of months ago, and the NHS decided they didn't need to replace her. Helen suspects the pregnancy was purposely timed, and respects Maxine's well-planned reproductive decision to avoid this particular part of the development process.

Nothing gets decided about the basements, and the call veers into ways to decrease space and cram in extra units. Pam asks whether people really need all that storage space when minimalism is so chic right now.

Helen clicks back to the news website and opens the headline article.

Lancaster's lost girls: Runaways, or something more sinister?

By J. Mitchell

Parents of missing teenager raise questions for Lancaster's police

Five years ago, the mysterious disappearance of 17-year-old Sadie Duncan shocked the market town of Lancaster. It was the end of August, and Sadie's suitcase lay half-packed on her bedroom floor, never taken to Leeds University as planned.

Sadie's mother, Charlotte Duncan, 45, still holds out hope that she'll come back home. 'Maybe she just didn't want to go to university. She was nervous about it. But she's just not the type to leave and not say goodbye, you know.' Tears slide down her cheeks, as they have every day for the past five long years.

The day she went missing was just like every other day, with nothing unusual and no arguments. Sadie went into Lancaster with her friends for a birthday drink and has not been seen since leaving the pub alone at 10.30pm.

With no sightings and very few working CCTV cameras in Lancaster's pedestrianised city centre, the hope of tracing Sadie's movements quickly faded. Her bank account remains untouched, her belongings and bedroom exactly as they were the night she disappeared.

Work of a serial killer?

'I think it was a serial killer,' says Charlotte's husband, Bill, whose hands shake as he talks of his missing daughter.

Bill continues: 'There are other teenage girls gone missing from roundabout [the local area]: Preston, Manchester, and one from Garstang a couple of years ago. They're all our Sadie's age. The police call them runaways but most of the parents are like us, with good kids from loving homes.'

I looked into Charlotte and Bill's claims, finding a rate of missing teenagers slightly higher than the national average. Potential victims include Joanna Bamber, 18, from Heysham; Roberta Clarkson, 16, from Morecambe; and Anna Keyne, 18, from Caton.

Police refuse to comment

Lancashire Constabulary refused to contribute to this story, stating that they could not comment on an active or unsolved investigation. Does this mean that there is an ongoing investigation?

With little forensic evidence and no bodies, it's hard to determine if this is the work of a serial killer or just a coincidence that these girls have all disappeared within the same area.

Anyone with information about any of the missing women in this article can contact Crimestoppers on 0800 555 111 or email j.mitchell@lancasternews.com.

'Helen?'

She shakes her head, trying to forget the news story now rattling around her brain.

'Sorry – what was that?' she asks, minimizing the browser. 'The line went fuzzy for a second.'

Pam clears her throat. 'Craig was suggesting that nobody needs kitchen worktop space, because they just put their dishes in the dishwasher and they're all probably going out for dinner every night anyway.'

After more than an hour, she finally hangs up the phone with very little decided except for the date of the next conference call.

'What a waste of time. Glad that's over,' she says to the dog. 'Now to start actual work.' She opens her A1 folder of sketches, floor plans and sepia photographs of the old hospital, but something niggles. What is it?

She flicks back to the news article, skims the text, but can't find what she's looking for. When she read it the first time, on the call, there was something familiar.

She reads it again, but nothing resonates now.

She lets her eyes wander over the web page, blurring the words. And there it is, like mist burning off on a warm spring day:

The author at the top of the article. How does she know that name?

Thomas

'I reckon the blue flame would be the worst, though,' Maggie says, colouring in their Science homework; a flame to show when there's oxygen in the pipe (yellow and wavy) and no oxygen (blue and straight). 'You know, if we put one of Josie Steadman's plaits into the burner.'

'I bet Josie would be bald on one side so fast that you couldn't even put the fire out before all her hair goes.' Thomas laughs at the idea of Josie bald on one side of her head. It's the best type of giggling because he knows he shouldn't be laughing at all. 'It'd be funny, but we might get in trouble.'

'Yeah. I don't need any more de-merits this term.' Maggie looks at her new smartwatch she got for her birthday last week. Maggie's mum and dad don't need to be careful with money, and she gets loads of new stuff whenever she wants it. But she still prefers coming over to Thomas's house after school instead of going over to her own house.

'Why do you like coming to my house anyway? You've got a giant TV and a PS4.'

Maggie shrugs. 'Duncan and Sandy never let me play on it. And Auntie Janet lets us do whatever we want.'

He supposes that's true: even when Mum's at home, she's busy with house stuff or Important Top-Secret Research. Or falling asleep in front of their TV, which is much smaller than Maggie's.

Mum is sitting with them at the dining table, but she's not paying attention. The overhead kitchen light lights up her hair, so shiny it's almost like she's wearing a gold crown. She props her chin up with her hands and stares at an old book, newspapers spread around to cover every inch of the table. Her face is blank and her eyes unfocussed, like she's been hypnotised by that guy Derren Brown from the TV.

Mum looks up from her papers, frowning. 'Guys, you remember I asked if you could play outside while I finish this article?' She looks out of the kitchen window. The sky is blue tinged with pink and the oak tree in the garden looks dark against the bright sky. 'You've still got another few hours of daylight. Could you go to the play park? Take a torch so cars can see you on the way back – and look both ways crossing that road. Back at nine for bed.'

Maggie taps her posh watch. 'Back at nine, no problem.'

'Okay Mum!' Thomas pulls on his wellingtons and grabs the massive torch from the shelf by the door. Then he looks around the porch.

'What else would be useful?' He picks up Dad's posh bird-watching binoculars from the coat hook, the ones he's never allowed to play with because they're not a toy. 'If Dad's not coming back, he won't need them,' he says, watching Maggie's expression.

She scrunches her nose and shrugs. 'They're practically yours now anyway.'

He loops the leather cord around his neck and lets the weight of the binoculars hang from his shoulders. They're surprisingly heavy, but the cord feels soft against his skin, which makes the weight bearable.

Maggie leans over to whisper in Thomas's ear: 'I stole a penknife from Duncan's drawer this morning. We can cut up sticks and build a campfire for our den.'

Thomas unfolds his arms. He can't help but smile back; Maggie looks so excited and making a den does sound really fun. He nods. 'Good idea.'

He's always wanted a penknife, but Dad wouldn't let him; said it's too dangerous. Well, Dad's not here anymore.

They call goodbye to Mum and set off along the garden path and onto the road, which is too narrow to have pavements, so they walk single-file near the hedge, facing oncoming traffic like they were taught.

'Where are we going, then?' asks Thomas, as they walk past the play park.

Maggie stops walking and grabs his arm. 'Oh my God, I can't believe I didn't tell you yet. I didn't want your mum to hear, because she'd not let us go out if she knew.'

She pauses for dramatic effect and Thomas frowns. 'We're not building a den in the woods?'

Maggie jumps up and down with excitement, her heels bouncing off the pavement. 'We don't need to *build* a den, because there's a whole den ready out in some trees, and no one goes there anymore.'

Maybe it'll be a little tumbledown shed, like the one their Grandpa has on his allotment. It would be fun to have one like that of their own. Or a treehouse, that would be even better.

Thomas is getting excited. 'We can hang posters and play noisy games with no grown-ups to tell us to keep the noise down. And maybe next summer when it's warmer, we can have sleepovers out there and keep each other awake telling ghost stories! I hope the roof doesn't leak. Grandpa's shed roof does.'

Maggie shrugs. 'Duncan told me about it. He said your Dad took him there once.'

A thrill of excitement; this is his Dad's secret, too. They've never had a secret together before. He skips a little. 'I can't wait to tell him we've been there! I wonder how Dad found it.' Thomas peers into the hedge alongside them, checking for creepy stuff. 'This den's not, like, haunted or anything? Where is it?'

'In the woods, near the old asylum. The one that's falling down. Properly hidden in the trees, though. Barely anyone knows it's there anymore because everyone's forgotten about it.'

'Is it a shed?'

'It's an old caravan. Someone dumped it years ago.'

Thomas knows he should feel excited, but there's a part of him deep in his stomach that feels afraid and hopes they don't find it. It's probably mouldy and damp. If they don't find it then they can have fun exploring the woods, but they don't actually have to go inside and get all dirty. And in the future, they can talk about that fun day they went looking for the caravan and didn't find it, instead of talking about that time they found a caravan and Thomas didn't want to go inside. Yeah, Thomas hopes they don't find it.

He slows his steps a little and fiddles with the strap on the binoculars. They're actually quite heavy. Maybe he could hide them in a hedge and pick them up on the way home.

'What if someone's living in it? It could be some homeless guy's house or something.'

Maggie looks at him, wide-eyed. 'That would be so cool.'

Thomas doesn't say anything to that. He doesn't think that would be cool.

'Duncan says they used to play poker there, it was their gambling den. Some kids from his school used to go there but no one uses it anymore.'

'Why not?'

Maggie looks at Thomas and purses her lips. 'Probably because they're too old and boring now.'

Thomas feels a gnawing, uncomfortable clenching in his gut, like when he's on a long car journey and is worried he needs to pee. 'Yeah, but why, though?

'Doesn't want to share the fun, I bet. He made me promise I'd never try to find it.'

Helen

Helen's cutting cloves of garlic when the doorbell rings. Her fingers are sticky with residue.

'Zoe, can you get that please?' she calls up the stairs, where Zoe's packing her bag to stay overnight at her Dad's.

No answer.

'Zoe? The door.'

Still no answer. Helen can hear Zoe wandering around, and the low thump of bass on her stereo, but either Zoe didn't hear or she's choosing to ignore her.

Helen rinses her hands and walks to the door while she dries them on a tea towel. She pulls open the front door. Tony's standing on the step, his face yellow in the porch light.

'You're not my daughter,' he says with a chuckle. He's grinning; clearly he heard her shouting for Zoe. He's teasing, but Helen's not feeling jovial this evening. She steps aside to invite her ex-husband into the house. 'She's still packing her bag; you might have to wait a while.'

'That's not unexpected.' He steps into the hall and picks up the ballet shoe, examining its stains with a curious look on his face. 'I won't ask.'

'Alfie brought it home.' She tells him about the Lune Hospital while Tony examines the shoe.

'Sounds like your kind of project, cool architecture with a side of local history.' Tony drops the shoe back onto the carpet. 'Need to wash my hands now, though. Train your dog not to pick up rubbish.'

'He's untrainable,' she jokes, and Alfie wags his tail as she ruffles his ears.

He rinses his hands in the downstairs loo and follows Helen into the living room, where he throws himself onto the sofa and puts his feet on the coffee table without removing his shoes. Helen winces but doesn't say anything. Let Melanie whine about shoes on the coffee table in their own house.

For a moment, Helen feels light, more carefree. She doesn't have to nag another adult about anything ever again if she doesn't want to. Her only responsibilities are to herself and Zoe, no one else. It's quite liberating, given enough distance from the pain of a divorce. And it did need four years of distance to really appreciate.

'Fancy a glass of wine while you wait?' she asks, waving her own glass of red at Tony through the doorway from the kitchen.

Tony gives her a thumbs up. 'Just a little one; I'm driving.'

She hands him a glass and sits next to him on the sofa.

'How are you doing?' he says in that voice he reserves for friendly concern, as if she's ill or someone's died.

She can't let him use that voice on her, not anymore. 'Really great, thank you. Never better. Looking forward to a night in on my own, actually. I might open another bottle.'

He chuckles. 'Good for you.'

'How about you?'

'I suspect we'll have our hands full with the twins and Zoe all night. I think they're dying to play some new game with her.'

Zoe enters the living room in a cloud of perfume, her hair backcombed and a huge amount of eyeliner on her lower lashes.

'Hey, panda-eyes!' teases Tony.

Zoe ignores his remark. 'I can't play with the twins tonight, I'm afraid. I have plans.'

Tony's face falls, and he looks like a young man again, the young man Helen met years before. 'But you're coming over to ours to stay,' he says firmly.

'Well, no one asked me what my plans were. And I have plans already, so yes I'm sleeping at yours but I'm not staying in.'

Tony sits forward, lowering his feet onto the floor and setting down his wine glass where his heels were. 'Yes, you are. We have a standing arrangement with Melanie and the twins.'

'I'll have dinner with you guys, but I'm going out later with my friends. It's been arranged for ages.' She sits in the armchair and pulls her denim skirt down her thighs to cover some skin.

Tony shakes his head and looks at Helen, his eyes pleading with her to fix this somehow.

Helen shrugs. This one's Tony's to fix; Helen has to battle with Zoe's teenage strops most days, and now it's his turn.

Tony stands up and drains his wine glass, grabbing his car keys off the table. 'Come on, then. You're at least having dinner with the family before you go anywhere.'

'That's fine,' states Zoe. She stands, pulling down her skirt again and shouldering her backpack.

'Did you bring clothes for college tomorrow?' asks Helen. 'Wouldn't want you to have to wear that outfit in class.'

'Yes, Mum.' Zoe leans down and kisses Helen on the cheek.

'Bye, love you,' calls Helen as Zoe head out of the door. 'Be careful, Zoe, okay?' she calls, remembering that newspaper article. Outside, there's a slam as Zoe gets in the car and closes the door behind her. Through the passenger window, Helen can see Zoe's face lit up blue by the light on her phone as her thumbs tap on the screen to share the injustice of being a teenager.

Tony turns around and frowns at Helen, rolling his eyes slightly.

'Find out where she's going and who with before you let her go anywhere. And make her wear jeans if you can.'

Tony salutes and follows Zoe out of the house.

The front door closes behind them and the house is quiet. Helen glances at Alfie, who's on his bed looking at her, his head resting on his paws.

'Peace at last, Alf.'

Him

'Petra?' he whispers. No response.

He stops in the hall, silent, listening. Nothing. He moves down the darkened corridor, his footsteps echoing on the wooden floorboards. The kitchen is dark, blinds drawn against the daylight, a plate waiting to be washed by the sink.

Even though he didn't choose it himself, this house is ideal for his purposes: at the end of a quiet street where everyone is too concerned with what others think of them to notice what is actually happening around them.

It was his childhood house, where he learned to be the person he is now, under the firm guiding hand of his mother. For him, it is the place where he sleeps, the place where he stores his belongings, but it is not his home. She had an inkling of the full depths of who he is, he suspects. Enough to teach him how to hide it, to use it. She showed him how to keep his intense anger inside, to store it and channel its power for useful purposes. He will always be grateful to her for the lessons she taught him, even though the process of learning was painful.

He has lived alone since his mother departed. The mere

thought of sharing his space with another makes him shiver. But Petra is different.

He opens the back door, stepping out into the garden. It's a small patch of grass bordered by high wooden fences on either side, with man-height hedges to block out the neighbours.

'Petra?' He hears a bell tinkling and a muffled mew. Petra emerges from under one of the bushes, her tail upright, mouth stuffed full of something furry. She meows again. He is always surprised by how loudly Petra can call while her mouth is full. She's a beautiful cat, larger than a normal tabby. She looks more like a miniature leopard than a domesticated feline. She drops her prize at his feet.

Petra has caught a vole. It tries to scuttle away, dragging a broken leg. Its black eyes shine with fear. She's clearly been playing with it for some time. Domestic cats can play with an injured animal for hours before killing them.

Petra reaches out with her paw, pinning the creature to the patio. She looks up at him, seeking approval.

He understands feline emotions, they're so legible. He moves his features into a smile, sure the cat can read his expression too. He reaches down to stroke Petra's neck, behind her ears. She pushes against his hand, brushing his palm with her whiskers, acknowledging his superiority.

'Good girl, you've brought home a plaything for us.' He settles on the step, leaning against the doorframe. There's going to be a nice little performance. Petra likes to play with her food.

The cat lies down, tucking her front legs underneath her and smothering the vole. She can probably feel it wriggling under her chest. He imagines the cat's satisfaction at feeling the creature's futile twitches; the mastery of knowing there is no way she can be thwarted.

Petra watches him, her steady gaze trained on the human's, eye to eye. He respects this cat more than any human. She knows her own mind, asks for nothing, does whatever she wants, and causes destruction without the encumbrance of remorse. Remorse is a waste of time. It's a weakness, a pointless construction of the inferior brain. The big cats feel no remorse; you don't see a lion apologising to the disembowelled zebra, crying over its bloodied corpse. No. The lion is a survivor, fighting to get what it needs and consuming where it can.

One could argue that the domestic cat is an unnecessary killer: with a bowl full of cat food on their owner's kitchen floor, why do they slaughter unsuspecting and undefended rodents and birds? Why torture them before they put them to death? But he understands and respects that. It's entertainment. Instinct. Desire. And all without remorse.

Petra digs her claws into the fur of the vole, tossing its broken body into the air. It lands on the concrete with a small thump. The helpless creature tries to get away, but now both of its rear legs are broken and it drags the back half of its body behind it along the patio. Petra watches the painful progress, letting the vole believe it has a chance of escape. She follows slowly, legs retracted into her body, muscles taut, stomach and head close to the ground. A little killing machine.

He leans forward, hands on his knees. There's a delicate trail of blood spotted across the flagstones, and Petra releases the vole for long enough for him to see that the small intestine is hanging out of a gash in the abdomen. Nice work, cat. The vole lies on its side, belly heaving with its last breaths. Its eyes still sparkle. He stands up and walks over to the creature.

'My turn,' he says to Petra. The cat steps back to watch. She respects her master.

He steps forward, placing the toe of his boot on the vole's head. Transferring his weight into his right leg, he prepares to press down on the skull, anticipating the crunch through the sole of his boot.

The vole's whiskers shudder, nose still sniffing the air in its last moments. Its eyelid twitches, its black eye shines. If he moves closer, he would see his own face reflected back at him in that vole's eye. He'd see the grimace on his face as he took its life.

The muscle in his thigh flexes and he's ready to stomp, to crush the bones.

He sucks in air through his teeth with a hiss. 'No.'

Something stops him at the last moment. He lifts his foot off the creature and stands, hands on hips, staring out into the garden, the grass high and waving in the breeze.

He nods at Petra and leaves her with the vole, still shivering on the patio. Let nature take its course today.

There's no time to waste; it's time to make some plans. He needs to get the wheels turning faster on his next victim. Years of waiting; years of biting his tongue, doing as he's told. The meek good-boy who never put a foot wrong. A servant.

***

He enters the house through the patio and gathers two surgical gloves from the kitchen cupboard where he keeps his cleaning supplies. He pulls them over his hands and flexes his fingers until the fit is snug. From his bag he removes his most recent plunder: a stolen baseball cap and woollen gloves. He lays them out on the kitchen table, the clean oak his mother used to polish every Sunday.

Next, he picks up one of the gloves, pinched between his thumb and forefinger as if it's poisoned. He pulls it over his surgically-gloved hand, testing the fit. They're slightly large on him, which is fine – better that he can wear the surgical gloves underneath: uncontaminated DNA can mingle with the blood of victims to produce the perfect frame.

Inside the hat, loose hairs and skin cells hide in the folds of the material. He sits for a moment, staring at the ring of dried sweat and the back of the embroidered letters inside. Then: an idea. He climbs the stairs and opens the door to his mother's bedroom.

The air smells of her talcum powder and Chanel No. 5 perfume, which he still sprays into the air every month or so when the scent starts to fade. Everything is as she left it when she went to hospital and never came home again: the chintz bedclothes are perfectly smooth, with one cushion positioned in the centre of two pillows. The dressing table is framed by a row of her 'lotions and potions', as she called them: face moisturiser, night cream, serum, face powder, and many other creams, powders and gels of unknown purpose.

He sits at the dressing table, where his mother sat for hours as she rolled curlers in her hair or wrapped it around tongs for a night out. She was glamorous in her youth; she knew she was beautiful, and she liked to attract men to her 'like bees around a honeypot'; another one of her little phrases.

She liked to entice men and see what she could get from them, how far they'd go to win her favour. Her son was no exception. She was proud of how men strove to impress her; she played a game to win their hearts and then stomp on them. A game that she showed her son how to play, on a different scale.

She liked to toy with men's hearts – particularly those who were easily won and easily hurt. She liked those who didn't question what she wanted from them: the ones less clever than the rest, or those who thought that attractive women owed them attention. She taught him not to push, not to question her, to give her the respect she deserved.

His fingers stray to the raised scar on his left forearm, the white circular burn, like a button to push when he wants to remember. He still loves her, even now. Misses her presence around the house, even though part of him sighs with relief every time he returns home and remembers that she's no longer here. That she can't hurt him now.

She taught him well, although she was a brutal teacher. His own methods take his mother's approach one step further. He likes those who are easily tricked, enticed away from their friends, into a car, down the dark alley. They deserve to be taught a lesson. They shouldn't be so stupid. They should sense the danger in him because it leaks from his every pore: if he can feel it, why can't they? They deserve their fate, just like his mother's men deserved to be cheated out of whatever they would give her.

He picks up the lotions and potions, feeling the weight of the pots and the cut-glass bottles. His mother's hands once held those jars too, not so many years ago. No one else has touched these objects. Just him. He's careful, placing them back in the exact position, lining up the edges where the ring of dust begins. He was a careless child once. He's not careless anymore. The silver scars threading across his palms tell the story of a boy forced to pick up the jagged shards of anything he broke. But he's not angry. He's grateful.

He opens the top drawer, where her silken undergarments are laid out in folded rows. Pinks, creams, light blues – all pastel colours. No black or red; his mother wasn't a whore.

He reaches to the back and finds what he knows is there: a pair of sheer stockings in a light colour, like skin.

It seems a shame to take them from his mother's drawers, as if his collection will be incomplete now. He shakes his head. His mother has no use for a pair of stockings now, and she would understand.

Staring at his reflection in the dressing table mirror, he pulls the end of the stocking over his scalp, making a tight hat from the material. There. Now he's protected from the baseball cap and the flakes of someone else's skin and dried sweat. He ties a knot into the leg of the stocking and cuts off the remaining fabric with Mother's nail scissors. Then he pulls the hat onto his head, tucking the stocking away and out of sight.

In the mirror, he doesn't look like himself anymore.

'Hi,' he says to himself in the mirror. He smiles a little, practicing a friendly, open expression. He lifts his eyebrows up from their usual hooded frown. The smile doesn't reach his eyes. Then again, it never has. Even in the old school photos stacked in the dresser drawer, never hung on the walls. She wasn't like other mothers, with school portraits on proud display. They weren't a normal family, inside their house with the doors closed and curtains drawn. Even then, he was pretending to be normal to the outside world, just like now.

He nods at himself in the mirror, smiles once more. His teeth look nice and white. 'Nice to meet you.'

His voice seems to echo, even though the room is furnished and carpeted. It's been a long time since someone spoke out loud in here.

'Okay' he says to himself. 'Tonight, we'll go out and paint the town red.'

Anonymous: How to get away with murder

By Urban Dark Reporter

*Anonymous contributor claims to advise readers on the best techniques for committing horrible crimes**

* Editor's note: This article is for entertainment purposes only; Urban Dark Reporter accepts no responsibility for any harm caused by following the directions outlined below.

Inspired by Leonard McVitie's lesson plan (check back in a few days and all will be revealed), here's an imagined syllabus for a willing pupil:

Location, Location, Location

Find a location with no connection to you; remote with no danger of being overheard. Your prey can run away, but you'll soon catch them nearby with no witnesses. If you're indoors, ensure it's easy to hose down, and be ready to abandon it if it's compromised.

Frame someone else

Plan in advance: select an unwitting person and plant evidence throughout their life. Sow seeds of doubt in the minds of their loved ones, charm their wives and children, go for dinner, and all the time, remove things and leave things behind. Steal their underwear, the hair from their hairbrush, their soiled clothes. Secrete tokens from your victims in a place they won't be found until a police search, even a box of trophies if you can bear to part with it. They'll be hard to leave behind but you will always know where they are.

Choose your victims

The ideal prey won't be missed. However, children are easy to grab and transport, and most of them follow instruction from adults. Adult males are available and incautious, often putting themselves in risky situations. Teenage girls won't fight, and often don't recognise a threat until it's too late. And they can't take their booze. Adult women are a viable target but you must ensure vulnerability and lack of self-defence skill. Avoid fat ones of any demographic. They're hard to transport, difficult to undress and disposing of their bodies is annoying.

Destroy all the evidence

If there's no body to find, there's no murder investigation. After death, a body is a big sack of meat between 5 and 6 feet long, and it is difficult to transport. Transport to the kill site while still alive. After death, chop it up into small pieces. Do that naked if you can: clothing fibres get everywhere. Work fast before it starts to smell.

Don't get caught

The most admirable hunters were never caught: Zodiac, Jack the Ripper, Gilgo Beach Killer. But even better are the ones we don't know about: who covered their tracks so well that no one realises there's a serial killer at work. In my town, there's no police investigation. No missing persons posters. No one looks for my victims, because no one knows they're even missing. Clean up your mess and leave no trace.

A clean getaway

Be ready to abandon your life as soon as your crimes are discovered. Waste no time. If you have followed my instructions then you, too, can flee without repercussions.

Comments:

1488-HH: LOL avoid the fatties. That's some advice everyone should take in all situations

OGmagus: This is DARK. Has anyone called the police on this guy?

DDT: This is disgusting and should be taken down immediately. I used to come to this site for the interesting snippets of 'little-known' Lancashire history, but this post proves that this site has gone to the dogs. You're going to lose a lot of readers over this.

Phoneguy: I have several books on hiding evidence. While all of them have useful ideas, guidance on outdoor, structural, and away-from-home hiding places is always the most useful. You simply must have some carpentry experience and a lot of patience.

> Rogersmith52: I suspect you're talking about publications from Paladin Press? Interesting yes, but not well written. In many cases they've deliberately withheld information to prevent being liable for readers' crimes. Defeats the purpose, surely?

420blaze: So how do you get rid of a body though? Like ... meat grinder? Wood chipper? It's all very well telling us to get rid of it, but I need some concrete tips here. And wait though, if you do it naked doesn't that mean you leave skin flakes and pubes and stuff?

> Urbandarkreporter: The police may not be looking for you, but we are.

Combaticus: Unsubscribed. This website needs to be shut down.

Zoe

'Mum'll say I need to know where you're going tonight and who with,' says Dad.

Zoe's phone vibrates in her jeans pocket, but she can't check it easily, not without Dad getting pissed off. She glances at the clock on the wall above the oven, a giant train-station-style clock that she knows Melanie probably bought in TK Maxx thinking it looked real classy. Wrong.

'You can call her Helen, Dad. I'll know who you're talking about.'

It's nearly seven, and Dane said he'd pick her up about ten-past. Maybe that's why her phone is buzzing; maybe he's outside, waiting for her. She jiggles her leg under the table, jiggle jiggle jiggle. It gets some nervous energy out, but also she read in a magazine that it helps you lose weight if you're always fidgeting. Maybe if she jiggles her leg enough she can burn off the milkshake she had with Abbie today when they should have been in IT class. Abbie had wanted to talk to her about something, but they got distracted by a comment from Abbie's most recent Instagram stalker.

Melanie sees her looking at the clock and smiles at her. Zoe doesn't smile back. Mel doesn't notice, she's already too busy trying to get Bennie to eat a chicken nugget. He won't open his mouth and keeps turning his head away and shouting 'noooo'. It's quite funny to watch.

Dad cuts a piece of chicken nugget and offers it to Lucy, who opens her mouth straight away because she's never said 'no' to a morsel of food in all three years of her life. Bennie wriggles off his chair, trying to climb down. 'No, baby. It's dinner time,' Melanie begs her son. 'You still need to eat. Just one nuggie.'

Zoe winces at 'nuggie'.

'So?' says Dad.

'Oh, the pub. With some friends.'

'And Dane?'

She nods.

'How old is he again?'

'Fifty-seven.'

Melanie looks up at Zoe, eyes wide, and then quickly gives Tony a sharp look as if to say 'and you're alright with this?'

Zoe suppresses a grin.

Tony shakes his head and pats Melanie's free hand. 'And how old is he really?' he says in a calm voice.

Zoe laughs. 'Twenty-four. Same age gap as you and Mum had. And you guys were really happy for years.' She sneaks a glance across the table, but Melanie doesn't react.

He nods. 'Which pub?'

'None of the bad ones,' says Zoe. Having a former police officer for a Dad has some advantages and some disadvantages. She knows which rough places to avoid, but she also knows he hates her going out drinking when she's still underage. Him and Mum did it when they were the same age though, so he can't say much.

'Don't go to the Phoenix. There's some really rough types drink in there.'

'Ew, that's a smelly old man pub anyway.'

'Be back by ten.'

Zoe opens her mouth wide in shock. She's gutted. She needs to stay out as late as Abbie, otherwise she'll have to leave Abbie and Dane alone in the pub. 'Abbie gets to stay out as late as she likes.'

'You're not Abbie.'

Even though Abbie insists she doesn't fancy Dane and is back with Max, she probably wouldn't say no if she got the chance. Abbie's the kind of best friend that's really fun, but you wouldn't pick her as your first choice for help in a life-or-death situation. Or go to her for advice. She'd ditch you in a second. Only a good friend for a fun situation.

Zoe can feel her face getting hot. She jiggles her leg some more and the table wobbles. 'Come on, Dad. This isn't fair. It's better if we stay in a group instead of all separating anyway.' She's quite proud of that point.

'Okay, half ten, then. You've got college tomorrow, mate.'

'Not your mate.' Zoe's phone vibrates again in her pocket. There's a text from Dane, from ten minutes ago: 'I'm outside', and another from just now: 'You coming? Or shall I go without you?'

Her heart sinks. She shoves down the last couple of mouthfuls of food, grabs her handbag and rushes out of the door, calling 'bye' over her shoulder.

The air smells of bonfires. A sudden gust of wind grabs at a kite caught in their silver birch, the kite's white tails flapping against the greying sky like they're begging for rescue.

Dane's waiting on the drive in his old Mercedes, playing weird jazz music on the stereo that she has to pretend she likes so he thinks she's cool.

'Took you long enough,' he says as she gets into the car, slamming the door hard behind her.

Zoe ignores him and slides into the bucket seat. Dane inherited the old car from his Grandpa, and he's absurdly proud of it. He waxes and polishes it once a week, and watches loads of YouTube videos about car maintenance. To Zoe it's just an old car with a funny smell inside and a tendency to struggle climbing steep hills without a jerky gear change halfway up.

She leans across and kisses Dane on the mouth, but he doesn't respond straight away. She pulls back, stung. 'Fine,' she says, folding her arms.

'I've been waiting for ages,' he says.

'You were early.' She shrugs. Tonight isn't starting off well. 'Sorry, okay? I can't help it if I have to justify all my actions to my Dad before I go anywhere. He even made me get changed.' She points at her jeans. 'I'm lucky to get out at all, really.'

'I nearly left without you.'

'Why are you so desperate to get to the pub anyway? It's only Abbie and that lot.' She watches his face carefully when she says her friend's name, but he doesn't react.

Dane sighs. 'I don't like waiting around. And I'm not used to parents like yours anymore: it's been a while since my mum cared about stuff like that.'

'Coz you're old,' Zoe jokes.

'Yeah, yeah.' He starts the car and checks his mirrors. 'It's nice that your mum and dad worry about you.'

She kisses him on the cheek and he smiles as he pulls into the road.

She wants tonight to be fun, for her friends to be at their best, and for Dane to see her surrounded by people who like her and think she's cool.

'Who else is going?' asks Dane, his tone friendlier now he's made it clear he was irritated. He's kind really, and a sulk never lasts long.

Zoe looks out of the window, watching the dark outline of hedges pass by the car as they whiz through the countryside into town.

'Who's going ... erm. Well, Abbie and Max—'

'Back together?'

'Yep, for now.' She puts on a light-hearted voice. 'Oh and watch out for Abbie; she likes older men. Like you.' She laughs and gives him a playful poke, hoping he'll tell her that she has nothing to worry about, that Abbie's dull, that Zoe's perfect.

Dane doesn't respond to the bait. He's met Abbie before, but not Abbie's long-suffering boyfriend Max. Dane actually met Abbie before he met Zoe; Abbie was the one who introduced them to each other. Abbie likes to joke that she would have got together with Dane first if she hadn't been back together with Max in an 'on again' section of their 'on again, off again' relationship. Zoe doesn't think that's a funny joke.

'And we invited Phil and Freya, but I don't know if they're coming. If Phil's there then Freya probably will be, too.'

'Which pub are we going to?' asks Dane.

Lancaster is small for a city, but there are a lot of pubs. Some good, some bad. There are some cool student bars but they are the ones most likely to ask for ID, and it's another few months until Zoe turns 18. Most are 'old man pubs' with sticky patterned carpets and a betting machine in the corner flashing its lights. Some are rough like the Phoenix, with frequent fights and a bouncer on the door even on a Tuesday night. Zoe's friends don't go to those pubs; they go to the pubs that don't check your age, the ones which accept the fake IDs Max buys on the dark web for a tenner.

'We're meeting at Richard the Lionheart, but we might go somewhere else once everyone's there. Max likes their pool tables.'

Dane nods. Zoe thinks he'll get on well with Max. She hopes so: if the two guys become friends, then Dane won't flirt back if Abbie tries anything. Not that she would in front of Max. Zoe hopes.

She reaches out to hold Dane's hand, but he only gives her fingers a squeeze and then lets go, resting his hand back on the gearstick. Zoe puts her hand back on her lap and looks out of the window.

Dane slows the car as they pass some children walking down the lane.

'Stupid kids,' he mumbles, skirting the dark silhouettes walking along the verge. 'What are they doing out here in the middle of nowhere?'

Zoe leans forward, peering into the dusk. It's a boy and a girl, about 10 or 11, wandering along the road in the dark. 'I can barely see them. They should have a torch or something.'

Dane passes them and speeds up again once they're clear. Zoe turns in her seat to look back at them, watching them grow smaller in the back window until the car drops into a dip and they disappear out of sight. Where are they going, she wonders? There's nothing along this road – no houses. And no pavement. She shakes her head slightly and turns back to face forward.

'They're gonna get killed.'

Thomas

As the sun sets beneath the horizon, the air turns chilly and a breeze picks up, bringing with it the scent of burning from the allotments alongside the train tracks. About a mile along the road, Thomas and Maggie reach a narrow lane that branches off, away from streetlights and into the darkness. Tall hedges line both sides, so big and wild that they look like they're reaching into the air to break free and turn into trees.

The lane stretches ahead into the distance before it disappears over the crest of the hill. Over the hedge to their left, thick trees grow tall and close together, all different types.

They wander along the hedge, looking for a gap they can squeeze through and into the woods. Finally, Maggie stops and peers into the tangle of hawthorns and some other hedge plants Thomas doesn't know the names of yet, even though he got a Collins Gem book of plants from Grandma last birthday.

'Here!' she says, and drops down to her hands and knees, head and shoulders disappearing into the bushes. She struggles and squeezes and there's lots of rustling, and then she pulls back and looks up at Thomas, her brow furrowed with irritation. Her cheek is scratched, and her hair is everywhere, with leaves and sticks caught in her curls.

Then her face breaks into a grin. 'I'll have to use the penknife!' She reaches into her coat pocket and pulls out her brother's stolen knife.

Thomas opens his mouth in surprise. It isn't a little Swiss Army knife like he expected, but a huge flip-knife, the blade at least 5 inches long when she opens it. Thomas's eyes widen and he freezes.

'Woah, that's massive, Maggie. That's not a penknife.'

'Isn't it? Oh.' Maggie plunges back into the bush, her hand ahead of her with the knife ready to chop through the hedge. After a minute or two, she inches forward and disappears into the darkness.

'It's like a fish knife or something. My dad has one for cutting the guts out of fish he catches.' Thomas gets down onto his hands and knees and follows her through the small gap, eyes tight shut so he doesn't get poked in the eye.

It's a tight squeeze, and twigs catch in his hair and on his duffle coat. He shoves the binoculars into his coat so the lenses don't get scratched. The ground under his knees is muddy and damp. Soil oozes between his fingers and under his nails. The earth smells fresh and good, though, and this is an adventure, even if they're trying to find an old caravan that's probably full of drug addicts, and even if Maggie has a scary knife in her pocket.

In the woods it's darker than it was out on the road, and it's hard to tell whether the sun is fully set yet or not. They'll have to keep an eye on Maggie's posh watch to make sure they don't stay out too late.

'It's seven-oh-three,' says Maggie when he asks her for the third time.

'OK. Tell me when it's eight-oh-three, okay?'

Maggie claps her hands. 'Auntie Janet won't notice if we're a bit late back. She's busy working. Or she's fallen asleep on the sofa. Either way ...' Maggie holds out her hands palm-up and shrugs, looking like Bart Simpson about to do something naughty.

They pick their way through the trees, their footsteps thumping on the pine needles and rotten leaves carpeting the forest. The ground feels springy under Thomas's feet, as if he could bounce up and down on it like a bed.

'Do you know which way we're going?' Thomas asks.

She shakes her head. 'Just gonna wander around until we find it. If not tonight, we can always come back another day and keep looking. It's not going anywhere.'

They walk in a straight line from the hedge, and Thomas pays attention to trees they pass, noting any distinctive markings in the hope they can find their way back to the gap in the bushes.

The forest light brightens as they emerge from the trees into a large expanse of waist-height grass, like a meadow. Saplings pop up here and there, tendrils reaching for the sky and blowing about in the wind. And there in the distance is the old asylum, silhouetted against the dark sky, with empty window frames, dark stone and roof spikes.

Thomas draws in his breath. Maggie stops walking.

'Wow. It looks like Wayne Manor in Batman!'

Thomas nods.

'Pass me your binoculars, will you?' Maggie holds out her hand.

Thomas unloops them from around his neck and hands them over, grateful to get rid of their weight. He wonders if he can persuade Maggie to carry them for a bit.

She holds them up to her face, peers at the building, her only movement the tip of her finger as it twiddles the focus to get it just right. 'It's blurry, I can't ...' Her words trail off.

'You can't what?'

'It's okay, I can see now. I can see—' she stops talking. She still doesn't move, the binoculars held firm to her eyes.

'What, Maggie? What can you see?' He tries to grab the binoculars but she wrenches them away, focused back on the derelict building.

'Get off,' she hisses. 'Shut up for a sec.'

Thomas folds his arms. 'I carried them all the way here and they're mine. Give me a go. What are you even looking at?' He looks up at the building, which seems to glare right back at him. He shivers. 'Come on, Maggie.'

She lowers the binoculars and Thomas reaches for them, forgetting his plan to get her to carry them home. This time, she hands them over quickly.

'What did you see?' Thomas holds them up and looks through them, but all he can see is the building, bigger this time, and he can't get the lenses to line up with his eyes properly. And everything's blurry.

'I thought I saw something in a window up at the top. A face.' Maggie says quietly.

Thomas lowers the binoculars and stares at Maggie. His

skin prickles with goosebumps, the hair standing on end. 'What? Really?' He shivers.

Maggie's eyes are wide, the pupils enormous. Her cheeks are pale, her skin the sickly white of milk. But she's smiling. 'Really. But then I looked and looked, and I think it was a trick of the light or something.'

Thomas takes a big breath and lets it out slowly. He can't work out if she's kidding or not. There's a part of him – now that he knows Dad's been to the caravan too – that wonders if he's been here recently. Maybe he's here now, somewhere in the woods. Dad likes going for walks at night, says the air smells fresher when it's dark. Thomas scans the windows, but each frame is blank and empty; nothing moves in the asylum.

'Wanna go in?' asks Maggie.

He shakes his head. 'No way. Not tonight.'

She raises her eyebrows at him, like she's daring him. 'Maybe tomorrow then.'

'Let's find our new clubhouse and then we'll have an exploring base.'

'Clubhouse. I like that' says Maggie. 'I was calling it a den, but clubhouse is even better. We could be spies and that's our hideout.' She turns back to the forest, ready to find the caravan again.

'Exactly,' says Thomas, relieved that tonight they won't be breaking and entering as well as trespassing. He loops the binoculars back around his neck.

Maggie's really adventurous because of her brothers: they throw her around and play rough, give her scary dares and fall out of trees. She's brave and doesn't think about danger.

But Thomas isn't like that; he doesn't have brothers, and he likes being safe. Thomas has never broken a bone, whereas Maggie, Sandy, and Duncan seem to be always getting x-rays for stuff.

Mum's got enough to worry about without Thomas doing anything scary too. But now Dad's gone, maybe Mum doesn't have time to worry about Thomas. Maybe now's the time to become more like Maggie and less like Scaredy-Cat Thomas.

They turn back into the woods. It gets darker and darker the deeper they go into the forest. Big, gnarly trees covered in moss and thick bark which feels rough and scaly under his fingers as he brushes past, like stroking a crocodile or an alligator. He's looking at a tree like that when Maggie shouts 'There it is!'

It's a caravan in the middle of a small clearing, with a narrow track leading to it. Thomas has no idea how someone got it this deep into the wood, maybe years ago there was a lane and it got swallowed up by the trees.

Moss and algae have stained the once-white caravan walls to leaf-green, and it sinks on one side where a tyre is gone from one wheel. There's a window, but the glass is just as green as the rest of the outside. It doesn't look like much light gets in. Thomas draws a deep, shaky breath.

Maggie has paused too, to Thomas's surprise. She's staring at the caravan. Now that they found it, the reality is more daunting than exciting. It looks a bit too grubby and damp to be a great clubhouse for spies, that's for sure.

Next to the door, bright red graffiti makes shocking contrast with the green moss of the wall. 'MINE!' is scrawled in scarlet paint, which drips from the letters like something in 'Goosebumps'.

'Go on then,' says Thomas. He needs Maggie to be the brave one and then he can follow.

She takes a step forward, leaves rustling as she moves. Crows caw above their heads, and Thomas peers through the trees up to the grey sky peeking through the canopy.

Maggie reaches for the caravan door, hooking her fingers behind the recessed handle. Thomas winces at what could lurk behind that door: germs, insects, slime ... bad guys.

She pulls and pushes at the door, tugging at the weak handle until finally she loosens it from the frame with a crunching noise. Even once the seal has broken, it's not easy; the hinges are rusty and it's almost like the door was never supposed to open at all.

Thomas joins her and both of them lean back with all their weight, but it doesn't budge.

'Try pushing,' he pants.

After three sharp shoves there's a cracking, splintering noise as the hinges come to life. A blast of damp air hits them in the face, filled with the stench of mould.

They look at each other. Maggie's eyes are wide and her half-smile tells Thomas that they've reached the limit of Maggie's bravado.

It's dark inside the caravan. Thomas's heart is beating hard and he's having trouble getting enough air inside his lungs.

'It'll be fine. It's not scary. It's just an old caravan. Someone used to have holidays in here. Holidays are fun. Not scary at all.' Maggie's jabbering.

He concentrates on breathing steadily so Maggie doesn't hear that he's scared, and he reaches into his pocket for the torch he took from home. 'Here,' he says, handing it to Maggie.

She puts one foot up on the step into the caravan.

'Wait!' shouts Thomas, throwing his arm out in front of her. 'Shine the light in first, look around a bit from out here. We need to make sure it's safe.'

She clicks on the torch and shines it into the darkness. Thomas crinkles his eyes up so they're almost closed, ready to shut them immediately if there's anything scary. He peers into the caravan through his eyelashes.

Maggie raises her foot up on the step and leans right in, blocking Thomas's view.

'Hey, I can't see!' He nudges in beside her so they're shoulder to shoulder in the doorway, following the torchlight.

'Woah,' whispers Maggie.

Zoe

There's a sharp bite to the autumn air as Zoe and Dane cross the car park towards the Richard the Lionheart. It's usually full of college kids, so it's not an old man pub, but the decor is similar: scuffed leather bar stools, a quiz machine and that stale-boozy smell that hovers over everything. The barman is youngish, about the same age as Dane, and the jukebox has all the right music on it. Zoe's certain that Abbie would have arrived earlier than everyone else so she can pick the first five songs and look cool sitting there tapping her cigarette on the table as everyone arrives.

Zoe hangs back and lets Dane go in first. She hates walking into a place first, likes to sidle in behind someone and make an entrance in her own time.

Abbie's a dancer, and even now she's standing at the jukebox choosing songs, doing ballet-style leg stretches under the pretence of absent-mindedness. But actually she has a ferocious and constant awareness of how she looks to others. Her long red hair reaches down to her waist, and she's constantly flipping it around or pulling it up into a ponytail only to take it down again a short while later.

There's a stranger standing close next to her, helping her select songs. He's wearing a baseball cap and isn't bad-looking, for an older guy. He's not as old as Zoe's Dad, but he's definitely at least 10 years older than Dane. Maybe he's Abbie's type 'on paper': she's dated older guys in the past, while her and Max were broken up. Abbie's pointing at the song list, chatting with the guy when Zoe taps her on the shoulder.

'Zoe! Dane! Darlings!' Abbie runs over and throws her arms around Dane, kissing him on both cheeks, continental style. Yep, there's an unlit cigarette between her fingers, Zoe notices. What a poser.

Dane looks awkward, as if he's not sure what to do with his hands, Zoe sees with a twitch of a smile. He does like Zoe best. He does. It's her he's going out with, not Abbie. And he *could* have gone out with Abbie, if he wanted to. He said to Zoe that Abbie is too immature, even though she's six months older than Zoe. But to someone who's twenty-four like Dane, they all must seem immature sometimes, even when they're as mature as Zoe.

'And Zoe, my fucking darlingest,' Abbie turns her attention to Zoe and does the same two-cheek air kisses but doesn't throw her arms around Zoe and pull her body close, like she did with Dane.

'Fucking darlingest,' Zoe repeats, her eyebrows raised. Abbie likes to shock people, and her newest approach is outrageous swearing. 'Nice to see you too, Abs.'

Abbie blows a kiss to jukebox guy, leading them to the table she's occupied in the corner, as if she's the host for the evening. Max is there, sitting next to their coats and looking a little gloomy.

'Hey Maxie,' says Zoe, sitting down next to him at the table. There's a half-drunk pint of Guinness on the table in front of him, his hand wrapped around the glass.

Abbie and Max are an odd pairing, Zoe has always thought. They've been together since they were about fourteen, which is practically forever compared to everyone else's short-lived loves at this age.

Max is quiet and gentle, with a curly mop of dark hair always falling over his eyes. He's into geek stuff: graphic novels, Marvel, Star Wars, and Star Trek, all the stuff that doesn't get you the girls usually, but it suits Max. He's an amazing artist, and he's always carrying a sketchbook where he's drafting his own graphic novel, something about multiverses and a little boy who turns out to have superpowers. Zoe hasn't read it, but she's seen the drawings and they're fantastic.

'She's going to break up with me again,' says Max, quietly.

When Abbie and Max first got together, Abbie was quieter and less arrogant. If they met now, Abbie wouldn't look twice at Max because she'd think she was out of his league. That's probably why they keep breaking up.

But if Zoe had to choose, Max is a ten-out-of-ten person, whereas Abbie maybe gets a seven. And Abbie's got some weird competitive thing with Zoe, where Abbie tries to charm and flirt with every boy that Zoe likes until the boy has a crush on Abbie instead. Dane is one of the only boys this hasn't yet worked with, but Abbie's still trying hard.

'Surely not,' she reassures Max. 'She'd have told me if she

was, and she hasn't said anything.' Zoe looks up at Abbie, who's back pushing jukebox buttons with one hand and flicking her hair with the other. She knows she's on show, and sure enough: jukebox guy is leaning against the bar, watching.

Max shrugs. 'You saw her flirting with that guy. There's something going on with her. Probably for the best anyway, long term.' He drains his Guinness just as Dane returns to the table carrying a taboo and lemonade for Zoe, a lager for himself.

'Pint, mate?' Dane says. 'Didn't realise you were running on empty.' He nods at Max's drained glass.

'Please.' Max smiles and nods, and Dane returns to the bar, sidestepping Abbie's ballerina impression as he passes.

'We were never going to last forever,' shrugs Max.

Zoe puts her head on his shoulder. 'You're better off with someone who treats you nicer anyway.'

Abbie announces herself with a cough and throws herself into the chair next to Zoe, the one she'd wanted Dane to sit in so they could hold hands.

When Dane gets back carrying Max's pint, he has to sit on Abbie's other side. Abbie can barely suppress a smile and Zoe thinks she sees her shuffle her chair slightly closer to Dane's. Zoe takes a big gulp of her drink. Tonight's going to be a long night if Abbie's in this kind of mood.

As soon as Dane sits down, Max leans forward in his seat, looking each of them in the eye in turn. 'What did you guys think of the article I sent?'

Abbie groans dramatically and covers her face. 'Not this again. Get a life, Max.'

Zoe shakes her head and pats Max on the arm. 'It was really interesting. I had no idea about that guy.'

Dane nods. 'Me neither. Good article, mate.'

'Do you guys know anything else about the history of the Lune Asylum?' He points upwards, indicating the hill over the town where the old derelict hospital stands.

Dane and Zoe shake their heads.

Abbie slurps her drink and turns in her chair, gazing out across the bar as if looking for better company.

Max blushes but carries on. 'I found some stuff online about that old serial killer, McVitie, and kept looking into it. It's how I ended up writing the article, there's so much stuff because he was so prolific. So much writing. He was this *insane* creep, like totally psycho. It's taken them years to catalogue everything at the library.'

Abbie faffs with her hair and exhales loudly. 'No one cares, Max.'

Zoe flashes a look at Abbie. She's creeped out by Max's ghoulishness, but she doesn't want to hurt his feelings. She opens her mouth to reassure him, but Dane's faster: 'This is fascinating stuff, mate.'

'But there's something else I found too. There was a serial killer they never caught; in Lancaster about 20 years after him too—'

'They *always* say stuff like it's a serial killer, Max. That's how these newspapers get readers: by making shit up.' Abbie folds her arms, a triumphant smile on her face.

'That isn't even the thing, though.' Max's eyes are wide, the pupils huge. He looks really intense. Although he's into the true crime stuff, Zoe's never seen him like this. Usually, Max talks in a tone that implies he can't believe that these kinds of monsters exist. It's like he wants to understand them, but can't, no matter how much he learns about them. But tonight there's an extra intensity and glee to him as he talks, his spine straight and body held unnaturally still. Zoe can't look away. She doesn't want to hear, but she feels compelled to listen.

'The police never caught the one in the '80s. He got away with it. They called him Mr X.' Max grins, leaning across the table. His eyes flick from Dane to Zoe and back again.

'That's a creepy name too.' Zoe frowns. Something about this Mr X thing sounds familiar, like she's heard about it before. But she can't have: she's never been interested in crime and would have shied away from any TV documentary or article. Must be a weird déjà vu.

'How many victims do they think he killed?' Dane's leaning forward in his seat.

'They have no idea. Maybe around 15, maybe twice that. It's all pretty much undocumented by official sources, because he left so little evidence behind. The police tried to keep it quiet because they knew so little. But I follow some local crime forums and stuff—'

'On the *dark web*.' Abbie interrupts, in a voice similar to Christian Bale when he says '*I'm Batman.*'

Max barely notices Abbie's interruption. 'Sometimes, yes, on the dark web.'

Abbie lets out a 'humph' and turns back to stare out at the pub.

'They're amateurs, the other people on the crime forum,

but they're using FBI techniques. Like the Behavioural Science Unit: they look at the crimes and come to conclusions about the person who committed it. And link them together. And they think Mr X might have learned some techniques from McVitie – the lunatic guy I wrote my article about.'

Dane nods, enthralled. 'How is that possible? If McVitie was locked up?'

Max shrugs. 'That's what I want to find out: what's the connection? They can't be the same age, because when Mr X was operating, McVitie would have been in his seventies. Too old for hauling bodies around.' Max laughs.

Zoe pulls a face at him. 'Creep,' she mouths.

Dane nods. 'So, we know that McVitie died in the asylum, but what happened to Mr X?'

'Mr X is dead.'

Zoe laughs. 'You sound very sure about that.'

'Yeah, how do you know? He could still be out there, is all I'm saying. Like the Original Night Stalker; just in retirement.' Dane says.

'If Mr X is still alive, where has he been? Why did he stop? People like that don't just stop killing; something happens to stop them, forces them to stop.'

Abbie groans again. 'Come on, guys, I didn't come here to play Detective. I came here to get drunk and have a laugh.'

Zoe glances at Max. His cheeks are red; she can't tell whether he's embarrassed or angry. She tries to catch his eye and smile at him, but he doesn't look up from his pint. Although she feels bad for him, she doesn't want to talk about murdered girls, just as she doesn't want to get his weird texts in the middle of the night.

'Let's play a game,' says Abbie. She looks around at the rest of them with a glint in her eye. 'Let's play "I have never".'

Dane and Max groan in unison, probably for very different reasons.

'Come on, Abbie,' says Max. 'I'll summarise how that will go. I've done nothing, you've done everything, and Dane's done some stuff Zoe would rather not know about yet.'

Dane laughs loudly and Zoe forces herself to join in, slightly late.

Abbie's smile falters. 'You don't know everything about me. None of you do.'

Zoe looks at her, an eyebrow raised. What's that about? Abbie does thrive on secrets, but usually those belonging to other people, exchanged like currency.

Abbie picks up her glass. 'I have never ...' she runs her eyes across each of them, probably assessing who she wants to fuck with tonight.

'... picked up a stranger in a bar.' She takes a gulp of her drink to indicate she actually *has* done that and looks around expectantly. 'No one? You're all liars. Dane, I bet you've picked up your fair share of pretty girls in bars?'

Dane blushes and shakes his head. 'I'm not telling.'

'That's not how you play the game! You have to be honest!' Abbie's starting to sound a bit whiney and Zoe feels a little sorry for her. She's trying to liven up the night the only way she knows how.

'How about we play a different game?' suggests Zoe, trying

to redirect Abbie away from whatever course she's steering them on.

Abbie shakes her head and ignores Zoe's suggestion. Her eyes are glazed and Zoe realises that Abbie's had a lot to drink already. When Abbie's drunk it's almost impossible to stop her trajectory into destruction, like a homing missile.

Abbie stands up and smooths down her skirt. 'Nope, I want to play this one.'

'Where are you going?' asks Max, not raising his gaze from the table.

Abbie ignores him and looks around the pub, until she seems to notice something by the bar and smiles. Zoe leans around Dane to see what Abbie's looking at. It's the jukebox guy from earlier; looking over at them, a faint smile on his lips.

'Come on, Zo,' Abbie reaches for Zoe's hand.

Zoe looks at Abbie, puzzled. 'What are we doing?'

'You didn't drink. You've never picked up a stranger in a bar.'

Max closes his eyes and groans quietly. Like Zoe, he knows Abbie well enough to understand that she's on a chaos mission and nothing will divert her. She wants to turn everything upside down, manufacture drama and destroy anything that gets in her path.

Abbie takes a few steps away from the table, walking towards the bar. She turns back to Zoe. 'Bet you we can get his number.' She holds up both hands, palm out like someone's training a gun on her. 'Just getting his number; nothing else!'

'What's going on with you, Abbie?' Zoe looks at Dane and shakes her head, trying to communicate an apology for Abbie's behaviour. He must think they're so immature.

Dane won't meet her eyes.

This is awful. Zoe just wants to go home. She doesn't follow Abbie, and stays sitting at the table, staring into her drink. She's pissed off with Abbie, and worried about things with Dane, but there's also a weird niggle in the back of her mind: where has she heard of Mr X before?

Lancaster's Predator Professor: Uncovering the archives of Leonard McVitie

By Urban Dark Reporter

Second in a series of articles exploring the newly catalogued archives of Lancaster's most prolific lunatic.

Like many of you, I was intrigued by the recent article about Leonard McVitie, written by one of my anonymous UDR colleagues, so I decided to do some more research into his life. Until now, little was known about McVitie: medical files are destroyed, Lune Hospital records are sealed, and little remains of court documents. As soon as McVitie was determined 'not guilty by reason of insanity', he disappears from the legal system and public written records. There was no traditional trial, no determined sentence. They locked him up and threw away the key, for the safety of society.

What does this mean for us scholars of insanity? Until recent months, it meant that McVitie was forgotten by everyone but those who lived or worked in the asylum from the 1950s to the 1980s, most of whom are still bound by patient confidentiality.

But what happened after the trial? After he was caught, charged, and incarcerated, McVitie lived for another 26 years. What was he doing for all of that time?

As far as anyone knew, very little remained of McVitie: his body cremated, the ashes unclaimed; his few belongings destroyed. Until at some point two years ago, a young archivist began work at the John Rylands Library, new to the job and eager to get their teeth stuck into a meaty new project. In a dark, forgotten corner of the stacks, he or she found a collection of dusty boxes, uncatalogued, marked only with the initials 'LH' for 'Lune Hospital'. No one knew what the boxes contained or how they got there.

What the curious librarian found was McVitie's entire archive, donated to the Library anonymously and promptly forgotten, until now. So, to the question of 'what was McVitie doing while he was incarcerated?' we now have the answer:

Creating his legacy. Making himself immortal. And it's all there in the archives.

More to come soon.

Comments:

DDT: Locking him up -- why not just hang him!

1488-HH: I see the Daily Mail readership have found us.

Phoneguy: Sad about his unclaimed ashes and stuff. Collectors would pay good money for those relics now.

Thomas

There's another door at the far end of the caravan, jammed shut. Thomas tugs at the handle, leaning with all his weight, but it won't budge. He wanders around, prodding at cupboards and shelves in the kitchen area, which takes up the wall opposite Maggie's sofa.

'Must be locked,' Maggie looks pointedly at her notebook.

'Maybe it's a toilet or a little bedroom or something.'

Maggie shrugs. 'Or full of treasure.' She's sitting cross-legged on a ripped sofa which runs along one wall. 'I'm calling this meeting to order,' she says in her most important-sounding voice.

Thomas tugs on a drawer handle and finds it's not a drawer at all: it's a big flat block of wood that slides out and creates a table. Then a leg folds out from below to prop it up. Clever.

He pulls it all the way out and props it up from underneath.

'I said—'

'I heard you,' says Thomas. He flattens both hands to the wooden surface and jumps up, pushing himself up onto the table. It creaks a little under his weight but stays sturdy. He shuffles around and sits with his back against the caravan wall. It's slimy and damp, but that doesn't matter because his coat is thick.

'So the first order of business. Our new spy agency needs a codeword,' says Maggie as soon as Thomas is settled.

He shifts his weight a little and the wood creaks. 'How about Skywalker?'

'That's what I was thinking too,' says Maggie, writing it down, tongue sticking out of the side of her mouth with concentration. 'I've written it backwards in case the notebook falls into the wrong hands.'

'Like a proper spy,' says Thomas. 'So, what are we actually doing here?'

'I was hoping you'd ask that,' Maggie says, in a slow voice. She pauses for a moment, thinking. 'We need a mission. A mystery to solve.'

Thomas is quiet. The idea of this clubhouse was much better than what they've actually found. The damp smell is starting to make his chest hurt, and his bum is getting damp and cold.

He doesn't know why, but he's got the same feeling that he gets when he's in the waiting room at the doctor's surgery: a gnawing dread, like something horrible is about to happen. And he doesn't want to touch anything because it all looks greasy and germy.

There is something he really wants to suggest, and still might. But first he needs to work out whether Maggie will laugh at him or not.

'Well, Agent Maggie—'

'*Special* Agent.'

Thomas tries not to roll his eyes. 'Special Agent Maggie.'

'Thank you.'

He does roll his eyes this time. 'Anywayyyyyy,' he says. 'I have a real mission for us.'

Maggie's mouth twitches and she looks a little excited, even though she's trying to hide it. 'Oh yeah?'

'I want us to find out where my Dad went.' He reaches up to push his glasses up his nose, before he realises he's not wearing them. He scratches his eyebrow instead.

Maggie purses her lips. 'Okayyyyy.'

'What?' Thomas asks. 'That's a mystery I actually want to solve.' She's really annoying. He pauses. Maybe he just needs to change it around a bit. 'The proper mission could be to get him to come back. He's been gone for ages now, and Mum won't tell me where he is.'

'I don't know,' Maggie says, in a quiet voice. 'Can he just come back like that? What if he's stuck somewhere, with no trains or something?'

Thomas folds his arms. He's spoken with Dad on the phone a couple of times, once on Thomas's birthday and once on a Saturday afternoon when Dad was somewhere very noisy; it sounded like he was watching a football game and not really in the right mood to talk on the phone.

After that particular phone call, Thomas ran up to his room and broke off the left arm of his old Transformers toy. Breaking it felt good in that moment but as soon as the arm crunched in his hand, Thomas was flooded with a terrible feeling of regret and guilt, which was worse than the original sad feeling he was trying to make go away in the first place.

Maggie folds her arms too. 'That's not a mystery. I think we should think bigger.'

'Think bigger,' he repeats quietly, frowning.

'Yeah, I think we need to get into that asylum. See what's hiding in there.'

Thomas swallows as acid rises up in the back of his throat. 'See what's hiding in there,' he repeats, as the hair on his arms stands up in the cold. Maggie's weird choice of words repeats in his head. 'What do you mean, "that's not a mystery"? Why is it not a mystery, where my Dad went? It's a mystery to *me.*'

Maggie looks up from her notebook, eyes wide. She doesn't move, and looks like she's been caught by a teacher, passing notes at school.

He jumps down from the table, his boots crashing onto the floor of the caravan with a big *thump.* 'Maggie,' he says, in a firm voice. 'You know something about where Dad is.'

She shakes her head. 'No, I don't know anything, Tom, I promise.'

He walks over to her and stands over her where she's sitting on the sofa. She looks up at him, her eyes shining in the amber torchlight. He can't tell if there are tears gathering or not. He makes a fist. 'Tell me what you know, or I'll never talk to you ever again.'

Zoe

At the bar, Abbie's giggling and tossing her hair. The guy in the baseball cap seems to enjoy the flirting. A new drink has appeared in front of Abbie and she's sipping from it while maintaining eye contact, a flirting trick she taught Zoe last year.

The guy looks up, over at the table where Zoe's sitting with Dane and Max.

The boys are talking about comics and superheroes. Zoe had no idea Dane knew anything about comics, but they're pretty engrossed in whether Christian Bale's Batman would beat Ben Affleck's Batman in a fight. They're ignoring Abbie's behaviour, which is probably the best approach.

At least they've stopped talking about murderers. She hopes Dane doesn't think Max is too geeky or boring. Or weird.

'And Squirrel Girl would beat everyone!' shouts Max, and a laugh explodes from Dane, a loud, happy laugh Zoe's never heard him make before.

Zoe's keeping an eye on Abbie. Even though she wants to get away from this situation as fast as possible, she knows it's not safe to leave her friend. Plus, it's great that Dane and Max are getting on so well.

Max checks his phone. 'Phil and Freya are at the Mousetrap; they've got a good table near the arcade machines.' He drains his pint and puts the glass back on the table. 'Fancy getting trounced on Street Fighter 2?' he asks Dane.

Dane grins. 'Absolutely.'

'Mousetrap has all the good ones: Galaga, Punch-Out!!, and even Michael Jackson's Moonwalker.'

'That sounds awesome,' says Dane. 'Let's do it.' He turns to Zoe. 'Zo? Fancy that?'

'Zoe! Get over here!' Abbie shrieks across the pub.

Zoe looks up. Abbie's grinning and the guy has a wide smile on his face. Abbie's beckoning her over. Zoe looks at Dane. 'I'll just go and see if she's okay.'

Max just shrugs, but Dane nods and carries on the comic book chat. 'So what about Cavill's Superman versus pre-Crisis Superman?'

Zoe pats Dane on the shoulder. 'I'll leave you to it. We can see you guys at Mousetrap once I've tamed Abbie, okay?'

Dane nods. 'See you in ten minutes?'

***

Up close, the bar guy is definitely older, but does have a slightly handsome look about him, a bit like Paul Rudd.

'Hey Abs,' she says, glancing at the guy, who is smiling in her direction. 'The guys have gone to meet Phil and Freya.'

He holds a drink out to her. 'Your friend says you're a

taboo and lemonade girl,' he says. His voice is soft, with long Lancashire vowels.

'Thanks,' she takes the drink. 'We're actually just about to go somewhere else.'

'We'll go find them after this drink.' Abbie raises her glass to toast.

Zoe resigns herself to an extra few minutes before they can join the boys. She raises her glass and takes a sip.

'I'm Paul,' he says, making eye contact with her from under the brim of the hat, which Zoe can now read the slogan on: 'F.B.I. female body inspector.'

'Nice hat,' she says with a grimace.

The guy laughs. 'It's not mine. I'm wearing it to win a bet with a friend.'

'It's totally disgusting,' sneers Abbie. 'I can't believe you'd walk around wearing something so misogynistic.'

Paul laughs and agrees with her. 'He said I couldn't pull it off. But you two are talking to me, so I guess it's not as repulsive as my friend thought.'

'Pretty repulsive though', says Abbie, giggling into her drink. 'I don't even know why someone would make that. And then you paid money for it.' She mimes gagging on her fingers. She's leaving the mischievous, flirty stage of drunk and is rapidly entering the insulting stage. This is a familiar pattern to observe with Abbie: the escalation of hostility to men she's enticed earlier in the night. Almost as if she eventually detests any man who is interested in her. Especially poor Max.

It's happened before: Abbie flirts her way into the sights of a guy, drags Zoe along with her and then a couple of drinks later, she's rude to the guy and Zoe has to apologise, make up for it and restore the bruised egos Abbie leaves in her wake. It's an annoying pattern. Zoe plans to talk to Abbie about it in the morning when Abbie's sober.

For now, though, in the harsh glare of Abbie's snark, the man's attentions turn to Zoe.

'Well, it was nice to meet you, er ...'

'Paul,' he says, a sparkle in his eye as if she said something funny.

'Paul,' she repeats. 'But we're having a night out with our friends, so we should go.'

'Don't escape so quickly, Zoe.'

She flinches at his use of her name. It's too familiar from a stranger, like he's taking something from her.

He continues: 'I'm only just getting to know you both.'

'Yeah, Zo,' says Abbie. 'The conversation's barely getting started.' She wiggles her eyebrows at Zoe, clearly referring back to her earlier challenge.

'Tell me about you, Zoe. Where are you from, what do your parents do, what do you want to be when you grow up?' He rests his elbow on the bar and cups his chin in his hand. The muscles on his bicep pop out, veins threading under the skin.

She gulps the drink, trying to finish it so they can leave.

Abbie takes over, her eyes twinkling with mischief as she knows how annoyed Zoe will be. 'She's from around here, her dad's a policeman and her mum's rebuilding that creepy old mental asylum in Flagstone Woods. And she wants to be a kept woman.'

Zoe glares at Abbie, not caring what the guy thinks of them anymore. 'Shut up, Abbie. None of that is right, anyway.'

The guy's staring at Zoe, as if Abbie just told him she was next in line to a throne or something. 'Flagstone Woods, eh? Your mum's, what, a builder?'

Zoe gives a non-committal shake of her head. 'An architect. Come on, Abbie.'

'An architect. Working on the hospital redevelopment, I guess?'

'Mmhm.' Zoe taps Abbie on the arm. 'Let's go meet the guys.'

Abbie shakes her head. 'They ditched us. Fuck them.' She turns back to her drink.

'They didn't ditch us; we're going to meet them.'

Abbie shrugs. 'Probably both jealous because we're talking to other guys. I can't be doing with that kind of negativity.'

Zoe purses her mouth. Might Dane be angry? It's not like she was flirting or anything.

He shrugs and slides another drink to Zoe and one to Abbie. 'One more for the road, girls. Then you can go find your Prince Charming.'

Abbie grins. 'I never say no to a free drink. Let's pick some more songs on the jukebox! Wanna dance?' she asks the guy.

***

One drink later, Zoe's legs are wobbly, and she holds onto the bar for support, closing her eyes for a second. 'I feel a bit weird,' she says, trying to enunciate her words.

The guy slides a bar stool over to her and she climbs onto

it. 'Sounds like you can't take your drink, young lady.' The room around her shifts and spins, like she's on a boat.

She does a quick calculation in her head; she's had about four drinks. One from Dane and one, or two – she's not sure now – at the bar with this guy and Abbie. Not enough to feel like this. She's so tired.

But there are empty glasses in front of her. More than she remembers drinking. She looks at Abbie, who's half-swaying, half-leaning against the FBI-hat guy, her eyes almost closed. Abbie looks just as tired as Zoe feels.

Zoe rests her elbows on the bar and puts her head in her hands. She could close her eyes for just a minute, try to stop the spinning and the tiredness. The jukebox music sounds weird in her ears, like she's under water or it's slowed down.

Where's Dane? Mousetrap. Not far.

'I need to go,' she slurs, and slides from the barstool. She grabs her handbag and chucks her phone inside. She feels like she's floating. Holding her head up is difficult, like it weighs a hundred pounds.

She walks carefully towards the back door of the pub, struggling to walk straight and stay upright. 'Need to find Dane.'

'Let me help.'

She feels an arm around her shoulders, propping her up and walking her towards the exit. Then everything goes black.

Helen

'You wouldn't believe what your daughter's done,' Tony says, when Helen picks up her mobile.

'*Our* daughter,' says Helen. She's in the bath, trying to make the most of her night at home alone, but not managing it. The idea of the evening was more idyllic than the reality: her bath water is cold, and her fingertips are beginning to crinkle.

'Yep. But she's just as obstinate as you were at this age, so I'm giving you full ownership today.' His tone is light-hearted, so Helen can tell it's fixable.

'Hang on a sec.'

She switches the phone to speaker, sets it on the side of the bath and dips her head underwater, running her hands through her thick hair and feeling it float around her face. The water dulls her hearing and her heartbeat thuds in her ears. As she stands up from the bath, water pours from her hair and runs rivulets down her back.

Wrapped in a towel, she picks up her phone and trails damp footprints along the corridor to her bedroom. She props up pillows onto the headboard and settles onto the bed.

'Okay, what's the little rebel up to?'

Tony's exaggerated sigh tells Helen that whatever he is about to moan about isn't an emergency. Zoe's being Zoe, winding up her Dad and doing what she wants to do.

She knows her ex-husband well, and he's about to launch into a long-winded explanation of his frustration with Zoe. And he'll expect Helen's sympathy, even though she deals with their daughter's teenage tantrums and drama every single day. It was worse a couple of years ago; seventeen-year-old Zoe is much easier to deal with than fifteen-year-old Zoe, but Tony won't know that because he was immersed in baby twins back then and had very little time for his oldest child.

'Well, that's just it. I don't know. She's gone out, says she's gone to the pub with some friends.'

'Hmmmmm. She did she say she was going to do that. Which friends? Which pub? Did you ask?' Helen tucks her feet under the blanket and settles in for a long chat. She can hear the kids in the background, their high-pitched chattering to Melanie, and Melanie's lower-pitched replies.

'Of course I asked. She said she's with her boyfriend, Don?'

'Dane.'

'Yeah, that's the one. He's fifty-seven years old apparently.'

'That's about right. Who else?'

He pauses for a long time. 'She did mention someone ...'

Helen runs through the mental list of Zoe's friends. 'Sarah?'

He's still quiet.

'Abbie?'

'Yeah, that's one. Don't think she mentioned any others.'

'Okay, well make sure you wait up for her. I'm not sure about that Abbie. Bit of a troublemaker, I reckon.'

'Takes one to know one.' He chuckles. 'But yeah, I'll wait up. She promised she'd be back by half ten anyway.'

'That's good. If you're lucky she'll be back by midnight,' Helen laughs. Tony joins in.

There's whispering on the other end of the phone. 'Gotta go, time to put the kids to bed.'

Helen's used to this; when they're getting on best, Melanie's always hovering nearby, ready to pull Tony back and away. It wouldn't matter if it was only Helen, but Melanie's just as weirdly jealous when Zoe needs her Dad.

'Wait, there's something I need to ask you about.'

Tony's quiet on the other end of the line.

Helen is unsure whether to ask – whether she wants the answer. 'I saw an article in the newspaper today, some investigation about some missing teenage g—'

'That journalist's sniffing around again, is she? Janet Mitchell.'

Helen suddenly realises. J. Mitchell – the author of the article. *Janet.* Of course. That's why the name sounded familiar. 'You know her?'

'Well, I've not met her. But she's been pulling stories out of her arse for months. One of my old colleagues told me about her the other day. No substance to any of it.'

Helen giggles. 'This is so funny, she—'

'She's a doorstepper, nothing more. Worse than the paparazzi. Has a bee in her bonnet about the local force, has had for years – even before I retired. Thinks they're all incompetent and wants to *expose* them, or something. She's really ramped up her game lately too.'

'Her article said there's a serial killer, after teenage girls.'

'Is she still on that? Absolute nonsense.'

'Ah, well. I guess I can ask her myself.'

'No evidence at all—' Tony stops talking. He's just registered what she said. 'Ask her yourself? What?'

'She lives next door. I knew I recognised the name when I saw the article earlier. I didn't know she was a journalist.'

Tony chuckles to himself. 'Good quality neighbours you have over there.'

Helen thinks about the family next door: an adorable little boy, with blue-framed glasses that magnify his blue eyes. And Janet: always gives a friendly wave. 'They're fine, thanks.'

Tony splutters. 'Sure, until you get involved in a scandal, she'll be all over it. And none of what she writes will be accurate. Or true.'

'Well, luckily I wasn't planning to participate in any scandals soon.'

He's not listening. 'Oh, and the husband too. We had him for questioning as a suspect for some serious shit a few years ago, when I was in the force. Couldn't pin it on him, but right place and right time; no smoke without fire.'

She has a vague recollection of the husband but hasn't seen him around for a while. Good-looking guy, although not Helen's taste: tattoos and muscles. She sits up, pulling the towel tight around her chest. 'Alright, thanks for ringing. Text to let me know when Zo gets in.'

Helen drops her phone on the bed and folds her arms across her chest, chilly from sitting wrapped in a damp towel. Zoe's responsible and Dane will look after her, but this age is tough on Helen. Zoe tests the boundaries all the time and Helen wants to let her.

But Helen remembers what it's like to be seventeen. She remembers the stupid decisions and dangerous choices she and her friends made. Sleeping in the back of a hippy man's van on the seafront throughout the summer of 1983 was one particularly low point. He sold cannabis to local teenagers and she thought he was dreamy. She's lucky nothing terrible came out of those bad decisions. She wants to let Zoe make some mistakes, but none drastic or unfixable. And she doesn't want to cling onto her too hard, because that's even more dangerous, making kids lie and pull away even faster. It's a tough balance, and a tough age.

She texts Zoe: *Have a good night. Be safe. Go home when you said you would – Dad's worried. Love you x*

Her thoughts drift back to the faces of the missing girls in the Lancaster News. She can't shake the story from her head. All so young, skin still smooth, long hair worn thick and loose, smiles still hopeful.

She hopes they were runaways, not something worse.

Him

Even when she slips into unconsciousness, she seems to possess an unnerving control over her body. She's easy to pick up and slide into the boot of his car. Her legs tuck neatly under her body and she curls up, like a sleeping child on the bare metal of the stripped-back car. Her breath steams from her mouth.

There's a flutter of excitement in his chest as he looks down at her. She's perfect, just as he expected when he first saw her.

It is all working out very well tonight. He had waited outside the pub, skulking around the car park in the dark waiting to see who went in. No need to commit to entering until there's a viable target, he's very clear on that.

He settled himself on a stool, watching the quiet one in the mirror behind the bar. The quiet ones are always the most fascinating: they suffer in silence but fight hard, clinging to life for longer than the others. You really see the light in their eyes fade away as they die.

The evening passed quickly, watching these teenagers and their interactions. The curly-haired boy out of his depth, struggling to keep up with his feisty and unpleasant girlfriend.

He'll soon outgrow her. The older guy, new to the group and not fitting in, and unsure whether he wants to anyway. He sits apart, joining in the conversation but never driving it.

He is a good judge of character and can assess a situation accurately with just a glance. The prey doesn't stand a chance against a hunter like him.

He drank more drinks than he intended, blending into the background, watching this group. Watching Abbie attempt to control everything around her: the music, the conversation, her friend and the boys. And when her iron grip on everyone started to slip, she began to act out and flail. That was when she wandered over to him, quietly minding his own business at the bar.

Even then, though: at that stage it wasn't the right environment for him to make his move and start the hunt. Abbie's too easy, like bait tied to a stake.

But then she called over her friend. Zoe.

Pretty, apple-cheeked Zoe who's quiet in a powerful, controlled way. Zoe has no fight to impress, doesn't talk to be noticed. She's confident that she'll be noticed for herself, not for her bids for attention. He likes the way she moves, gracefully and with purpose. Just right. Even then he didn't intend to do anything; not with the two guys hanging around. There will always be others: other girls, other days. His thumb moves to the circular scar on his arm: his mother taught him patience, to wait his turn and bide his time.

But then Abbie said the words that sealed little Zoe's fate. *She's from around here, her dad's a policeman and her mum's rebuilding that creepy old mental asylum in Flagstone Woods.*

And he knew why this girl looked familiar. And Abbie delivered her to him.

And then the boys left, and everything shifted. It was a gift. This opportunity was just too good to miss. Little Zoe was all-too-quick to accept an extra drink, and then her eyes glazed over. She relinquished all agency as her friend stumbled around the car park, staring at her phone, mumbling about getting a taxi home.

***

Tonight will be excellent fun, he can tell. It's been too long since he had one like this, clean and untainted.

To an ordinary male, he's sure she would look sexually enticing, particularly with her dark hair all ruffled and her cheeks reddened with alcohol and benzodiazepine. To him, she is alluring in a different way. She's the most expensive dish on the menu, and he's selecting her for consumption.

Her wrists are tender and thin, incapable of much physical strength and unable to fight back if he pinned her down and crushed her windpipe with his thumbs. Her skin is so white it's almost see-through. It would tear like the skin of a peach if he bit into it.

'You're such a pretty girl,' he whispers. 'I bet you're exactly right.'

He has no idea what will happen next; it's out of his hands. If he's lucky, he'll have her all to himself. He closes the boot lid and sits in the driver's seat.

He glances into the rear-view mirror to check the girl's

companions haven't returned, but they're nowhere to be seen. His reflection in the mirror reminds him he's still wearing the repulsive baseball cap on his head. He rips it off and throws the hat out of the window onto the tarmac of the car park. Next he removes the stocking from his head and puts it in his pocket to dispose of later. He rubs his hands over his scalp as if to erase the hat's presence.

Even if her mother never finds out where her precious little girl went, he will know. *If you take something of mine, I'll take something of yours* – that's the way it goes. So, he did.

Zoe

She opens her eyes and it is dark all around her. She's so tired. Her eyes keep closing even though she doesn't want them to. She wants to be awake.

Where is she? It's freezing cold and she can't stop shivering, her teeth chattering and her muscles almost frozen in place. Her mouth is dry and there's the faint tang of vomit lurking at the back of her throat.

She tries to sit up but it's hard, her body doesn't want to obey her instructions. She tries again, but she bangs her head on something and slumps back down.

It's noisy. There's a rushing noise, like a river. Like water?

Like an engine.

Is she beside a road?

Her brain just won't work. It's worse than the most intense hangover she's ever had.

Beside a road in a box.

A box? Why would she be in a box? Why would she be beside a road?

She's lying on hard ground, like metal covered in harsh scratchy carpet. It's definitely not a bed.

So tired. She could just go back to sleep for a while.

The rushing noise sounds like an engine – is she in a car? She looks around but she can't see anything in this darkness.

She's getting jostled around and the rumbling has muffled, but she's moving more even though there's less sound. She's still in the box.

Jostle jostle jostle.

Her eyes float closed once more.

Thomas

Maggie's ignoring Thomas, clutching her notebook and writing as fast as she can. Her pen is clutched in her balled fist, the way teachers tell you not to.

'So, what do you know about Dad?' he asks, pacing the caravan.

She stops writing and shakes her head. 'Nothing. No one tells me anything, same as they don't tell you anything either.'

He reaches the far wall, the one with the locked door, and turns back to Maggie. 'But there's something.'

A small smile crosses Maggie's lips. Thomas frowns. How can she be smiling about this?

'Look, I might have overheard some stuff. But I don't know what any of it means. I'll tell you – and we can talk about Uncle Tom – but you have to agree to something first.'

'Agree to what?'

'I'll tell you what I know if we can go into the old creepy mental hospital tomorrow night.'

Thomas shivers. He crosses to the caravan window and presses his face close to the glass. It's getting dark, and all he can see is the tops of trees. His stomach feels acidic. He doesn't want to go inside that building, where there's probably mice and cobwebs and everything rotting. But his Dad, his lovely Dad who used to play football with him in the park and was supposed to help with homework and give him advice about how to be braver and better and bigger ... he's gone, and Thomas wants to find him. That's more important than anything else. Thomas shrugs. It isn't easy to talk with his throat feeling scratchy. 'Fine.' He swallows. 'We'll go in the asylum tomorrow.'

Maggie grins.

'Now tell me what you know.' He sits back on the table, his feet swinging in the air.

'Right, well, my mum said something about him going down somewhere. She said he would be away for a while,' Maggie shrugs. 'But Duncan said it's nothing to do with holidays. He says that Uncle Tom didn't want to go.'

Thomas breathes in, his ribcage expanding as he draws air into his lungs. *Dad didn't want to leave him.* Maybe he's coming back. It's as if his chest was tied up with rope, and someone just untied him. But then another thought occurs to him. 'What, like, Mum made him go?'

Maggie shakes her head. 'You can tell Auntie Janet is sad. I don't think she wanted this. *And* you're poor now. You weren't poor when your Dad was here, and I don't think Auntie Janet would have wanted that to happen.'

Thomas frowns. He doesn't like Maggie saying it like that. *You're poor.* Her posh watch glints in the torchlight and he wants to hit her. Not enough to hurt her, but just enough to make himself feel better.

'When did you last see him?' she asks.

'Summer holidays, I think.' His voice is quiet.

'Right. So, it's October now, and that's about, what? Two months ago? Three? Maybe three.' She counts on her fingers. 'He could be anywhere by now.'

Thomas folds his arms over his knees and digs his chin into his wrist. He remembers the night his Dad came into his room to say goodbye. It was dark and Thomas was asleep, that deep, deep sleep when you first go to bed, where anything could happen and you'd sleep through it. Dad had to shake him a lot to wake him up, and when he finally did wake up, it was difficult to make sense of anything Dad said, but he thinks Dad might have been crying. It was all scrambled up with his dream, where someone was shouting 'Thomas! Thomas!' over and over while Thomas paddled closer and closer to a waterfall and could feel himself getting dragged downstream.

'Thomas?'

'Hm?'

Maggie's looking at him with a frown. She must have asked a question he didn't hear. 'And then I heard Grandma say that Uncle Tom just has something wrong with him and needed to get it out of his system. That he'll be fine when he comes back. She thinks he'll be back in time for Christmas.'

'What could be wrong with him, though? Nothing's wrong with Dad.'

Maggie shrugs. 'I don't think they want us to know everything that's going on,' she says in a low voice.

Thomas scuffs his shoes on floor, pushing his toe into a

little hole in the lino. 'I heard Auntie Julie tell Mum that Dad wouldn't come back if she didn't fight for him. She doesn't look like she is fighting much. She's too busy working.' She should fight, Thomas thinks. It was more fun when Dad was around. Everyone laughed more, Mum wasn't so tired, and Dad helped Thomas with his Maths homework when it was too hard. Since Dad's gone away, no one has time and Maths isn't going very well.

Maggie closes her notebook. 'Look, I don't know anything. But Duncan said something weird about it.'

'Weird how?'

She's quiet, and unusually for Maggie, doesn't seem to want to talk any more. She looks at her feet. 'I didn't understand what he said, but it was something like how everyone thought he was the golden boy and the mighty have ... fallen?' Her voice goes up at the end of the sentence like a question, but Thomas doesn't know what she's asking.

Dad is so much fun, always playing jokes and acting like a kid too. Mum says he needs to grow up, but Thomas disagrees. Maybe that's what Duncan meant; like he's a golden boy: like a kid.

Maggie shakes her head, with a sad look on her face. 'He said that Uncle Tom's not as great as everyone thinks he is.'

Thomas balls his hands into fists and hits his own thighs. 'What? That's rubbish. How could Duncan say that? Dad's really cool. He's the reason we found this clubhouse. Duncan's an idiot, and he's telling lies.' His thighs ache where he punched himself.

Maggie's wrapped a curl of hair tight around her index

finger, and watches as the tip of her finger turns red, then purple. 'Anyway, that's all I know.'

Thomas opens his mouth to ask Maggie again; to make her promise she doesn't know anything else. But he stops, and listens. The caravan's thin walls let in a lot of sounds, like crows cawing from their perch in the trees above.

Maggie puts her finger to her lips, she can hear it too.

The faint rumble of a car engine hums in the distance.

Zoe

She's not afraid yet. She will be soon.

Something bad is happening, but her brain is just operating at, like 7 per cent battery – like when her phone battery runs low, the display dims and all the apps start to shut down – that's how she feels. Her brain has closed the app she needed to feel anything except sleepy, cold and slow. She'd be fast asleep again by now if it wasn't for this jostling.

Then the jostling stops, and she can finally get some rest.

But the lid of the box opens and it's that creepy guy from the bar, the one Abbie knew. His hat is gone, and his face is meaner, like he was pretending to be nice before. And he's right there, looking down at her in her box and she knows.

She knows what's happening now.

But still she doesn't feel scared. She just feels tired. But she knows she needs to do something.

Do something.

Do something, stupid.

This is bad.

Act.

Her limbs won't move.

She breathes in hard.

She screams the loudest, most blood-curdling scream she's ever screamed. She screams until her lungs are raw, her throat burns, and her mouth is dry.

Thomas

A piercing scream fills Thomas's ears, ripping the smile off his face. It's too loud and so quick, and then it's over as suddenly as it began.

Then there's silence. Thomas opens his mouth to say—

And then a slam of a car door. Very close.

Maggie stops giggling and they both hold their breaths. The silence is so thick it almost hums.

'What was that?'

'Switch off the light.'

She fumbles with the torch, but she can't seem to get her thumb onto the switch. The light hits the ceiling and threatens to shine at the window as she wrestles with it. Giving up, she thrusts the beam into her chest, stifling the light with her jumper.

A small ring of light shines around the torch until Maggie manages to finally extinguish the bulb. Her eyes are wide and white, glinting through the darkness. Her pupils are huge, darting around trying to see in the dark.

Thomas is unable to move. He strains his ears to hear anything, but after that screech and bang, everything is silent.

Thomas and Maggie stare at each other across the caravan; all he can hear is the sound of their ragged, panicked breathing.

'Let's go. Let's go. Oh my God, let's go home,' whispers Maggie.

Thomas loops the binoculars back around his neck and slides off the makeshift table, careful to make as little noise as possible when he lands. Maggie shoves her notebook into her pocket and grabs Thomas's hand. Maggie's breath flutters against his cheek as she whispers in his ear.

'Just open the door and run for it,' she says. 'Don't look around and don't stop.'

He nods, unable to speak. He puts his hand on the door handle and moves it slowly, wincing at every squeak and click as it turns. Maggie points at the path through the woods, the one they came through earlier, what seems like hours ago now. Thomas nods again, and then they run fast and straight like dogs let off their leads.

They hare into the darkness of the trees, and Thomas doesn't stop to close the door, or even check where the screaming came from. He doesn't look back.

DAY TWO

Helen

Helen opens a browser and types 'Lancaster missing girls' into the search bar. Pages and pages of results: teenagers missing, then found; girls from Lancaster, Pennsylvania in the United States; girl kidnapped, girl found safe; sighting of teenager; girl found dead.

She's about to search for Janet Mitchell's articles, see how much of a hack she really is, when the office door opens. 'Morning, Helen,' a voice chirps.

Helen alt-tabs to an Excel spreadsheet, and columns of numbers obscure her search results. There are no answers there. It's a deep hole with no way out. The footsteps approach her desk; she looks up.

It's Diane, Gary's assistant, carrying a stack of paperwork, an ingratiating smile on her face. Helen feels her facial muscles slacken. She nods hello.

'Just got these forms for you to fill in. If you could get them completed and back to Gary, photocopied, by lunchtime, that would be great.'

'Mmmhm,' Helen mumbles.

Diane hands over the papers. Her long nails are painted

dark red, perfectly manicured. 'A couple of us are going out for a drink after work tonight if you fancy it?' she asks.

Helen looks down at her own dull fingernails, preparing a polite refusal, but as she opens her mouth to reply the phone begins to ring. She gives Diane an apologetic smile and shrugs.

'Good afternoon, NHS Property Services, Helen speaking.'

'Ms Summerton?'

'Yes. How can I help?'

Diane pats the pile of paperwork with a red-tipped hand and leaves the office. Helen waves vaguely at her departing back.

'Apologies for disturbing you at work.' The voice on the other end of the line sounds throaty. 'Zoe's file had this listed as an emergency contact number.'

Helen's muscles freeze. She inhales sharply through her nose.

'This is Kevin Byass, Zoe's Principal at Lancaster College.'

Helen's terrified that something awful has happened. 'Is everything alright?'

'Not quite. I'm calling to discuss Zoe's attendance record.'

Relief. Not exactly an emergency. 'Right. Is there a problem?'

'Zoe didn't attend today's History revision session. You might know, the college monitors student attendance closely and as soon as it falls below eighty-five per cent, we take action.'

Helen looks up, her gaze travelling across the room. Norah is talking on the phone, Tina filing her nails. The other members of the Planning Team must be out for site visits. At the end of the room, she can see Gary through the glass window of his office, his back to her.

'Oh dear.' She doesn't know what else to say. 'It was a revision session; are those compulsory?'

A sigh rattles down the line. 'Yes. And Zoe's attendance of my History class last term was approximately sixty per cent,' says the headmaster.

Helen remains silent.

'We sent a letter home last month.' He pauses, expectant.

'I did receive that. I'll talk to her again when she gets home.'

'She needs to focus at this time of year.'

She sits up straighter and rolls her eyes. 'Yes, I know. I'll tell her again.'

'She's a good student, but it seems her attention has been elsewhere for a couple of months.'

She feels a prickle of irritation. Even years after leaving school herself, a reprimand from a teacher still makes her flushed and awkward. Her voice has a cold edge: 'I will talk to her. Thank you for calling.'

She hangs up, returning to the reports, but she can't concentrate. She pulls her mobile from her handbag to phone Zoe and have a go, give her the usual lecture.

But her phone says four missed calls: one from the College, three from Tony.

She opens a new text message. It's from Tony:

Call me back please. Urgent.x

This isn't good. Why didn't he call her work number if he couldn't get through? 'Arsehole,' she says.

She tries to call him, but it rings and rings until it hits voicemail.

Then she tries Zoe: straight to voicemail; it doesn't even ring.

'Fuck,' she says, louder than intended. She tries to focus on her computer, but finds herself staring at the screen, her eyes unfocused, while she mentally runs through what could be happening. Her breaths are short and shallow.

Zoe probably left her phone charger at home before she went to her Dad's and didn't charge her mobile overnight. The battery's dead. It's happened before.

And non-attendance at the History session, that's normal too. Just teenagers being teenagers. But still, Helen can't concentrate. She needs to do something; staring blankly at her PC screen while obsessively calling Zoe's voicemail isn't enough.

Gary pokes his head out of his office door and scans the room. His gaze lands on Helen, and she knows he'll head over soon to ask about her progress on the paperwork.

She sends Diane a quick email, promising the completed forms in the afternoon, and leaves the office carrying a folder of papers so she looks like she's going out to a meeting.

She finds herself on a picnic bench on the edge of the Lancaster Canal, around the corner from her office. A barge floats past; the captain smiles and waves at Helen. She nods to him and looks back at her phone as the boat continues under the stone bridge. A crowd of ducks gather at her feet as she calls Tony again. No answer.

'Jesus, Tony, answer your phone.'

A group of daytime drunks sit at the next bench along the canal, a Staffordshire bull terrier running around their feet and barking. One of the men looks up at her voice, then looks away again quickly.

She calls Zoe's mobile, still voicemail. Zoe has probably

been skipping classes to spend time with Dane or bunk off with Abbie. Abbie's influence has been sinking Zoe's grades for the past year. That must be it. Hopefully that's all it is. But Helen can't quell the rising panic. She has so little control over Zoe's life. She doesn't even know where her daughter is half of the time, or who she's with.

The bull terrier climbs out of the water and shakes, spraying the drunks with stagnant water. The drinkers jeer and one of them lobs an empty can at the dog, causing the dog to skitter into the path of the passing cyclist.

The cyclist swerves towards the water, missing the dog and veering dangerously close to the edge of the canal bank. 'Watch your dog!' calls the cyclist as he rights himself and continues along the path.

The drunks laugh. 'Fuck off!' one of them shouts, sticking two fingers up at the cyclist as he pedals away from them.

Helen tries to remember how to breathe. In, out – big, deep intakes of air to compensate for her shallow gasps of the last ten minutes.

'She's fine. She's probably fine,' she says to herself.

One of the drunks looks over at her, points and says something to the rest of the group. They giggle and stare at her. Helen shuts her eyes and turns back to the ducks.

Zoe got drunk with her friends last night. She'll be lying in bed at Tony's, nursing a stinking hangover and refusing to get up to go to college. Tony's probably calling to whine about their daughter's bad behaviour and ask for Helen's advice.

Finally, her phone screen lights up with a call from Tony.

She presses the green 'Answer' button and before she can say anything, the tremor in Tony's voice confirms her worst fears.

'What's happened? Is everything alright?'

His breath hisses along the line. 'Oh, God, Helen. She didn't come home last night.'

Zoe

It's like she's inside a dirty fish tank, or under water in a pond. The walls emerge from the darkness as the sun rises, October light gradually filling the space with a strange, blue-green hue. The light is green because of algae or moss – green stuff, anyway – growing over the rounded window panes.

Zoe aches all over. What happened last night? It's a minute or two before she remembers anything at all, and then the night comes back in quick bursts of images. With each flash of memory, her heart beats harder and faster. Abbie, Dane, and Max in the pub, and Abbie being difficult; Abbie talking to the guy at the bar who bought them drinks; feeling drunker than she'd ever been in her life, then blackness. Nothing.

Something awful happened.

Terrible.

There's this anxious, nagging feeling in her gut that just won't go away. Like the 'What did I do last night?' feeling of a hangover, but a thousand times worse.

The rounded plastic of the windows looks like she's in a caravan. But why is she in a caravan?

Where's her phone? She pats her jeans pocket where she always keeps it, but the pocket is empty. It must have fallen out somewhere since the pub. Since ... flashes of memory: a man's face, an arm around her shoulder.

Her mouth fills with saliva, as if she's about to vomit. She swallows, feeling her throat muscles push the bile and spit back down into her stomach. Her skin prickles with a mixture cold and fear, hairs standing on end.

Her arms hurt so much. She tries to stretch them, but they won't move. Her breath catches in her throat. There's something around her wrists. Her hands are tied together behind her back. She feels sick with fear, but her stomach feels so empty that she knows that even if she retched and retched nothing would come up.

She looks around the room again. It's definitely a caravan – the ceiling curves away at the end in that rounded way that caravans have. But no one's had a holiday in this caravan for years. It smells of decay and damp and it gets in her throat and nose.

Her mouth is so dry, but there's no water here – not even a sink with a grimy tap. Her tongue feels like sandpaper. She tries not to move it inside her mouth.

She pulls at the cord around her wrists, testing the strength of the knots. The knots are tight, and it seems like the rope is tied around something behind her.

She seems to be on the floor, lino cold and damp against her back. She sits up slowly, dizziness causing the room to spin around her as she raises herself upright. She twists around, trying to see what she's tied to. If she can just loosen the knots and stand up, she might be able to get out of this somehow. Hopefully.

Either way, she can't just sit here and wait for something to happen to her. If she has any kind of chance of getting out of this, she has to do something, and do it soon.

She takes a moment to sit still, listening. The wind rustles through leaves outside. She must be in a wood. But there's no other sound. Somewhere remote, then. She's safe to move.

She shifts forward a few inches, tugging at the rope. Her arms burn from being restrained behind her for so long.

The rope is looped around an oven door handle. If she can yank it hard enough, she can probably knock the oven door loose to open it and gain some distance. She shuffles forward; her arms pull the rope taut behind her. She hears the oven creak as she pulls. She shifts forward further, her arms pulling backward and sending streaks of pain up her arms to her shoulders. But she keeps moving. A sore arm is better than getting murdered.

Panic rises up in her throat, fizzing and burning, like acid rushing through her whole body. She closes her eyes; there's no time for that. Focus.

When she reaches the limit of the rope, she jerks forward, yanking at the ropes in a desperate effort to open the oven door. Sharp pain shears through her shoulders and upper arms as she pulls, still tangled up by the rope. She's still tied.

She sits for a minute or two, waiting for the pain in her arms to subside. She gently lifts one shoulder after another, testing the joints to ensure her shoulders are still in their sockets. They're painful but operational, no damage done.

It's still quiet. No one's heard, and no one's coming for her. Not yet, anyway. She breathes, like Mum taught her when she used to graze her knees and she was in pain: take a breath in, and out. In, and out. Keep breathing, one breath at a time and eventually she'll find a way out.

It seems like her wrists are tied together with one piece of rope, which has around half a metre of slack running between each wrist. She's limited to a small radius around the oven, but its open door means she can move further around the space.

She takes another breath, tries to remember more from the night before. She goes back to the beginning: remembers eating dinner with Dad and Melanie, the kids whining and fussing. In the car with Dane, driving through the dusk to the pub. Walking across the car park, into the doors of the pub.

Oh.

There's another flash of memory from last night.

The doors opened and there, directly across from the entrance was Abbie standing at the jukebox picking songs, just as Zoe thought she would be. But there was one detail that Zoe hadn't predicted.

Oh, my God. Abbie standing at the jukebox with the man, picking songs together. Laughing. Their shoulders touching.

Abbie knows him. Abbie knows the guy who drugged Zoe; the monster who tied her up and trapped her here.

Thomas

'Who's heard the phrase, "Here be dragons"?'

A few hands go up, Maggie's included.

Thomas lifts the lid of his desk to hide from Mr Ketteridge; he doesn't know the answer. There are his glasses, in his desk next to his Luke Skywalker pencil case and Spider-Man rubber, right where he left them yesterday. He puts them on and shuts the desk lid.

'It means there's monsters in that part of the country!' shouts Simon Tindall, who has trouble waiting for his turn.

Mr Ketteridge shakes his head.

Maggie rolls her eyes. 'No, it *doesn't*.' Thomas can feel her wriggling, trying not to blurt out, but the need to share what she knows must have got the better of her.

'Go on then, Miss Everett.'

'People wrote that on maps when they didn't know what was in that place. They hadn't been there, so they hadn't mapped it yet.'

'Very good, Maggie,' says Mr Ketteridge. He calls her Maggie when he's pleased with her and Miss Everett when he isn't. 'Map makers used to draw pictures of sea monsters and dragons in areas of the map where they didn't know what was there. And they'd write things like "Here be lions" or "Here be dragons".' He pauses and looks around the whole class, holding eye contact with each person for a moment before moving on to the next one. 'People are afraid of what they don't know.'

Maggie looks at Thomas then, her eyebrows raised. She's trying to communicate something.

'I just remembered a thing,' she whispers to him, too loudly again. 'It's really important.'

'A lot of mapmakers made mistakes, and those mistakes were passed from map to map, often for hundreds of years. And sometimes you can tell a lot by what's *not* on a map.' Mr Ketteridge starts talking about people who believed in dragons and sea monsters and it's really interesting, except that Maggie keeps poking him in the ribs.

'Tom, listen,' she hisses.

'Shhhhh,' says Thomas, straining to hear stuff about sea serpents and basilisks and explorers from the olden days.

Maggie shoves him, hard, and he slides from his chair and off the other side. 'OW! Maggie, you DICK!'

'MR MITCHELL! MISS EVERETT!' shouts Mr Ketteridge. 'I've been trying to ignore your misbehaviour, but this is just one step too far.'

'But Sir! I didn't do anything!' Thomas climbs back onto his chair, glaring at Maggie.

Maggie sucks in her bottom lip and chews on it, her cheeks turning red. She sits up straight in her chair and stares at her hands on the desk, fingers laced together like she's been as good as gold.

'Go and stand outside in the corridor,' he says, and Maggie pushes her chair back and sighs like Mr Ketteridge is the one behaving badly.

'But Sir—' starts Thomas.

'Maggie, outside. Thomas, you stay where you are.'

Thomas closes his mouth and stares hard at the top of his desk, where he carved his initials a few weeks ago.

'This is your fault,' Maggie whispers as she brushes past Thomas, and drops a scrunched-up piece of paper into his lap.

Maggie storms out of the classroom and closes the door hard behind her, not a slam to get her in more trouble, but hard enough for Mr Ketteridge to know where he stands with her. Thomas bows his head and unfolds Maggie's note. 'Knife lost. Need to go back. Tonight.'

His stomach twists and his skin goes cold and clammy. He really, really doesn't want to go back to that caravan in the creepy forest, even though he promised. That was before.

'Thomas?'

He'd rather give Maggie all the pocket money he's ever saved up in his entire life so she can buy a new knife for her stupid brother. Yep, that's what he'll do. He's got at least £54 in his money box. Maggie can have it.

'Mr Mitchell!' Mr Ketteridge is standing in front of Thomas's desk. Thomas crumples up Maggie's note and drops it on the floor, nudging it away with the toe of his shoe. He looks up at Mr Ketteridge, whose yellow waistcoat seems to have a tea stain on the chest about the size of a man's thumb. The tweed suit and waistcoat outfit makes him look a bit like Toad from The Wind in the Willows.

Mr Ketteridge's eyes flick to the floor and back to Thomas. 'Am I going to have to send you out into the corridor too?'

Thomas shakes his head. 'Sorry, Sir.'

'What's wrong with you two today?'

'Nothing, Sir,' says Thomas, sliding his foot to cover the note under his desk.

'Hummph.' Mr Ketteridge rocks forward on his heels and turns back to the whiteboard. He draws a compass on the board but doesn't fill in the eight points. 'Copy this and complete the compass points,' he says to the class, and walks out of the classroom to talk to Maggie.

A few minutes later, the door opens again. Mr Ketteridge steps into the room, holding the door open as Maggie sidles through it. Her cheeks are still a bit pink.

'Right, everyone. How'd you get on with the compass?'

Maggie climbs into her chair and doesn't look over at Thomas until they leave the classroom at the end of the lesson and go into the playground for lunchtime.

***

'I don't want to go back. Forget the knife.'

'No,' says Maggie, panting. She's jumping over a skipping rope, her voice staccato by her leaps into the air. She's pretty good at it, and sometimes crosses her arms over and loops the rope or jumps extra high to double-spin the rope under her feet.

'I can't believe you left the knife behind. I remembered the binoculars, and they were massive and heavy.' Thomas folds his arms.

'We ... Have ... To ... Get ... It,' she expels a word on every jump, which is annoying because Thomas wants this conversation to be over, with a quick and easy decision to abandon the knife. Then they can join the massive game of tig that just started in the main quad.

Maggie stops skipping, the rope slumped at her feet. 'We made a deal. I kept up my side of the bargain: I told you what I know about your Dad—'

'Not much, that's what you know.'

She shrugs. 'Doesn't matter, you still agreed.' She folds her arms and looks at him, thinking. 'How about a new deal? I'll do my best to investigate and find out more about where your Dad's gone.'

Thomas opens his mouth but Maggie holds out her hand, palm up.

'I'll ask loads of questions. And I'll tell you everything I find out. And in return we're going exploring and back to get the knife.'

'I told you, we'll put together our pocket money and buy a new one for Duncan. He'll never know what happened.'

Maggie shakes her head, flips the rope over her head to the back of her heels, and carries on jumping. 'It's ... a ... special ... knife,' she pants.

'Special how?'

Her foot tangles in the rope once more and she stops, letting the handles slip from her hands onto the cracked tarmac.

'Grandpa gave it to him. It's engraved with a special message.'

Thomas sits down on the ground and puts his head in his

hands, pushing his glasses into the bridge of his nose. 'You can't be serious.'

'I am serious.'

'Fuck,' says Thomas, for the first time in his life. He has said bad words before, like 'dick', but never the F word. It makes him feel more grown up.

Maggie sits down next to him. 'Yeah.'

'But you heard it last night, right? The scream? There's something bad happening there. Someone screamed, really loud.'

Maggie shrugs and examines her palms, picking a piece of grit from her skin. 'Could have been a fox, or someone playing a game, or anything. Doesn't *have* to be something bad. Listen,' she says, holding out her hands towards the rest of the playground.

Tig has started and kids are screaming as Josie Steadman grabs for them, her long plaits flying behind her as she runs. 'I can hear people screaming right now. It's not something bad.'

Thomas feels sick. 'But last night it sounded like something bad. Something really bad.'

He sinks his head back into his hands and listens to the playful screams, which sound totally different to the piercing shriek they heard in the woods last night.

Maggie shrugs. 'I'm going back. Tonight. If you don't come, then I'll go on my own.'

Thomas speaks through his hands. 'Fine. We'll go back.'

Him

The smell hits him as he opens the door.

Damp, mould, and piss.

There's a scrabbling sound from the darkness as the girl sits up. He pauses, waiting as his eyes adjust to the darkness. Four rooks observe from the branches above the caravan; his only witnesses.

After a moment, he makes out her shape on the floor. 'Not exactly where I left you, then?' he whispers.

'Fuck off,' she says, her voice tearful and congested. It's probably hell on the lungs, all the mould spores floating through the air in here.

She's dislodged the oven from its cavity, dragged it into the centre of the space. She pulls herself into a sitting position, her eyes watching him as she moves. Her pupils glint in the light from the doorway. She's more alert than he expected at this stage. Good for her. He likes a bit of fight in them.

'Sleep well?' he asks.

Her expression changes from watchful to furious, but she doesn't respond.

'I bet you're hungry,' he says and then pauses.

After a minute, she breaks the silence. 'You have food?'

'If you're well behaved,' he lies, using a familiar phrase from his own childhood. He hasn't brought anything.

'What does "well behaved" mean in this context?' she asks in a cold voice.

He smiles. 'Oh, I do like you.' Usually they're begging and crying by now. This one's steely. He appreciates her quiet anger; it's admirable in a way.

She shifts her position. She's leaning against the wall, her arms behind her. He moves to the sofa and sits, resting his hands on his knees and looking down on the girl, like a king from his throne looking down on his subject.

'Your name's Zoe,' he says.

She nods.

He laughs, a sharp guffaw that fills the caravan with sound.

She sees his empty hands and her eyes widen. 'Don't you at least have some water?' she asks, her voice cracking with emotion and self-pity.

'Now you sound just like the others. I'm disappointed in you.' He stands and crosses the caravan towards her. He stops when his feet are a few inches from her and reaches down to the back of her head, cupping her frail neck. She flinches and moves her face away, a shudder wracking her body. He takes a handful of her hair, still tender, still slow. Her hair is between his fingers, tendrils caught around his hand. Her breathing is rapid; she's not used to such a touch.

'What are you doing?' she asks, her voice trembling. 'Get away from me.'

She tries to kick him, but he steps back and she misses.

He brings back his fist and plunges it towards her stomach. She recoils, shrinks away from him, but the blow doesn't come. He stops just at the last moment, hysterical laughter bubbling in his throat.

She looks up at him, confused. He strengthens his grip on her hair, pulling it tight. But not too tight. The threat often has more impact than the act itself; he knows this from experience.

'Let go of me,' she shrieks, as if she can request him to stop; as if she has any power over her own destiny. She has none. It's all in his hands, literally and otherwise. In this moment, her life belongs to him.

He laughs in her face, his spittle spraying her cheeks. He leans down even closer, his forehead pressing against hers, pushing her against the wall.

She digs her fingernails into his forearm, tugging at him, trying to wrench him away. But every time she pulls at him, she causes him to yank out more of her own hair. He lets go, fingers still laced with strands of hair.

She wasn't ready for the release of tension: her head snaps back and her skull slams into the floor. The noise is louder than he expects, the caravan echoing with the force of the blow to her head. He pauses with gleeful surprise.

She makes a strange noise, a mixture between a shout and a scream. He closes his eyes, relishing the sound of raw desperation.

He hears movement and opens his eyes to see she's stood up. She must have somehow untied her rope. At the same moment, she lifts her leg, her knee smashing into his balls.

He doubles over with the pain, his eyes screwed shut, breaths fast and short. 'You little fucker,' he hisses.

She runs to the door, uttering little sobs. He straightens up and hobbles across the caravan, adrenaline overriding the pain.

She tries the other door, the bedroom door. He freezes, watches to see what will happen. If anything will happen.

She wrenches at the handle, smashes her fists on its surface. The door shakes in its frame, but the door doesn't budge.

She runs back to the door that leads outside; howling, banging on the wood. She can't get out. It's bolted, the lock too stiff for her cold fingers. She turns her head to look at him, still wrenching, pulling and pulling at the immovable bolt lock.

'Get away from me. Get the fuck away from me you fucking psycho.'

Nothing moves; there's no way out for her.

He chuckles. He's won. They both know it.

He grabs her shoulders, tripping her and she sprawls along the floor, face smashing into the lino. He winces at the crunch of her nose.

In the moments before she attempts to stand, to continue her pathetic escape attempt, she drags herself along the floor away from him. Just like Petra's vole last night.

He stands above her, watches her try to crawl away. Time seems to move slower in moments like this. She must have untied herself overnight, waiting for the moment to reveal she was no longer bound. Clever little thing.

There's a throb of pain in his testicles, blossoming up into his stomach. A reminder.

Energy surges through his body like petrol through an engine.

He grabs her discarded rope in both fists. His hands are shaking but he's still in absolute control. A laugh escapes from his lips. He is panting and his heart is pumping. He feels so alive.

She moans, turning her head a little as if she is sleeping. He stands over her, one foot on either side of her torso. He gets down to his knees, straddling her chest. In any other circumstance, for any other person, crouching in this position would seem erotic. And he supposes it is, in a way. It is erotic and fascinating for him in the same way that children enjoy coating their hands with glue and peeling it from their skin; or putting raspberries on their finger ends and slowly plucking them off with their teeth, one by one. Or picking a dried-up scab from a grazed knee.

He pulls her arms behind her back and loops the rope around her wrists, tightly this time, and crosses the ends, pulling it taut into a secure handcuff knot. He can almost feel her wrist bones crumple under the pressure. Almost.

Her eyes fly open and her hands begin to flail, grasping at the rope, at his hands. Her movements are pointless; she is helpless against his strength. Her legs kick out, pawing the ground.

'I was going to move you somewhere more comfortable,' he whispers in her ear.

A noise emerges from her throat, a gasp combined with a croak.

'But I think we'll leave you here for longer. Let you think about what you've done.'

Soon, the hands stop grasping, the arms stop flailing. Her legs stop kicking. She realises that fighting is pointless.

The girl belongs to him. She's totally, utterly his. He wishes this feeling could last forever.

Helen

The clock says 1pm. Zoe's been out of contact for around fifteen hours.

Helen returns home to a quiet house. Alfie greets her in the corridor with a wagging tail. In the living room, one of the sofa cushions is warm where he slept away the morning. She looks over at him.

'Sneaky dog.'

He wags his tail.

'Where's Zoe, Alfie?' she asks, dialling her number and getting sent straight to voicemail again; the phone is still switched off. Helen swallows her panic, replacing it with irritation. Irresponsible. Thoughtless. Selfish. A normal teenager.

She dials the office and Diana answers, giving her usual lengthy intro spiel. 'Lancaster NHS Property Services, Diana speaking, howmayIhelpyoutoday?'

Helen pats the sofa next to her, inviting Alfie to join her. He leaps up immediately and snuggles into her side, the comforting biscuit smell of his fur filling her nose. 'Diana, it's Helen.'

'Helen! You've had a leisurely lunch.' Her girly giggle

resonates through the phone and Helen resists the temptation to hang up. 'Been anywhere nice? Think you'll wander back any time this afternoon? I still need you to look at those reports, I hope you haven't forgotten.'

'I won't be coming back in, I'm afraid.'

'Why ever not? Ooh, Helen, what's the gossip?' Diana loves scandal, gossip, and drama. If there's none, she'll invent it.

'Family emergency,' she says, and realises she's never used that excuse before in a genuine situation, until now. There were the intense hangovers of her early twenties when she couldn't rouse herself from bed, and then there were a couple of days after Tony told her he was leaving, and then once more when she had a particularly bad bout of insomnia. But never for a real family emergency like this.

'Oh, dear.'

Helen can picture Diana looking around the open-plan office, widening her eyes at anyone who'll meet her gaze, pointing at the phone with her red-tipped fingernails and signalling 'scandal' to anyone who'll pay her attention.

'Anything you need to share?'

Helen pulls a face. 'I'm sure it'll be fine, but I can't be in the office for the rest of the afternoon. Can you please move any appointments and give my apologies for the staff meeting?'

'Do you know when you'll be back? I'll tell Gary.'

'No. Sorry. I have to go.'

Disappointment seeps down the line at the lack of gossip fodder. 'If you need to talk, you know where I am, love.'

'Ha.' The small mirthful laugh escapes before she can stop it. 'Thanks, Diana. I'll call tomorrow if I'm still off.'

She ends the call and stands up. Alfie leaps onto the carpet, following her with anticipation.

'Just settle down, Alfie,' she says as she walks to the telephone table by the front door. They barely use the table or landline phone any more now that they both have mobiles and contact lists. The red plastic phone looks lost, as if it's a prop in a film that never gets to play its role.

Inside the drawer there are various household odds and ends: loose buttons, biros long run dry, and there: the tattered address book. She hasn't opened it in years; all of her numbers are stored in her mobile now. But she does recall updating it five or six years ago when Zoe started secondary school, adding the phone numbers of new friends' parents each time Zoe attended a party or a sleepover.

She flicks through the pages, scanning columns of her own scraggly handwriting, suitable only for shopping lists and signatures. Here and there she comes across an entry in Zoe's careful pre-teen hand, recorded as she started to add her own friends to be just like Mum.

Eventually Helen finds the number she's looking for: Abbie's house. The ringing stops and a male voice asks 'Hello?'

She feels like a teenager herself when she asks: 'Is Abbie there please?'

Minutes pass, with silence at the other end of the line except for occasional footsteps and murmurs far away from the phone. As Helen's about to give up, the receiver crackles and a voice comes on the line.

'Hello?' Abbie sounds sleepy, her voice cracking like she needs water.

'Abbie, it's Helen. Zoe's mum.'

Abbie is silent for a moment.

'Abbie?'

'What happened?'

'I was calling to ask you that. Zoe didn't come home last night.'

'What? Oh shit.' Abbie's voice is slow, her usual enthusiasm dimmed and muted.

Helen frowns. 'I need you to give me all the information you can.'

'She didn't ... what?' There's a pause on the other end of the line and Helen hears Abbie, her breathing ragged like she's ill. 'I'm sorry Helen, I just can't think today. Last night was crazy.' The teenager laughs.

Helen raises her eyebrows, her mouth open in shock. She's just told this girl that her supposed best friend is missing, and Abbie's laughing. Laughing. Helen sinks to the floor, her back against the wall in the corridor. 'Look, I'm not interested in your drunken antics of last night, Abbie. I want to know where my daughter is.'

'I know, I know. I'm sorry. That's not what I meant.' She's talking really slowly, mumbling the words and pausing between each. She almost sounds like she's still drunk.

Helen makes a fist with her free hand, willing Abbie to talk quicker.

Abbie continues. 'Something weird must have happened; I don't remember anything after like nine o'clock and I don't remember how I got home, and I just woke up like ten minutes ago.'

A cold dread creeps across Helen's skin. 'Why don't you remember? Did you have a lot to drink?' She tries to keep the resentment from her voice.

'Not masses. Like, maybe five drinks. Maybe some shots.'

'How much did Zoe have? And when did she leave?'

'About the same. I don't know when she left. I really don't know anything.' Her voice cracks with emotion and it sounds to Helen like she might be crying now.

'Abbie, are you okay?' Helen asks through gritted teeth.

'I've never felt like this,' she says, sniffing. 'I can't think. Mum wants to take me to hospital.'

Helen uncurls her fist. 'Abbie, your mum's a doctor, right?'

'Mmhm.'

'And what does she say? Why does she want to take you to hospital?'

Abbie sniffs. 'She thinks this is more than a normal hangover, I guess.'

Helen leans her head against the wall in the corridor, feeling the bumps of the woodchip wallpaper pressing against the back of her skull. 'Did you take anything? Pills, or something? Did Zoe?'

'Nothing, no. We don't do that stuff.'

'Could someone have put something in your drink? In Zoe's drink?

'Oh fuck. Shit. Maybe. I don't know. I mean, Mum says I'm probably okay, like no lasting damage, but Zo ... maybe we were both roofied. I don't know. I don't remember anything.'

'You must know more than this. There must be something you can tell me.'

Abbie is silent.

'Who did it? Who was there?' Helen's barely holding the receiver to her ear. Alfie sticks his nose in her face, his wet nose touching her cheek. Helen presses her face against his fur. There's sniffing from the end of the phone, but no answer to her question. 'If you don't remember leaving, that means you don't remember what happened to Zoe?'

'I'm sorry. I have no idea.'

'Come on, Abbie. Give me something to go on. You were there.'

'Max and Dane might know something; like I said, I only just woke up so I haven't talked to them.'

'Right.'

'I'll give you their numbers, maybe she's with one of them. I really hope she is.'

'Yes.'

'She's probably fine, it was a quiet night in the pub, nothing happened and surely she's fine and just with Dane or whatever. I'll text you his number.'

Helen says goodbye and hangs up the phone. She remains on the floor, staring at the coat rack on the opposite wall. Helen tries to imagine how she'd react herself if a friend's mother phoned about her missing daughter. Even as a teenager, Helen would have been shocked and devastated. She would have told that friend's mother absolutely everything about the night: who they spoke to, what time they arrived and left, everything she could think of.

And maybe it's the effects of having a drink spiked, and maybe it's just who Abbie is, but Helen had to drag information from Abbie. Behind Helen's panic, the acid burning in her stomach and the clammy skin all over her body, something niggles about that call. Something lurks in the silences and hides behind the things not said. What is that girl concealing?

Zoe

Is it possible Abbie knows him, Zoe's kidnapper? Is she involved? Her friend is impetuous, irresponsible, and sometimes a total bitch, but surely she's not a bad person, not someone to give a moment of time to someone truly evil.

Abbie would have gone to the police as soon as she noticed Zoe was missing. The police are looking for her right now. They have to be.

But she's still terrified. What if that's true? What if Abbie *does* go to the police, they find the guy, arrest him, and he refuses to talk? He's the only human being in the whole world who knows where she is. She might die in this caravan, tied to a fucking oven door.

Zoe's mouth grows drier by the minute. She runs her tongue across her lips, which feel rough and puckered like the skin of an orange. She can't stop coughing, her throat too dry to soothe itself.

This monster. Who is he? What will he do? Just thinking about it makes her heart race and her brain fizz, unable to function through the pure fear.

A frisson of something hums at the back of Zoe's brain.

She keeps remembering Abbie chatting at the jukebox as Zoe arrived in the pub with Dane, Abbie's eyes flashing to the door, then turning back to the stranger. Then later, the way Abbie invented that weird game as an excuse to talk to him again. Forcing Zoe to follow her to the bar, to talk to the guy too. To flirt. As if Abbie was his procurer or something, providing Zoe to him like an offering.

It suddenly seems sinister, the mischievous glint in Abbie's eyes as she sipped at her drink, her eyes flicking from Zoe to the stranger and back again.

No, Zoe must suppress that and focus on other things, fighting and escaping her captor before he can hurt her, rape her, or worse. There's no evidence to suggest that Abbie is anything other than a stupid, brainless idiot who likes to cause drama.

This is ridiculous. If someone had asked her, just yesterday, which of her friends she'd suspect of aiding a kidnapper, well, none of them. But she's only known Dane a couple of months, no matter how much she likes him. Can you know someone that well in such a short time? And Max is the one with the creepy obsession with murder and torture. He reads all those creepy websites, talks about serial killers. Max, not Abbie.

Her kidnapper tied her tighter this time, but she can still wiggle her fingers and the blood flow to her hands is okay, thank goodness.

Behind her back, she moves her wrists back and forth, working the ropes looser and the knots further apart. She just needs a little give in them to be able to shuffle her bum back and over her hands. She's probably got hours to work at this;

it'll all be fine. She can do this, and she can be primed and ready when this monster returns for her once more.

She's not sure how long she works at the rope, but the shadows have changed on the lino since she started. She finally manages to separate her hands enough to edge herself backwards over her knotted wrists. Her arms and back scream with pain as she pushes her shoulder blades apart, but soon she manages to shove herself over the worst of it, and then her hands are in front of her once more. Still tied, but visible now.

She looks around the caravan, desperate for something to help her. And there – under the sofa, something glints in the half-light. What is that? She crouches leaning to press her cheek to the floor, the lino cold against her skin. It couldn't be ... is that a knife?

Under the one-inch gap between the sofa and the floor, she can see the curve of a wooden handle, the glint of metal hinting at a folded blade. She strains towards it, her hands bound together.

The rope around her wrists catches on the lip of the sofa; she can't stretch her hands far enough to touch it.

She just needs a couple more centimetres, but she just can't reach. She stretches and pushes and wiggles her hands, pushes the rope against her flesh until her skin is raw.

Her fingertips touch the cold wood of the handle, but she can't get a grip. She wriggles her fingers, but pushes the knife even further out of reach.

The knife remains inaccessible, taunting her with its promise.

She crouches on her haunches, hooks her fingers under the

sofa and tries to lift it, but it won't budge: it's built into the caravan, never meant to be moved.

She lies on the floor, staring at the weapon as the shadows get even longer, unable to untie herself further or get to it. The spark of hope that briefly rose in her chest fizzles into nothing.

For the first time, she thinks she might die. Her eyes fill with tears and she closes her lids. A tear slips from the corner of her eye and plops onto the floor. She tries to relax her muscles, trick her body that everything is okay, even when her brain knows it's absolutely not.

Something moves.

She listens hard, her ear pressed to the floor. Her heart pounds in her chest.

Sounds reverberate up from the caravan's floorboards, loud in Zoe's ear. Shuffling, like fabric dragging across the floor. Heavy breathing, the wheezing sound of an asthmatic dragging breath into constricted airways.

She holds her breath to hear better, her lungs burning with the effort. Zoe forces herself to open her eyes, and squints through the murky light.

The sound is coming from inside the caravan.

Across the room, a door handle moves.

She pushes herself backwards, into the corner.

Her whole body shudders with fear. She isn't alone.

Helen

Leave your message after the tone.

'Dane, this is Zoe's mum. Call me back urgently as soon as you get this. It is an emergency.'

She's shoved her panic aside in favour of action, although soon she's sure it'll rocket around the corner and hit her full in the face with terror very soon.

Max picks up on the second ring. 'Max, tell me what happened last night. Zoe is missing.'

'Missing? I don't understand. She was in the pub with us. Abbie said she went home.'

'Just tell me what happened, please.'

He makes an unintelligible sound: half-sob, half-gasp, then seems to pull himself together. 'Abbie was being ... well, Abbie. She wanted to get Zoe to pick up a guy in the bar.'

'What?' Helen picks at the corner of a loose strip of wall-paper, gripping it between her fingers and pulling it slowly away from the wall.

He sighs. 'Yeah ...'

'With Dane right there?'

'Yeah. Abbie's going through some stuff, I guess. I don't really understand her.'

Helen shakes her head, utterly baffled. Why would Zoe talk to another guy when her boyfriend was there with her? Why would Abbie want her friend to do that?

'Abbie decided that she was going to wind me up by flirting with "some guy" at the bar. Zoe went with her, I think to make sure she was OK and to try and get her to stop.'

'But where were you? And where was Dane? None of this makes any sense.' Helen runs her fingers through her hair and grabs a handful, tugging the strands taut and feeling the pull in her scalp.

'Dane and I stayed at our table. He's a pretty cool guy and seemed to know that Zoe wouldn't do anything, that it was all Abbie's usual bullshit.'

'But I don't understand. Zoe's dad said that Dane was supposed to bring her home at the end of the night. Why didn't he? Surely you two didn't leave them in the pub?'

'Me and Dane were both a bit annoyed by the guy; he kept looking over like he was showing off that he was the big man, talking to our girlfriends, buying them drinks. So, we went on ahead to another pub to catch up with some other friends. Zoe didn't want to leave Abbie on her own; we thought it was safer if they stuck together. The girls were supposed to meet us soon after, but they never came. We had a couple of drinks at the new place and when they didn't show up we went back to look for them. They were gone. The guy too.'

'Both girls were gone? But I spoke to Abbie, she's fine.'

Max is silent for a moment. 'We went back into the pub,

asked the bar staff if they'd seen them, and even went into the ladies' toilets but they weren't anywhere. Then we found Abbie in the car park, wasted. Stumbling around, trying to be sick. And she told us ...' His voice fades.

Helen closes her eyes. 'She said Zoe went home?'

'Yeah. Abbie was sure. Said she got in a taxi.'

'What? Why didn't you call me? Or Zoe's Dad? Or the police?'

Max's voice gets higher. 'We'd had a few drinks, we were pissed. Abbie was out of control, stumbling around and off her head. Dane was worried, but I guess he just thought Zoe had taken off. Abbie was no help, she could barely talk, and she couldn't answer any of our questions.'

Helen can't speak.

'I'm so sorry. I'll get in touch if I think of anything else that might help.' Max is quiet, and then whispers, 'We thought she must have just got a taxi home or something.'

'You stupid, stupid boys.'

Zoe

The door handle rattles, someone pushing at the door from the other side.

Still lying on the floor, her cheek pressed to the ground, Zoe slides backwards away from the door. Her breath comes in short bursts, so fast that she can't get enough oxygen into her lungs.

Stars spangle the edges of her vision, as if she's about to faint. She can't see what's coming towards her.

Not now, don't faint now. She can't lose consciousness at this moment, she needs to be alert.

A footstep.

She peers into the dusk, but the door doesn't open. They've been in there all along, lurking on the other side of the wall listening to her cries, her struggles to escape. And they've been deadly silent the whole time. Zoe's body shivers from head to toe.

She can hear breathing now. A raspy, dry breath: an asthmatic wheeze. It sounds like a narrowed windpipe: dusty and catching, air forced through a gap too narrow. Someone whose body is not used to walking; a straining, struggling breath.

To Zoe, it sounds like the breath of the dying.

The wheezing continues, like the bellows on a pair of bagpipes warming up to be played. In, out. In, out.

There's a scratching noise, like nails on a chalk board or mice in an attic. Almost scrabbling.

She scrambles to a sitting position, shuffling as far away from the door as possible.

The scratching becomes a scraping, loud and purposeful. But the door remains closed. Zoe watches the handle as it rattles and twitches, moved by whatever is on the other side of the door.

The scraping gets louder, as if the person in the other room is digging at the floor, at the door, at the walls. The sound fills Zoe's ears, and she curls into a ball, her hands over her head to protect her from whatever is about to emerge from the darkness.

She keeps her eyes open, peering into the darkness, never moving her gaze away from that door. No matter what is in that caravan with her, no matter how horrific, Zoe cannot get away. She's trapped in there with it.

The scraping stops. The air is silent, crackling with expectation. Zoe's heart thumps in her ears.

'Please,' a voice croaks, almost a whisper.

Zoe holds her breath, listening.

'Help me. Get me out of here before he comes back.'

Helen

Helen has never felt fear this intense. No amount of rationalising can make this nightmare feel okay. She knows there's something deeply wrong, like any mother would know.

She calls Tony again.

'Hi, it's me.' Helen squeezes her eyes shut.

'Helen! Hi! How are you? Any news?' Tony's use of her name tells her that his wife is in the room, listening. She imagines him turning to Melanie and raising his eyebrows.

Helen grimaces. 'Have you heard anything from Zoe yet?'

Silence on the other end of the phone. He's probably lowering his large frame into an armchair, frowning at Melanie. 'Nothing. How about you?'

Helen's breath shudders out of her lungs with a half-sob. She just shakes her head, even though Tony can't see her.

'Have you two been fighting or anything? Could she be in trouble at school?'

She puts her head in her hands, tugs at her hair. 'Shut up, Tony. Just shut up. This is serious and all you can say is maybe we had an argument. Shut up and *help*, damnit.'

Shouting feels good, really good. Anger is such a relief;

a break from the constant, seething nausea and anxiety churning in her guts.

'The new boyfriend. She's probably with him, right?'

Helen shakes her head. 'I spoke to her friends; the ones she was with last night.' Speaking slowly and clearly, she tells him about the guy who bought the girls drinks, the man Dane and Max left them with.

Tony's quiet, his breathing ragged on the other end of the line.

'How could they be so stupid?' he asks quietly. 'What were they thinking, just leaving her like that? Don't they know the dangers of—'

But Helen doesn't want to leave the anger just yet. 'Tony, she was staying with you last night. She wasn't supposed to be going out. You were responsible for her care.'

She's on her feet now, pacing around the room, gesticulating with her free arm. Her face is hot, and she's started to sweat. 'You're responsible for her care and—' Helen does a quick calculation. 'We haven't heard from her in over sixteen hours.'

Tony is silent on the other end of the phone.

Helen's voice gets higher and higher. 'Get off the line. I need to call the police.'

'Wait, Hels. Don't get dramatic.'

'Oh, fuck off. This is not the time for you to be patronising. She could be anywhere. She could be dead. This isn't dramatic; this is realist.'

Tony pauses for a moment and she hears him gathering himself, imagines him straightening his spine and squaring his shoulders. 'Right. Well, when you call the station, mention my name and let them know she's my daughter. They might send some higher-ups, often do when it's one of our own.'

'I'm going to phone 999, because that's for emergencies. I don't want any of your "mates rates" bullshit for my Zoe.'

Helen can hear murmured voices in the background of the call.

'Melanie says have you called her?'

Helen digs her knuckles into the corners of her eyes. 'Yes, thank you. Repeatedly and all day. Straight to voicemail.'

'And her friends?'

'Of course. Catch up with Melanie after our phone call is over, please. I'm not going to repeat it all again. None of them have seen her since she left the pub last night.'

'Has she stopped out all night before?'

Helen scoffs. 'No. Has she when she's staying at your house, Tony?'

'Okay, then.' He is using his pacifying voice; the same tone he uses on Zoe when she's having a tantrum. 'I'm sorry. You must be worried. I'm worried too, but she's a tough cookie. She'll be home soon, I'm sure.'

'I don't know why you're so sure. Blind denial won't help if she's in danger.'

Tony sighs. 'I thought you wanted me to get off the line?'

'Yes,' she snaps. But thinks better of it. 'Can you please get over here? Bring all Zoe's stuff, and then if the police come you can answer questions from the officers about what happened last night and why you don't know where the hell our daughter is.'

Zoe

Zoe's mouth fills with bile, on the brink of vomiting with fear. *Years*. That's how long this woman has been a captive here.

The door is still locked, but Zoe and her fellow captive sit on either side, talking through the wood.

'I lose track of time. It's been cold many times. Winter.' She doesn't always speak in full sentences, but she's coherent. Probably not used to talking with other people any more. Her speech is unnatural: sudden gasps and tics interspersed with eerie silence. Zoe can't relax, as every sound or scrape sets Zoe's nerves on fire with fear that their captor is returning.

'Does he keep you in here all the time?' Zoe's shivering, every muscle firing and jerking, her skin covered in goosebumps.

'Sometimes. Other times we go to the big house, up through the woods. When the coast is clear.'

Zoe crosses to the window. She presses her face against the glass and peers out into the trees. 'There are two of us now. We can overpower him and escape.' She turns back to the locked door, pulling at it once more. It doesn't budge. 'We have to.'

'There's no way,' the woman's doesn't sound like an old woman, but she doesn't sound young either. Her voice has the depth of middle-age, like Zoe's mum or a bit older.

'Why not?' asks Zoe. A sob creeps up her throat and she swallows it down. 'We have to try. I can't be here for years too.' She crosses the room and places her hand flat on the door. It's damp and cold. 'You can't stay here any longer. We need to get you out, somewhere safe.'

'No one knows me. No one misses me. No one's looking.' The woman doesn't sound sad as she says this, just states it as fact.

Zoe shakes her head. 'Well, people are looking for me. And when they find me, they'll find you too now. My friend was there, Abbie, she'll call the pol—' Zoe stops. *Will* Abbie call the police?

The woman breathes in sharp. 'Your friend?'

Zoe sits down on the floor, her back against the door. 'I thought she was my friend. But I've been thinking a lot in here.' She points around the caravan, even though no one can see her. 'I don't know if she's trustworthy.'

'Oh?' the woman shifts, her voice quietens a little as she moves away from the door.

'I keep thinking she might have led him to me somehow. Maybe even without knowing.'

The voice is loud again; the woman has moved back to the door. 'An offering.'

Zoe runs her hands through her hair, her fingers catching in the tangles. It feels like the whole world is broken and spiked, like she was wrong about everything she once believed in. Even if she gets out of here, how can she trust anyone again? How can she trust strangers, her friends, even her family? Abbie might be genuinely evil. At best, Abbie's destructive self-obsession put Zoe in this danger. Dane isn't looking for her; he just let her stumble into danger without a backwards glance. And Max – lovely, gentle Max – creeps about on the dark web reading about paedophiles and serial killers like Mr X. For fun. What kind of person does that for entertainment?

'An offering. Something like that, yeah.' She looks around the caravan, at the sagging sofa and damp-streaked walls. 'What's happened to you here?'

'He keeps me alive. The others die.'

She flinches. It's not a surprise, but the blunt statement fires deep into her stomach like a bullet. She scrunches up her eyes, turns her face towards the wall, but the question escapes her lips. 'How do they die?'

The woman shifts, her movements reverberating along the floorboards to where Zoe sits. 'They die in many ways. Awful, terrible ways. He doesn't work alone. He likes to share.'

The rumble of a car engine signals the approach of the monster. At the sound, the woman shifts again, her voice panicked. It sounds like she stood up. 'Don't tell him we met. He'll be angry if he finds out I talked to you.'

Zoe scrambles back to the sofa, away from the door.

'He wants to feel he's in control.'

The door creaks open and daylight fills the caravan. Zoe raises her hands to shield her eyes from the light.

'Untied yourself again, I see.'

'Fuck you,' she says, her voice cracking with thirst.

'Now, now,' he says, looming over her. She tries not to flinch. 'If you're going to have an attitude like that, I won't give you any of this water and food I brought you.'

'Fine,' she croaks. 'Give me the water.'

'Please?' he says.

'Fuck. *Please*.' And under her breath: 'Shitbag.'

He kicks her in the side. 'And use my name.'

'Paul.'

'Paul what?'

She can't remember.

He chuckles and throws a bottle of water at her head. 'Paul Herbert.'

She grabs the water and gulps it down, rivulets coursing down the sides of her mouth.

'Slow down, my pretty,' he hisses from his seat on the sofa. 'It's not good to rehydrate so fast. You might die.'

She stops drinking, breathing hard and fast. 'I might die anyway.'

He laughs loudly. 'Oh, you're not stupid, are you?'

'No, I'm not. I know that you won't get away with this.'

He laughs again, his chuckle slow and dry. 'Ah, now there's where you're wrong though. Because I have got away with it many times, and you will be no exception. I was born to do this.'

'Oh yeah? Bet your mum is really proud of you. Does she know what kind of freak you are?'

He rolls his eyes.

'They'll find me, you know. There were witnesses in that pub who saw you.'

'Your stupid friends?' he shakes his head. 'Too far up their own arses to see anything except their own colons. All they could describe was that stylish hat.'

'You think you're clever, but you're really not.'

'A lot of planning goes into a life like mine.'

'This isn't a life. You're an animal.'

He sniggers. 'Thank you.'

'Whatever.'

He stands up, his movements sharp and powerful. Despite her stubbornness, Zoe flinches and moves away from him, shuffling backwards under the table, trying to get out of his reach.

'No point struggling now. We're going on a little trip.'

He steps towards her. She shuts her eyes as tight as she can, and clenches her fists, ready to fight and kick if she can. But he leans down and wraps his arms around her thighs, lifting her over his shoulder as if she weighs nothing.

He steps down out of the caravan and into the woods of the early afternoon, which smell of moss and leaves, fresh and clean in comparison to the inside of that dusty, mouldy caravan. She takes a deep breath into her lungs, noticing the autumn sunshine filtering through the leaves onto the forest floor.

Zoe lifts her head as Paul carries her away from the caravan, sees eyes glinting through a smudged window as the woman watches Zoe get carried away.

Lancaster's Predator Professor:
Leonard McVitie's legacy

By Urban Dark Reporter

Third in a series of articles exploring the newly catalogued archives of Lancaster's most prolific lunatic. Today we speculate what made McVitie who he was, using three key papers from his 26 years of imprisonment in the Lancaster County Lunatic Asylum.

See also:

Investigating Leonard McVitie

Uncovering the archives

The archives of Leonard McVitie give us an unprecedented insight into the mind of a deranged serial killer, while also shining a light onto the low levels of supervision and the free reign that even dangerous criminals were given in the old model of institutional incarceration.

What we see when examining his writings is his feverish desire for immortality. McVitie worked hard to pass on what he knew. He wanted to empower another to control, kill, and impersonate as he had done so successfully for so many years. What isn't clear from his correspondence is whether he was successful at finding a willing protégé, and who that might have been.

1) The Memoir: what made McVitie into a killer?

Lucky for us, among his papers is an unfinished memoir. From those scrappy chapters, we can determine some details about his life before he began committing crimes.

As a child he attended boarding school, so his parents must have been affluent yet distant. He does not mention the name of the school, nor does he specify the name of his one close friend during those years.

It seems that he and this friend enlisted together in the British Army at the outbreak of the Second World War, where he developed his taste for killing.

It's also where he learned to assume others' identities: the real Leonard McVitie died in 1941 during Rommel's attack on Brega in Operation Sonnenblume. The man we now know as McVitie traded identity documents with a corpse; his original name lost to the chaos of battle.

Although it is not stated in McVitie's documents, he must have committed a serious criminal act which required this identity theft in combat. This probably marks his first murder.

2) The Lesson Plan: McVitie's immortal legacy

Amongst McVitie's papers is also what can only be described as a syllabus. This list of lessons and their contents shocked me to the core, and I can only skim over their subjects here: how to choose the best victim, disposing of a body, keeping your victims alive while in captivity. McVitie's pupil is unidentifiable, but we assume they were a fellow inmate.

See also: How to get away with murder

Somehow, even under the supervision of the Lune Hospital's doctors and nurses, McVitie was teaching another patient how to kill, and how to get away with it. We know the conditions in the hospital weren't great: overcrowding, understaffing, budget cuts ... and therefore it seems that McVitie was able to hand down this information to an individual who (we assume) was then subsequently released back into society.

3) The Handover

One theme which emerges throughout all of McVitie's writings is his fetishisation of the apex predator in nature, and his fixation on the 'lone wolf'. He seems to have corresponded with other criminals in institutions around the country, and although we don't have his letters, the archive does contain some responses. They are not friendly replies. The tone is defensive, seeming to reflect a competitive jostling for position which clearly McVitie prompted in his outgoing mail.

This assumption is confirmed with some barely legible notes in a notebook dated '1984' (McVitie died in Spring the next year). The first pages contain scrawled phrases indicating a territorial/ownership attitude, like 'There can be only one'.

Then, as if coming to terms with his imminent death, there is a draft letter to an unnamed recipient:

> *I am ill [illegible – 4 words], it is your turn to kill. I've taught you well; do not disappoint me. There can be only one, and I have chosen you.*

It's unclear if that letter was ever sent. The rest of the notebook is blank.

Comments:

1488-HH: Lol bet he learned some cool stuff from the Nazis

Phoneguy: Lone wolf and needs a follower? WEAK

Combaticus: I wonder what the missing four words said? 'And I have failed' would fit.

> Rogersmith52: That is unlikely, considering he didn't fail. He actually succeeded: he sought to pass on his knowledge so his skills weren't lost after death. So that suggestion just doesn't work.
> 1488-HH: Do you think Rogersmith52 can write a comment that isn't a sanctimonious mansplain? Get a life, dude. If I met you in real life I'd set you on fucking fire

Thomas

The doorbell rings as Maggie and Thomas are flicking through the kids' channels on Sky, looking for the best after-school shows. Maggie stops on a channel where a girl spies on her neighbours through a pair of binoculars, writing observations in a mini notebook.

'This is the film I was telling you about,' says Maggie. '*Harriet the Spy.* Harriet's the coolest.'

Thomas doesn't respond. He can't concentrate on anything, knowing they're going back to the woods later. He won't let Maggie go on her own. But his stomach is full of knots thinking about those woods where someone is screaming and anything could happen.

'You not going to answer the door?'

Thomas shakes his head. 'Mum'll get it. It's for her anyway.'

She pokes him, and points at the TV. 'Harriet spies on people. Makes notes. Solves mysteries. Just like us! Everyone's got secrets. Especially grown-ups.'

Thomas turns to look at her. 'Just leave it, Maggie.'

Maggie tucks her skinny legs underneath her and leans forwards. 'Leave what?'

He shakes his head, looking at Maggie. Her hair's wild after a day at school, sticking out at every angle as if she's been rolling down hills at lunchtime. 'I don't want to be a stupid spy, okay?'

She punches him in the arm, hard.

'Ow!' He says, rubbing his arm. 'I've said I'll go back with you and get the knife back. But after that I'm done. No club-house and no mysteries. It's dangerous and I don't like it any more.' He looks around the room and sees the pile of board games in the corner. He lowers his voice and looks at his feet. 'Can't we just play Monopoly or something? Something that isn't stupid and dangerous like breaking into derelict buildings full of murderers.'

'Fine, on one condition.'

He frowns. 'What?'

'Let's go find out who was at the door.'

***

They crawl along the landing to the top of the stairs and stick their heads through the bannister to hear the conversation below. They can see a sliver of the kitchen through the half-open door, watching Mum's feet pace back and forth as she makes tea. The visitor is a woman, their voices low murmurs over the sounds of the kettle and cups and saucers.

'Can you hear anything?' Maggie whispers.

Thomas shakes his head, holds his finger to his lips. He can hear little fragments of sentences:

… haven't heard from her …

... you might know something ...

... only seventeen ...

... police on their way ...

'Is someone crying?' Maggie hisses. It does sound like crying: a stifled whining sound, and the soothing tones of Mum's voice over the top, the same as when she's comforting Thomas after he's skinned his knees.

'They said something about the police.'

He hears movement from the kitchen, sees a foot through the gap in the kitchen door. 'They're coming out, let's go.' He doesn't want Mum's visitor to know they heard her crying.

***

When Mum calls them down to dinner ten minutes later, Maggie's still on about their plans to go back for the knife. 'Duncan said the old asylum's got security guards in it. Your Dad's friends with them or something, so he told Duncan when it's best to snoop around. A few guys take it in turns; they're there most of the time. So, if there was a murderer, we'd be able to shout and get someone to help us.'

They run down the stairs, stopping in the hallway bathroom to wash their hands. 'Did he ever go inside the asylum?'

She shakes her head. 'He said there was no way in when they tried – only small holes big enough for a kid to wriggle through. But that was years ago. One of his friends did once, though. I'll tell you about that later. It's a really cool story.'

Mum looks up as they enter the kitchen. 'What are you two chattering about? Putting together another scheme?'

'Yeah! We're spies and explorers!' shouts Maggie. 'Who was at the door?'

Mum's hand slows as she spoons lasagne onto three plates. Her mouth turns down at the corners. 'That was Helen from next door.'

'Why was she crying?'

Thomas glares at Maggie, willing her to shut up. 'We weren't spying.'

Maggie sticks out her tongue at him.

Mum looks cross. 'I should hope not.' She brings the plates to the table and sets them down. 'She's worried about Zoe, her daughter. She ...' Mum pauses as she sits down at the table and picks up her knife and fork. She looks tired, her cheeks sagging. 'Zoe didn't come home, and Helen wanted to know if I had any ideas about where she might be.'

Thomas remembers seeing Zoe sometimes when she's going to school; she's pretty and always smiles at him.

'Why would you know something?' asks Maggie. 'Because of your job?'

Mum's quiet, thinking about how to answer. 'She asked if I'd seen Zoe, or ... yeah, kind of because of my job. Sometimes I write investigations about missing girls the same age as Zoe. Trying to find out where they are.'

'Why aren't the police trying to find the girls?'

Mum laughs loud and short, but her face doesn't smile. 'Good question, Maggie. The police don't think there's anything bad happening. They say there's not enough evidence. They're wrong, and it's dangerous.' She stabs at her lasagne like she's trying to kill it. Her mouth is pinched and small, and her eyes are narrow. She puts her fork down. 'But yeah, my job is to find good stories to write and then, if they're interesting, newspapers buy them to print.'

Thomas doesn't want to talk about newspapers, and he doesn't want to talk about things that make Mum sad or angry. But he can't stop thinking about Zoe; she bought him an ice cream once, on a hot day last year when the van pulled up outside. It was a Twister. 'Mum, where do they think Zoe's gone?'

Mum looks sad again. 'I don't know. But I really hope it has nothing to do with the stories I write for the newspaper.'

'What did you say to Zoe's Mum?' asks Maggie.

Mum shrugs. 'I wanted to tell her not to worry, but that wouldn't be honest. I think she should worry. So, I told her that if the police won't help, she should do the investigating herself.'

Him

He can hear sobs from inside the car boot, but he's parked on the opposite side of the lane, away from the gatehouse and out of earshot from the office. The air smells of autumn bonfires as he opens his door.

The spiked parapets of the asylum loom behind the gatehouse, black outlines against the deep indigo sky. The lights are on in the security office and a stocky figure is silhouetted against one of the windows. He watches the window for a moment, as the figure paces back and forth in front of the window, arms gesturing as he talks to someone.

He opens the boot and the girl is lying on her side, her hands still tied in front. She stares at him; terrified eyes open wide, wide, wide.

There it is: fear. It's crawling all over her face and in her eyes, like a swarm of insects, and it's all because of him. Eyes wide, nostrils flared, goose-flesh on her cheeks and bare arms. It's an interesting thing to watch on someone's face, as he's never felt it himself. Fear is not an emotion he suffers from. He has nothing to lose.

A glove is shoved into her mouth, her lips sealed with duct tape.

She's panting through her nose and whimpering. Her hair is plastered to her forehead with sweat.

He leans down so his face is close to hers. She smells of urine.

'I can see I'm going to have to shut you up, aren't I?' he whispers. She closes her eyes and tears leak out of the sides, trickling down her grazed cheeks towards her ears. She makes some muffled sounds, trying to speak. It sounds like she's pleading with him. They always plead.

'No? Are you going to be quiet?'

She nods.

'Liar.' He reaches out and grasps her nose, blocking her nostrils. She whimpers again and thrashes half-heartedly, her chest heaving, straining to drag air into her lungs. He longs to wait, watch her stop struggling and know he's subdued her. Her face reddens, she thrashes, bucking with the need to pull air into her lungs. Her blue eyes roll back in her head, and then swivel to look straight at him again. They're clear blue, with small flecks of hazel, like freckles on her irises. The whites are bloodshot and tearful. She holds his gaze, steady and pleading.

He tries to hold on, fingers stiff and curled on either side of her nose. But almost against his will, hand shaking, he releases her mouth and nose. He can't do it.

She wrenches air in through her nose like a swimmer surfacing from a dive.

She shakes her head violently and tries to speak. She might be saying 'No, no', but it's muffled behind the layers of duct tape he wrapped around her face.

He laughs and ignores her, lifting her over his shoulder;

she barely weighs a thing. He can feel her shivering against his chest. He curls his arm around her legs. She's too weak now to fight him.

He watches from the trees as a security guard leaves the gatehouse and climbs into his car. The ancient Escort narrowly misses scraping the gatepost as it trundles away.

He carries the girl up the sloping drive towards the asylum. Tall trees create an archway above his head through which he occasionally catches glimpses of the moon. It's a bright night.

The asylum looks beautiful. The steep roof gleams silver in the moonlight and the dark windows watch him and the girl like the multiple eyes of a spider. He imagines the faces of the lunatics at the windows, staring through their addled minds. He loves all the words they used for the patients: idiots, imbeciles, feeble-minded. So descriptive.

He's calm, content. He can't help smiling.

She utters a muffled sob.

'You're a very lucky girl. You get to see the workshop. My murder castle. It's where we kept the others.' A damp patch on his shoulder indicates that she has urinated again. Not even this can diminish his mood; he'll make her pay for that later.

He walks past the front entrance, where a stone staircase leads up to the double wooden doors. They've been locked for years. It looks more like the sweeping entrance to a palace than a lunatic asylum, but he is not complaining. This palace belongs to him for now. Diamond Security has eyes everywhere, but he knows where to step to avoid the twenty-one CCTV cameras dotted around the asylum.

Around the corner of the main wing and through the

archway, set back into the wall, is a small door. This one isn't usually locked; people rarely get this far into the grounds before a guard shoos them away. The handle turns easily.

The door opens into a wide corridor. Cold air enters his nostrils; the kind of cold which is so permeating that it makes your lungs feel damp inside. Large windows line the wall to his right, moonlight filtering through the dirty glass and pooling on the scuffed linoleum. Along the corridor on the other side, doors stand open to offer a glimpse into what used to be offices and staff rooms for the nurses. When it was decommissioned, they released the lunatics into the community, sending them back to live with their families or into sheltered housing. Many dropped out of contact, and no one followed up. For some, that was a gift.

They emptied the asylum but no one paid attention to the details and the building suffered the same slapdash approach: each room retains an object or two that hints at the room's former incarnation. A coffee cup abandoned on a windowsill, its handle broken off years ago. An unravelled fire hose slithering across the floor. A hairbrush. A basket, probably woven by a long-dead inmate.

He pauses at one of the doors. 'This is one of my favourite rooms on the ground floor. I'm glad I can show it to you.'

The door stands wider than the others, shoved back on its hinges. Strips of wallpaper hang down from the high ceiling. A broken window faces out into the courtyard, glass shards in the frame casting jagged shadows across the room. The room is empty except for one item: in the far corner, facing the wall, is a single chair.

'See that chair? Sat there on its own, staring at the wall? I wonder who used to sit there. I wonder what was wrong with them.'

It's not a normal chair. Coated in bile-green NHS vinyl, the chair tilts back. And unlike a traditional recliner, black straps on the armrests are ready to grip around a person's wrists, restraining their arms. The same on the front two legs of the chair, to wrap around the ankles. Two more mould-mottled straps hang from the headrest, waiting to loop around someone's shoulders and hold the whole body tight and still. Helpless and bound.

He toys with the idea of tying the girl to this chair, spending time in this room where the walls seem to ooze with fear; but they only have a few hours before sunrise and there are much more practical areas of the asylum to utilise. His shoulder begins to ache from her weight. She's not as light as he thought.

The corridor opens out into the entrance hall, the other side of the grand doors. Up the stairs are the cells, the bedrooms, big dormitories, and the attics, many of which are blocked off with asbestos warnings which repel even the bravest intruders. There are even some old padded cells right up on the third floor, at the back of the building. The padding is cursory: just a layer of beige leather coating a normal stone wall. It would still be very easy to smash someone's skull, even against the walls of a padded cell.

They're not going up there tonight.

In the corner of the entrance hall is a door, almost hidden in the oak panelling. It creaks on its hinges, the noise echoing through the cavernous foyer. He switches on his head torch;

they're descending deep into the heart of the cellars where the moonlight does not reach.

The girl begins to thrash, kicking her legs and nearly sliding headfirst from his shoulder. He grasps her legs with both arms, holding her in place.

'Trying to make a run for it, little mouse?' he purrs. 'You'd never find the way out.'

She lets out a muffled scream from beneath her tape-gag.

He descends the stairs into the darkness of the basement. Down here are miles of tunnels spreading out in all directions; it might even be bigger than the footprint of the building itself. There is the morgue, and boiler rooms, huge storage caverns, locker rooms and so many other nooks and crannies that he doesn't think he could ever discover all of it no matter how many hours he prowls around down here.

He strides along the dark tunnel, his thigh muscles pumping as he pushes through a set of double doors, glass panes criss-crossed with wire, towards a barred gate. This is the asylum's dirty little secret: where they dragged the violent patients when there was nowhere else they could be adequately restrained. He has modified its contents, but it still fulfils its original purposes well.

The room is small, about four metres along each wall, with a low ceiling snaked with pipes and wires. Big storage units line up along one side of the room, with floor-to-ceiling slatted doors to conceal their contents. There's a metallic smell of dried blood. The walls and floor are tiled in white squares, and in the middle of the floor is a grate, presumably so the asylum staff could hose down the room when a patient made too much of a mess. A bath stands in one corner, thin lines of rust threading from the taps. It's a practical room which continues to operate long after the rest of the asylum crumbled into disuse.

He crosses the windowless room and lowers the girl to her feet, back against the wall. Her legs are shaking; she can barely stand.

'Let's give you a helping hand, shall we?' he whispers into her ear, and cuts the ropes encircling her wrists.

Before she can rub the rope burns, he pushes her into a chair, a twin of the green restraint chair from the room upstairs on the ground floor. He straps her thin wrists to the arm restraints. Her fingers flex and shake as she struggles against the straps. Her head lolls to the side, held up by the curved headrest, designed for control not comfort. Her legs shuffle as she pulls on the ankle restraints.

He stands in front of her and fastens another leather strap around her shoulders, securing her firmly to the chair. He pumps the pedal, raising it up like a dentists' chair. He'll be able to stare straight into her eyes as he cuts her open.

She watches him the whole time, dry-eyed. Looks like she's gathered some strength.

He considers pulling the duct tape from her mouth, letting her have some conversation before she dies. But he's made that mistake before and it's not worth the hassle; they always say the same things: *why are you doing this to me? Please, I'll do anything, just let me go. I won't tell anyone. I'm a good person.* Blah blah blah.

He couldn't stop this even if he wanted to. He crosses the

room and presses a button. Although he can't hear it down here in the basement, he knows that six storeys up in the asylum's tower the rusted bell rang once.

'She's ready for us,' he whispers into the darkness.

Helen

The doorbell rings and she springs to her feet, slamming the laptop shut and running to open the door.

'Oh, it's all of you,' she says to Tony, who's brought Melanie and the twins. Melanie's holding their hands: Lucy's already crying and Bennie looks like he's on the verge of tears. Lucy's face is red, her mouth open in an outraged square, moments from screeching.

'Yes, it's us.' He steps forward and gathers Helen in his arms in what she's sure he intends to be a comforting hug. Melanie shoves forwards into the house, dragging the whining twins behind her. Helen's not sure how much energy she has for this kind of bullshit tonight. Tired toddlers and jealous wives are beyond her capabilities when Zoe's God-knows-where.

'Have you called the police?' Tony asks.

Helen clenches her fists, continuing to channel her worry into frustration because it's a more functional emotion than pure, sheer, paralysing terror. 'Of course, I have. They're on their way round.'

'Which officers?' Tony clearly wants the best of the best.

Helen shrugs. 'No idea. You'll find out when they get here.'

'Wanna play in Zo's room,' whines Lucy. Bennie, sucking his thumb, nods wildly, his balled fist bobbing up and down with each nod.

Helen shakes her head at Melanie and, in a rare moment of empathy, Melanie raises her eyebrows in understanding. Melanie's immaculately dressed, her makeup flawless and her long blonde hair pulled back into a graceful bun, latest iPhone in her pocket. Helen feels a flash of irritation that Melanie found the time to do her makeup when Helen's daughter – Melanie's step-daughter – is missing.

'Come on kids, let's go and see if there are any choccie biccies in the kitchen,' says Melanie, and Helen suppresses another wave of irritation at Melanie thinking she can help herself to the contents of Helen's kitchen. But at least they're out of the room for a minute and she can think.

Tony throws himself down on the sofa, its old legs groaning under the force of his sudden weight. He leans forward and puts his head in his hands. Maybe he's finally starting to realise how serious this could be.

'Where is she, Tony?'

He doesn't say anything, just groans into his hands.

'What did she say last night? What kind of mood was she in?'

He looks up and sits back on the sofa. 'I've been over it a million times in my head. She was totally normal. A bit sulky and stubborn, but normal Zoe stuff. She said straight to my face that she'd be back for half ten, and she wasn't lying. She really meant it; she intended to be back.'

Helen draws a breath. 'Look, I found an article online; I really think—'

The doorbell rings again and Helen gets up to answer it, a tiny sliver of hope in her chest making her imagine that it could be Zoe standing there on the doorstep, even though Zoe has never rung the doorbell once in her whole life. She'd just walk in.

She opens the door to Dane, shoulders slumped, hands shoved into his pockets. Although taller than six foot, he looks small standing on the doorstep, his eyebrows knotted together in questioning anguish.

Helen resists an urge to slam the door in his face. She catches herself just in time. He looks worried, not guilty. And he might know something that could help.

'I've been trying to call her all day,' he says, holding out his phone as if this proves the truth of his statement.

She opens the door wider and steps back to allow him inside the house. She glances out into the street but there's no sign of a police car yet. She pushes the door closed and follows Dane into the living room, where he's already introducing himself to Tony.

Tony has risen from his reclined position on the sofa, and Dane is holding out his hand for Tony to shake. There is a slight hesitation, and Helen knows her ex-husband well enough to deduce his thought process is tracing a similar path to when she considered slamming the door in the boy's face. Tony takes Dane's hand and shakes it briefly, white knuckles betraying that although they're shaking hands, Tony's still making a point.

'What happened last night?' Tony asks, stepping easily back into the role of policeman.

Dane opens his mouth to answer, but is interrupted by Melanie, hovering in the kitchen doorway. 'Isn't it better that we wait for the police? They'll just ask all these questions again.'

Helen wants to hit her. 'We need all the information we can get, Melanie.'

Tony doesn't say anything.

Dane shrugs. 'I don't mind. I'll say everything as many times as is needed. I just want to make sure Zoe's okay.'

Helen makes her mouth smile at Dane, before it slides off her face with the strain of faking it.

Melanie slinks back into the kitchen, and Helen is glad she's gone.

'Why did you leave her on her own? Where did you leave her?' Tony still hasn't sat down, standing over Dane despite being at least three inches shorter.

Dane's large face looks blank and puzzled. His eyebrows knit together in the middle. 'I didn't leave her, she—'

'Rubbish!' shouts Tony.

He descends to the couch next to Helen and she jolts from his weight like a kid on a seesaw. There's a clatter from the kitchen and one of the twins starts to wail.

Helen puts her hand on Tony's arm. The muscle is tense and shaking with rage. 'Let him finish, Tony. We won't find out anything this way.'

Tony opens his mouth to argue and then closes it again. Helen nods at Dane for him to continue.

'Who were they talking to?' says Tony, at the same time as Helen says, 'Have you heard from Abbie or Max?'

Dane looks from one to the other of them, probably trying to work out which question he should answer first, wondering which question is more urgent and which of Zoe's parents would be angrier if their question doesn't get acknowledged.

He looks at Helen. 'I've spoken to Abbie. She's OK, but it really doesn't sound like she knows anything.'

Tony slams his hands on his knees, and Dane flinches. 'We'll have to get her here too. We will have questions for her. Well, the police will. Who were they talking to at the bar?' Tony asks.

Dane shakes his head. 'I don't know. Some guy. Older. Wearing a baseball cap.'

'"Some guy" isn't good enough.'

He looks down at the carpet. 'I know.'

Tony claps his hands. 'You'd better start thinking, wrack those brains of yours. First they'll look at you, they always look at the boyfriend first. Also, you were there that night. You're suspect number one.'

Dane looks even paler. 'I love Zoe. I'll do anything to see her safe.'

Tony ignores him. 'Next they look at the family, Helen. Me and you and Melanie. Our brothers, too; Zoe's uncles. Then they widen the circle: friends, friends-of-friends. That's it. There's no one else to look at.'

'What do you mean?' asks Dane. 'The guy, the guy from the bar—'

Tony shakes his head, holding up a hand to interrupt.

'Outside of those circles, they rarely find the perpetrator. It's very unlikely. The trail goes cold. If we don't already have eyes on the person who took her, we'll never find them.'

'We don't know what's happened to her yet. We don't know she's definitely been taken by someone.' Dane's eyes are shining with tears.

Helen puts her hand on Tony again. 'The police will have lots of questions. They might be able to draw more out of him. We shouldn't push too hard before they get here.'

'I'm asking the same questions they will,' says Tony.

Helen shakes her head. 'You're retired, a civilian now. And anyway, in this context, you could never be involved like that. It's not your case, you're the family of a potential—' she stops. She doesn't want to say it. Just like she didn't want to say the word 'kidnapped' on the phone to the 999 operators.

'A potential victim,' Tony finishes for her.

She shakes her head. Saying it out loud makes it real. And if she doesn't say it, she can still maintain that small kernel of hope that it's all just been a big misunderstanding and Zoe is absolutely fine and will show up at the door any moment with no idea what chaos she has caused. That little wisp of hope keeps floating past Helen's peripheral vision like the first snowdrops at the promise of spring. Please make it all okay, somehow.

They're all quiet for a moment, as they try to understand that this is their reality now. But it doesn't feel real yet for Helen, it's like a horrendous nightmare from which she still believes she'll eventually wake. Surely she must. It can't be true, it just can't. Zoe should walk through that front door at any moment, and it'll all have been a crazy, unlikely misunderstanding caused by over-paranoid parents.

But what, really, could explain this absence? Helen looks at the clock. Twenty-two hours with no contact. There's nothing that could explain this except something awful. Something beyond imagining; something that even Helen's overactive mind couldn't think up right now because it's too unbearable.

'Abbie said she thought Zoe got in a taxi,' Dane says, looking worried. 'But obviously, now we know what's happened ... she thinks the guy put her in his car.'

He clearly feels a huge amount of responsibility for this – and so he should, Helen thinks to herself, trying to suppress a flash of unhelpful rage. Zoe is younger than Dane, more vulnerable, under the legal drinking age and in Dane's care. He was supposed to drop her home at the end of the night and he just ... didn't. How is that even possible? Who does that?

The real answer, Helen knows, is 'anyone' – any irresponsible young person who's had a couple of drinks and was in a new relationship, who doesn't know their girlfriend all that well and maybe had a bit of an argument or something – you'd just wander home and plan to talk with them in the morning, not thinking that 'talking with them in the morning' might not be an option *because* you'd left them. She shakes her head hard to clear the thoughts.

The doorbell rings. 'That'll be the police,' says Tony, standing up to answer the door as if it's still his house.

Helen stays on the sofa, watching Dane for any sign that he knows more than he's letting on.

Thomas

Nothing bad happened last time. Maybe nothing bad will happen this time either. Every time he does something brave, he'll be less scared until he's courageous about everything.

It's darker tonight because clouds are covering the moon. The wind catches through the trees, rustling and shrieking as branches rub against each other above their heads. Thomas flinches at every movement, all senses on alert. He scans from left to right and back, looking for creatures hiding in the darkness, searching for the glint of eyes watching them.

Maggie doesn't even notice. She shines the torch under her chin, lighting up her face. The light bounces as they retrace their route from last night. 'Alright. This is a true story, Duncan told me. A ghost story.'

Thomas tries to swallow his fear and focus on what Maggie's saying. 'Duncan and Sandy must be awesome older brothers.'

Maggie groans. 'Whatever.'

He's pretty jealous of Maggie growing up with them. They give her their hand-me-down band t-shirts and share hand-me-down secrets with her, like the caravan.

Their footsteps echo through the darkness along the lane towards the wood as Maggie starts her story. 'A boy called Alan used to play poker with them in the old caravan. Our clubhouse now. He was friends with Duncan, Sandy and all their mates.'

Thomas nods.

'One day, Alan was exploring on his own when he met the ghost of a patient who never left when they shut down the asylum.'

Thomas smiles. He's not scared yet. 'This is silly.'

Maggie ignores him, continuing with the story. 'The ghost didn't like children playing inside the building because it was her home, so to teach Alan a lesson, she trapped him in a padded cell up on the third floor.'

'Wow,' says Thomas. The hairs on his arms are standing on end, and he remembers the windows, their weird glow as he watched them through the binoculars yesterday.

Maggie grins and continues with her story. 'The padded cells were where they kept all the really mad people, and they're padded so the crazies don't hurt themselves when they're bashing all over and running into stuff. And Alan was so scared when he got locked in. None of his friends knew he was there so no one knew to call for help or the police. Alan screamed and screamed for days but no one came to save him. He died of fright. Or went mad with it, one or the other – I can't remember what Duncan said.'

'Well, if no one came to save him and then he died, how would anyone know what happened?'

'Maybe he didn't die at that point. Maybe he died later.'

Thomas is quiet, listening to their footsteps and the crunch of leaves as they walk. A massive gust of wind pokes through the wool of his jumper and he tries not to shiver. 'What? When?'

'Don't know. Anyway. The end of the story is that now Alan's ghost haunts the asylum, crying and yelling for someone to let him out.'

Thomas's mouth opens. 'Maybe that was what we heard last night.' The spiked roof of the asylum's tower pokes through a gap in the trees. 'Creepy story.'

Maggie shrugs. 'We could go inside and find the padded cells, see if it's true. There might be scratch marks on the walls where he tried to claw his way out.'

Thomas shudders and shoves his hands in his pockets. 'That story's not true. Duncan made it up to scare you, stupid. Ghosts don't even exist.'

'Yes, they do. My mum's seen one.'

'I don't believe it.'

Maggie turns to face Thomas. 'Prove they don't exist then.'

He laughs. 'Yeah, right. How?'

'We could go up there after we get the knife. Nothing will happen, right? We'll explore a bit and then come home. You've already agreed to go inside. We made a deal. So, while we're there we'll go up to the third floor, do a ghost hunt for Alan.'

Thomas shakes his head. 'Mum would kill us.'

'She's already asleep. She'll never know.'

'No way.'

'You're scared,' she says.

'No, I'm not. But I think it's a stupid idea. We should get the knife from the caravan and then come home.'

'Scaredy cat.' Maggie pokes Thomas in the side until he wriggles. 'Anyway, it's what we talked about yesterday. Our first proper mission.'

The numbers on his watch are blurry, so he grabs his glasses from his pocket, puts them on. The lenses are smudged with fingerprints, but he can see that it's nearly ten o'clock. Mum thinks they're asleep, and they set up pillows under their covers to look like they're in bed.

'You're stalling,' says Maggie in a sing-song voice. 'Don't wimp out on me. Family stick together.'

Thomas takes off his glasses again and wipes them on his t-shirt. Maggie is getting annoying; he just wants her to shut up about it.

'If you come with me tonight, I'll implement Mission Two as soon as Mum comes home from holiday.'

'Mission Two?' He frowns.

'Operation: Thomas's Dad. Listen, clearly the grown-ups know more than they're saying about where he is. Even Duncan and Sandy. They're all hinting and no one's telling us anything. And if we can just find out where your dad is, we could maybe get a bus to go and see him.'

That's all he needs. He'll give Dad a hug and ask him to come home. 'Surely Dad would come home if I ask him. If he knows how much we miss him.'

Maggie nods. 'Yeah, exactly. If he's allowed. And I'll help you find him.'

He shrugs, trying to ignore his fear. 'Alright. We'll go

inside after we get your knife. See how brave you are then.'

Maggie claps her hands. 'Brilliant! I'm braver than you. You'll be running home and crying for your mummy.'

'Whatever.' Thomas switches off the torch.

They push through the trees, walking along the same path they followed last time, and eventually the trees thin out and they're in the clearing with the caravan.

As they approach the lopsided caravan, Thomas throws out a hand and stops Maggie. 'Wait,' he whispers, and they both stop, listening quietly.

'What?' asks Maggie.

'Being brave doesn't mean we should be stupid. We need to check,' he says.

'Don't be a wimp.' Maggie whispers, and he can see her grinning at him, her teeth glowing white against the darkness of the rest of her face, like the Cheshire cat in the *Alice in Wonderland* cartoon.

He shakes his head. He doesn't want to look like a wimp in front of Maggie, but the memory of last night's scream is still fresh. It was terrifying. 'We still don't know who screamed.'

'It was probably a fox,' she says, trying to sound like she knows best. 'Have you heard them? They sound like human screams. I looked it up on YouTube last night. It was the same noise.' She steps forward, quicker than Thomas would like.

He's happy to stand there for a minute or two longer, being careful. Sure, it could have been a fox. But better safe than sorry. He hesitates for a moment, and then runs to catch up with Maggie, who's already pulling the caravan door open.

They stand at the doorway, peering into the blackness. Something's different.

Thomas frowns and waits for his eyes to adjust.

'Smells funny,' says Maggie, stepping up into the caravan.

She's right. It's that smell from hospitals and vet surgeries: the unhappy smell which you can't place but creates a fizz-pop reaction in your brain like a match just struck.

'Wait,' says Thomas, and Maggie stops. He shines his torch inside, and both of them gasp at the sight.

The oven looks wonky, and the table is folded away; he's sure they left it out from where he was sitting on it. There's a glove lying in the corner that he doesn't remember being there yesterday.

'Someone's been here,' whispers Maggie. Her voice trembles, like she's a bit scared. Thomas is relieved that it's not just him, and Maggie being scared makes him feel a bit braver. If Maggie's scared, then it's his job to look after them both and make everything safe.

He shines the torch around the caravan. What *is* that smell? It's weird, a bit like toilets, and it makes him feel nervous, like something's wrong.

'No one's here. I think it's safe,' she says.

Thomas pushes down his fear, and both of them step into the caravan. He tugs on the handle; the locked door is still locked.

They both get on their hands and knees, crawling around on the damp floor and checking underneath everything.

'There's something here!' calls Maggie, her face pressed against the lino as she peers under the sofa.

Thomas skids across the caravan on his knees and shines

the torch around. Something glints on the floor, near the back, but it's too dark to see what it is.

Maggie stands up and tries to shift the sofa, but even with both of them and all their strength, still it won't move. They manage to lift it a few millimetres, and then Maggie gets back on the floor to peer underneath again.

'I think that's it!' says Maggie, reaching her arm under the sofa. 'Damn, too narrow. It's right at the back. Can you lift it any higher and I'll slide underneath?'

'I don't think so,' says Thomas. 'I'm pretty strong, but it's, like, attached to the wall or something.'

'Duncan's gonna kill me if we lose the knife,' whines Maggie.

'Maybe he won't notice if you don't say anything,' suggests Thomas. 'Just keep quiet and he might forget about it.'

'Just think of something, dummy.' Maggie looks grumpy. She sits back, folding her arms, and leans against the sofa with a big sigh.

'Fine,' says Thomas. 'Go and get a stick from outside.'

Maggie grins and rushes outside, returning in moments with a skinny branch. She lies flat on the floor again, ready to slide the stick underneath.

'One, two, three,' counts Thomas, and gets his fingers underneath the sofa and bends his knees like they were taught with lifting things in PE class. The sofa is really heavy, like it's full of a million rocks. He lifts it as much as he can – a centimetre, maybe more – and holds it still even though his arms are shaking.

Maggie flicks the stick underneath, and Thomas manages to hold it until she hooks the knife out.

'Got it!' she says, grinning her massive smile and holding the huge knife up next to her face. She looks like a crazy person and Thomas starts to laugh.

'You're a psycho,' he says, giggling at her.

'Yeah, I am! Now come exploring with me or I'll stab you in the foot.' She points the knife at the ground and laughs too.

They're both short of breath, like they've been running for miles and won a race. They leap from the caravan into the trees, inhaling the fresh air of the forest. This is a fun adventure; it's not scary any more, and there's no one else in the woods making scary screams. Must have been a fox, like Maggie said.

Now that he's proved how strong he is, Thomas wants to do more, to flex his exploring muscles as well as his arm ones. 'Come on then, let's go find the padded cells. We've got more exploring to do tonight!'

Him

His approach is as tight as the skin of a drum, learned from the very best. One particularly smug freak commented online that it sounded as if he imitated Robert Berdella, the Collector. They said the boning knife was Berdella's weapon of choice, and that his own methods of kidnap and dismemberment copied Berdella. There might be similarities, but he would never emulate such a clumsy oaf in his methods. Berdella practically laid a trail for the police right to his own front door.

The room is pitch dark except for the light from his head torch. Its narrow beam follows his gaze, slashing through the darkness and throwing shadows around the room.

He itches to act; to get started. He's waited long enough, followed the rules for too long.

He reaches into the tool bag and draws out the ivory-handled boning knife, and watches it glint in the light from the torch. The angled blade is smooth and clean. Beautiful. It's as sharp as possible due to his skills with a knife sharpener, honed over years of practice and his constant habits of preparation. It was once part of a set gifted to his maternal grandparents on their wedding day, and has their initials carved into the handle, textured under his thumb but illegible in this light.

He hears a squeak from the girl. Even with tape over her mouth, the little bitch will not shut up.

'Didn't I tell you to be quiet? Didn't I?' he strides towards the girl.

She screws up her face, turning her head away. She smells pungent, of stale sweat and urine and fear. 'Look at me. Fucking look at me.'

Her eyes are still squeezed shut and she won't listen. He slaps her once, twice, but she won't open her eyes. Her head is turned away from him, cheek pressed against the wall.

'You won't get away with that for long,' he warns her, but she doesn't listen. He'll have to make her look at him.

'You need to watch me.'

He prises her eyelids open, pressing his fingers into her eyeballs. Her eyes roll upwards, away from him. She knows what he wants and she's refusing, looking anywhere but at him.

'LOOK AT ME,' he screams in her face.

He lets go of her eyelids and she squeezes her lids shut again, twitching and scrunched.

'The worst is still yet to come, don't you understand? This part is a fucking walk in the park compared to later.'

He raises the sharp, pointed end of the knife to her left eyelid, pushing the point between the top of her eye socket and her eyeball. 'This is what will happen if you don't do as you're told.'

She's shaking, her breath coming faster and faster through

her nose. Holding her jaw with one hand, pressing her head back to the wall, he pushes lightly with the knife, but doesn't break the skin.

Not yet. Anticipation is all part of the fun, and damaging her at this stage isn't in the plan.

'If you're not going to look at me, I'm going to make you,' he whispers.

He grabs more duct tape from the tool bag and rips a one-inch length from the roll. Using his left thumb to hold open one eyelid after another, he sticks open her eyes with sticky tape.

'It'll be the knife next time, so watch yourself. And watch me,' he snarls.

Now her eyes are open open open.

Helen

'So, you were in the Richard the Lionheart.' Detective Constable Audrey Parks looks not much older than Zoe, but she's very serious and focussed on the case at hand.

Dane nods, and they go over the details once more. Helen stares at her hands circled around her mug of tea, listening with one ear while her brain thrums with fear. They've covered the basics: when they last saw Zoe, who she was with, where she said she was going. The hardest part was their questions about Zoe's relationships with Helen and Tony; did they argue (not much), had Zoe ever run away before (never), did she have any friends she might be staying with (none that they haven't already checked with). All infuriating questions, but Helen and Tony both answered politely and patiently, knowing that the quicker they give information the quicker the true investigation can start.

'And the last time you saw Zoe, she was talking to the guy at the bar too?' asks DC Healey, pushing the questioning ahead. Healey is Tony's age. The men haven't met before, but occasionally exchange pally looks to show that they both know the ins and outs of the police world more than all the other civilians in the room.

Parks flashes her colleague an irritated look; she clearly wants to operate at a slower, more careful pace than Healey.

Dane blushes and shifts in his seat, but Helen wants to believe it's due to nerves about the seriousness of the situation, not that he's hiding anything. She's trying to give him the benefit of the doubt.

He looks a lot younger, flanked on either side by these police officers. He sits on his hands, his shoulders hunched up around his neck, unsure of himself and awkward like a tall teenager. He's picking at a loose strip of skin at the side of his thumbnail, pulling and pulling until a line of blood threads the edge of the nail. Helen can't look away from Dane's bloodied, ragged thumb.

He's trying to give the answers he thinks the grown-ups want to hear, like a school child who's in trouble with the headmaster. He looked different next to Zoe: older and more sophisticated.

'Before you and Max left them behind, and went to another bar?'

Dane flinches, but keeps nodding.

The coffee table is laden with mugs of half-drunk tea gathered around the teapot, milk bottles and half a plate of biscuits. Helen hugs her cooling mug of tea to her chest, both hands wrapped around it while everyone talks.

Melanie flits in and out, refilling the teapot and stocking up the biscuit levels. She never stays in the room long; as soon as she leaves the kitchen, the twins start whining and causing a scene. Eventually she gives up and takes them upstairs to Helen's bedroom, trying to get them to nap.

'Can you describe the bar guy for us, Dane?' asks Parks, frowning at her colleague.

Dane rubs his forehead with his hands, crinkling the skin. Then he ruffles his hair, almost massaging his scalp to encourage thought. 'Um …'

Helen leans forward, every muscle in her body taut. *Come on, Dane. You've got to remember. For Zoe. This is too important to forget.* She wills him to remember anything useful.

'Just a normal dude, I guess,' he mumbles.

Helen wants to jump up and slap him around the head to try and knock some sense into his stupid brain. Think, you imbecile. Don't let my daughter be lost forever just because you couldn't make your brain work. She's shocked at the force of her anger. She manages to hold it in; says nothing, just clenches her fists and silently wills him to think.

'Can you remember his hair style?' prompts Parks, in a kind tone.

Dane perks up. 'He was wearing a hat,' he says, proudly. Helen's heart sinks. Anyone can wear a hat. He could look like anyone.

Parks makes a note in her book. 'What kind of hat?'

'It was black.'

Helen suppresses a growl of frustration. This is a waste of time.

'I'm going to need a bit more from you, here, Dane,' says Healey, and Parks flashes him another look.

'I mean, was it a woolly hat or …?' says Parks, wresting control back into her hands from Healey's.

'It was a black baseball cap,' says Dane, almost standing up out of his chair. 'Oh! And it said something on it. In white letters, but I couldn't read it from where I was.' he says, looking so proud of himself.

Helen shakes her head. It's not enough.

'He was taller than both of the girls, about a foot taller.' Dane's eyes are closed. He seems to have reached some kind of bank of memories, and Helen silently encourages him, barely moving except to nod her head along with his every word. 'And he ... I think his head was shaved under the hat. I don't remember hair. But there was something weird about him ... a kind of stony look on his face.'

Stony. Great. Thanks, Dane, thinks Helen. *What the fuck does that mean?*

'Great, Dane,' says Parks. 'I think we're just about done here.' Parks tucks her biro into the special loop on her notebook and closes the lid. Her face settles into a serious expression. 'Dane, I know you've co-operated and given us all the information you can. We'd like to continue questioning you at the station.'

Colour drains from Dane's face. He stares at Parks.

'You're not under arrest. You aren't obligated to come.'

Healey takes over. 'But it's in the interest of Zoe's safety, mate. And we can tell that's what you care about most.'

Dane nods slowly, as if in a trance. 'Of course I'll come.'

'Of course he'll come.' Tony slaps a hand on Dane's thigh. He sounds almost triumphant. 'He's got nothing to hide, have you, mate?'

Dane stands, looks around the room for his coat. He shakes his head, not speaking.

Parks stands too. 'We'll head back to the station with Dane

and get someone to send this information out to all units, make sure everyone's looking out for Zoe,' she looks at Helen, her eyebrows raised as if she expects a pat on the head. 'And we'll get a team out at the Lionheart to check out the area.'

Helen has run out of politeness. 'Is that it?' she asks, knowing she's on the verge of explosion. 'That can't be it. It's not enough.'

She's at the point where she can either burst into tears or start shouting, and she really feels like starting to shout would accomplish more than tears. 'We need to find my daughter,' she says loudly. 'You can't all go home and eat your dinner and go to bed. It's dark and raining and she could be anywhere, with anyone. She could be hurt.'

Parks nods, at the same time as Healey shakes his head.

'Absolutely,' Parks says, while Healey says 'Not at all, madam.'

'Neither of you have a clue,' she shouts, and Tony puts his arm around her. 'I've found more information in ten minutes on the internet by myself than you two have in the last hour of questions.'

'I'm sorry about this,' says Tony. 'Very stressful time, you know.'

'We totally understand,' says Parks. 'Don't we, Healey?'

Her partner sniffs reluctantly in agreement.

'We're going to do everything we can to find Zoe, Helen. Everyone in the department will be doing everything they can. We're going to make sure of it. We can tell that Zoe isn't the kind of girl to run off, and this a very high priority case.'

'Don't you need more information, like other cases? There

are others, I've found them online.' The police and Tony look at Helen with blank expressions, not understanding her question. 'Aren't there others?' Her skin prickles with goosebumps. 'Missing girls? Are there any—' she stops, almost unable to ask the question. 'Are there any other girls like Zoe? Because I've found articles—'

Parks reaches out her hand and puts it on Helen's. With that and Tony's arm around her, she feels propped and bolstered, like an old tree with limbs held upright with wooden posts.

'There have been a few similar cases.' She pauses and resets her face to a bright expression. 'But most cases like this are solved quickly, with the missing people returning or being found in the first twenty-four hours.'

'Being found ...' says Helen, and her skin crawls.

'With the child home safely,' adds Tony very quickly. He pats her shoulder again. 'Most of them come home safely, love.'

'Zoe's not what we would call a high-risk individual,' says Healey, scratching his stubble.

'You mean she's not a drug addict or prostitute, then?' asks Helen, deciding to dispense with any bullshit. 'What about the drugging? The Rohypnol. Dane told you about Abbie in the car park.'

The officers promise to contact the pub and Zoe's friends. Parks and Healey rise to their feet, clearly ready to leave before another outburst or tricky question.

Helen sees the police out along with Dane, and when she returns to the living room, Tony and Melanie are readying the twins to leave, shoving their arms into jackets and finding scattered shoes while the kids whine and wriggle.

She stops in the doorway, watching them, the happy family. 'Told you they'd look at the boyfriend first,' Tony says, pulling a woolly hat onto Bennie's head.

She brings her palms to her face, cooling her hot cheeks. 'Dane's got nothing useful to say. He can't help them.'

She closes the front door behind them with dread, turning back to face the silent house and Zoe's empty bedroom.

Him

He doesn't like the noises she's making. Her feet stamp on the tiles, pawing the ground. It's boring and repetitive, just like all the others. He wanted this one to be different, to keep that spark and fight for longer. But he made the mistake of removing the duct tape from her mouth, and now she whimpers and screeches, like a dog.

He presses the electrodes into her temples, standing over her with his legs straddling hers. The machine whirrs, ready to blast electricity into her brain. He's wanted to try this for weeks, ever since he found the machine in the back of a storage cupboard and hooked it up to an old battery.

Her face is coated in a sheen of sweat and tears; liquid trickles down her oily cheeks. He pushes his face against hers, burying his nose in the matted hair behind her ear, breathing her in. He catches a vague hint of the perfume she applied hours ago, masked now with the animal stench of fear.

'Ready?' he whispers, his hand on the dial.

Her whole body shivers as he stuffs a sock into her mouth. 'Stop you biting your tongue. I'm not all bad.'

The sock muffles her howls.

He presses his nose into her soft cheek. He opens his mouth and pushes his teeth into the skin of her face, the beautiful layer of muscle which coats the cheekbone. He doesn't bite; he rests his teeth on her skin, feeling the tension, testing the strength. Her rounded cheek fits nicely into his mouth.

He increases the tension, closing his jaw slowly, slowly. He doesn't break the skin; it's strong and elastic, a thin layer of muscle and nerves. He could bite down hard, wrenching his head away and tearing her face.

But she's shaking violently and whimpering too. It's just boring, all this whining. It's time to move this forward, really push through any hesitation he might have and prove he's capable of this. He can do it; he's been waiting for this his whole life. Coached into it. Everything he's ever learned has been leading towards this event.

He stands back, looks at her reclining in the restraint chair, eyes taped open, tears running down her cheeks. He feels nothing but contempt.

'Blast off!' he yells, and turns the dial to 'MAX'.

Sparks. Shrieking. Then nothing. The ETC machine stops humming.

'What the fuck?' The battery blew out. It didn't work.

The girl still watches him, breath shaking as she huffs through her nose.

He kicks the leg of the chair and swears. Fine. It was only a whim anyway. He's played for long enough and now he's ready to begin the final act.

He draws the boning knife across her throat, scratching lightly across her neck. A promise, not a real injury. Little drops of blood pool along the cut, each growing larger until the membrane bursts and they trickle down her neck to bloom into her t-shirt. He watches as the rivulets stain the girl's pale skin.

She's breathing heavier and heavier, until some snot splatters from her nostrils and speckles his face. He pulls back, disgusted.

He's wants to slice her throat like a pig in an abattoir. He imagines pressing in hard, feeling the blade scrape against bone. But first, he looks at her one last time, and her pinned eyelids and tear-soaked face, her stained clothes and the shaking, panicked breaths shuddering out of her nostrils.

Soon, she'll stop making noises, she'll finally be quiet. And even as she dies, she won't be able to close her eyes.

But still he doesn't make the final cut. What is he waiting for? Get on with it. His hand twitches, knuckles white as they grip the knife handle.

He knows what this will be like, how it was for the others. There'll be the promised surge of euphoria, as he imagines a heroin addict might feel after a long-awaited hit. His heart will pound, the blood pumping through his veins. But then, disappointment and disgust with them, with their weakness and how they die so easily, with so little fight.

He fills his lungs with air tinged with the hint of death.

'Stop.'

His hand freezes. The voice is clear, familiar. He turns to face the figure in the doorway, her white nightgown glowing ghostly blue in the torchlight.

She holds out a hand towards him. 'Don't do this.'

She'll try to stop him, but he's ready to fight her. The knife is still in his hand, poised to cut. This is too important, he's waited too long. Nothing can get in his way.

He tightens his hand around the knife handle, resolves to ignore the protests. He closes his eyes for a moment and reignites the feeling he held a moment before: anticipation, readiness.

And then there's another noise from further away, deep in the building. They both turn away from the girl, towards the door, straining to hear the sound. Someone else is here. Someone uninvited.

Zoe

Paul pushes the woman out of the way as he rushes from the room, plunging his two captives into darkness; his headtorch was the only light source.

His footsteps recede as he runs along the corridor, on the hunt for the origins of the noise. There's a distant metallic *clang*: the slam of a door as he shuts them in. No chance of escape.

She releases her breath in a huge rush, the breath she was holding in her lungs as he pressed the knife to her throat. That could have been her final breath. She was moments from death. Her whole body is shaking. As she tries to calm herself, Zoe manages to spit out the dry, wadded sock that the man had crammed into her mouth.

'You saved me,' she whispers into the darkness to the woman, whose voice she recognises from the other side of the caravan's wall. 'You got here just in time; he was about to kill me. Are you okay?'

She can't hear anything, the silence heavy in her ears. A blast of cold air hits her in the face, along with the stench of body odour.

She caught a glimpse of the woman before the light went out: framed by a wild tangle of dark hair, she has the face of someone who was once beautiful. Large eyes, wide open and clear, sharp cheekbones, and lips pulled up into a gentle smile, the smallest glint of teeth.

The woman is wearing a gown, once white but now closer to grey. It reaches her knees; either a nightgown or a hospital gown, Zoe couldn't tell which.

Long, long fingernails: so long they're almost hooked.

'Hello? Please! Can you unfasten me? Quickly. I'm strapped to the chair.' Maybe Paul knocked her down as he ran from the room; although she's tall, Zoe can tell the woman is weak from years in captivity here. Her legs and arms are spindly, like a plant kept from the light. Perhaps she's lying on the floor, just on the other side of the room, unconscious or losing blood from a head wound, as Zoe stands there, helpless in the dark with her arms fastened to the wall. 'Are you hurt?'

Now she can hear her: the woman's raspy panting echoes through the room, closer now. 'I need to find a light.'

'Thank God you're alright. I thought he might have hurt you.' She tries to see movement in the darkness, but there's nothing, not even a pinprick of light.

'You're so brave.' Zoe can hear her shuffling around, moving things. 'Hurry please. He's tied me up, I can't move. And he's done something to my eyes, they're taped open.'

'I'm going to find a light.'

'Quickly, please.' Zoe pulls at her arm restraints. 'Untie me and we can get away before he comes back.'

'He's bad.' The woman sounds upset, her voice shaking with emotion. 'Very bad.'

Zoe nods in agreement. 'He's evil.'

A door opens and closes, and Zoe is left in silence.

Thomas

'ATCHOO!' Thomas sniffs as hard as he can and wipes his nose on his sleeve. There's a tickle in his nose that feels like he could sneeze again at any moment. He tries to stifle it, holding his nose.

Facing the reality of the derelict asylum, Thomas's new-found bravery has already started to falter, but Maggie's set on finding the padded cells from her brother's story. They begin to climb the stairs, their feet imprinting in the dust. Halfway up, they take the left branch of the staircase to the first floor.

The moon shines through a window on the floor above, lighting up the hall below in eerie silver. Maggie climbs the stairs ahead of him, Duncan's folded knife creating a bulge in the back pocket of her jeans. She's humming to herself as she climbs.

There's sudden clunk from below, like an object falling or a door slamming, and it's over as quickly as it began. Maggie stops singing.

'Did you hear that?' he asks.

They look at each other, eyes wide. Nothing moves.

No matter what made that noise, if there's someone else

inside this building with them, Thomas and Maggie must hide. They'll be in so much trouble for trespassing, for breaking into private property. He knows that kids can't go to jail, but there are other punishments for this kind of crime. They're criminals. He feels a moment of frustration: Maggie has made him a criminal.

They need to hide.

Thomas drops, flattening himself to the stairs as much as he can, the treads digging into his tummy. He switches off the torch and clutches it in both hands.

His heart pounds in his chest and he tries to quieten and slow his breathing, but the harder he struggles to breathe slowly, the more air he seems to need.

'Get down,' he whispers. He shuffles towards the bannisters, where he can see down to the main entrance. His nose starts to run; he's desperate to sniff or blow.

Maggie sees he's lying down and copies him, looking confused.

'I heard something,' he whispers, although he's not sure now if he imagined it or not. The air is thick with silence now, oozing into his ears like maple syrup.

Maggie's face goes pale. 'I think I did too,' she says.

The children press their faces to the gritty wood, staring at each other. Maggie's eyes are big and round, the whites glowing in the silvery moonlight. Their breathing is fast and ragged as they try desperately to be silent. Thomas covers his mouth with his hands. Dust from the stairs tickles his nose and he pinches his nostrils so he doesn't sneeze again.

Slow footsteps echo from the hall below. Maggie's hand grips onto Thomas's arm; he can feel her shaking. 'Is it a ghost?' Her words are a barely audible whisper.

He shuffles closer to the edge of the stairs, where gaps between the railings give a view over the wide expanse of entrance hall. He peers down, pushing his face between the spindles. A figure crosses the hall, pausing every few steps.

A sneeze threatens to explode out of Thomas at any moment. He holds his breath.

The man is wearing a head torch strapped around his shaved head, the light obscuring his features. His skin shines in the moonlight.

Thomas continues to hold his breath as the man crosses the hall, disappearing out of sight down the corridor which Maggie and Thomas had walked along moments before. The sounds of echoing footsteps slowly fade, followed by a door creaking open and closed. Then there is silence. For a moment, Thomas and Maggie do not move.

Thomas slowly uncurls his fingers from around the stair spindles and turns his face to Maggie. She looks pale. He reaches out and puts his hand on her shoulder. 'It was a man.'

She nods. 'What was he doing?'

Thomas shrugs. 'I don't know. He had a torch on his head.'

Maggie giggles. 'What a weirdo! Maybe he's stealing stuff. My mum said that's pretty common in old buildings like this, that people see them as easy pickings. Like your—' She stops talking, pulls her lips in tight. She leaves a silence for a moment before she carries on. 'Let's go see where he came from.'

'What? No way. Let's just go home.'

They descend the stairs, and Maggie finds a door to the

right of the main staircase, standing slightly ajar. Thomas shines the torch inside, the weak beam illuminating a set of stairs disappearing downwards into darkness.

'A basement or something,' Maggie says.

Thomas looks down the corridor into which the guy just disappeared, and points after him. 'He's blocked our exit: that was our way out. We can't go back that way, it's where the man went.'

'It doesn't look like he's coming back yet,' says Maggie. She points down the steps into the basement. 'Maybe we can get out this way and go home.'

'I don't know. It's so dark down there.'

'We're armed.' She pats her back pocket. 'And we have a torch.'

He shakes his head.

'There's probably a way out down there. A fire exit or something.'

Thomas stands up straighter, frowning. He wants to be braver. But he also wants to get out of this building. 'Come on then.'

Thomas goes first, shining the torch on the stairs by his feet so Maggie can see where to step. Maggie reaches forward and puts her hand on Thomas's shoulder, reminding him of pictures of blind soldiers they saw in history class.

The air in the basement smells even more damp and cold than on the ground floor. The walls seem to be painted dark red, with pipes and cables running along the ceiling like a nest of snakes. Their footsteps echo as they walk, and somewhere far ahead they can hear the dripping of pipes.

The temperature drops as they descend, and Thomas shivers beneath his woollen jumper. He thinks he can hear Maggie's teeth chattering. 'You cold?' he whispers.

Maggie shakes her head, hugging herself. 'I'm fine.'

The corridor stretches out of sight in two directions, further than the beam can reach. To the right, illuminated by the torch light, is an old fire hose, beginning to uncoil. Shadows along the walls indicate where doorways into rooms and further corridors might be.

The silence feels heavy inside Thomas's ears. 'This way, I reckon.' They turn right, Thomas shining the torch at their feet. 'Don't trip on the hose,' he says as they pass.

They creep by closed doorways, most of them blocked off with rusting bars, like prison cells. They approach what appears to be a dead end, a door standing open to the side.

Behind him, Maggie's footsteps stop.

Thomas slows and turns back, shining his torch down the tunnel. The light catches Maggie's face, reflecting in the whites of her eyes. Her skinny arms hug her body as she shrinks into the wall. She looks like a hare caught in the headlights of a car.

He's never seen Maggie look this afraid before. It's contagious, and his heart begins to beat hard in his chest. 'I don't want to go much further. I don't think there's a way out this way.'

'Me neither.' says Maggie.

'I'm not having fun any more,' he whispers.

Thomas sees a tear slide down her cheek.

She raises her hand to shield her eyes from the torchlight. 'We saw the guy leave. There's no one down here but us.'

She sounds like she's trying to convince herself as much as Thomas.

He lowers the beam. 'Alright,' he sighs, trying not to show his relief that they can leave without it being his decision. He looks down to the dark end of the tunnel. 'Let's go back. There's probably a way out; there has to be. OK?'

Maggie nods, sniffing back the tears.

Thomas takes her hand and they turn to retrace their steps back the way they came.

As they turn, Thomas's torchlight catches in an open doorway, illuminating a nearby room, and everything inside. Every horrific thing.

As soon as the light touches the walls, his grip on the torch loosens and it slips from his grasp. The torch smashes into pieces on the tiled floor and the light disappears.

Thomas squeezes his eyes closed, but the image he just saw will not disappear: the tiny room, dried blood pooled and clotted on the tiles, splattered up the walls, and a set of footprints trailing out and back along the tunnel down which Thomas and Maggie had just walked. And a body in a chair, its mouth a gaping hole and huge eyes wide open, wider than a normal human being.

Thomas is breathing too much, his face hot and sticky with sweat. He grips Maggie's hand until she whimpers and pulls her hand from his.

'What's wrong? What is it? Where is the torch?' asks Maggie, she crouches down to try to find the lost light.

'No,' he croaks, grabbing her under the arm and pulling her into a standing position. 'Don't. It's gone.'

He hears her turn to him. He imagines her quizzical expression even in the darkness, her frown of non-understanding. She didn't see what Thomas saw. She doesn't know.

He tries to slow down his lungs and swallow the nasty sting of sick rising in the back of his throat. He wants to lean against the wall and steady himself, but it feels like everything in the world is coated in blood. He can't touch anything. Nothing is clean, not even him and Maggie. They will never be clean again.

Maggie pokes him in the arm. 'What did you see?' she asks, quietly. She has stopped crying; he can hear it in her voice, but there is a tremor of fear in her words.

He shakes his head into the darkness. 'It was nothing,' he starts to say. Even though he doesn't feel sad, he feels as if he might start to sob and he isn't sure why. He swallows again, his mouth dry. 'I'll tell you later. We need to go now. I want to go home, too.'

But then there's a groan from the room behind them. It's so quiet he almost doesn't hear it. His whole body freezes.

'What was that?' hisses Maggie.

The groan again, louder this time.

'Thomas, what was that?' her voice is shaking and he can feel that she's about to run. She's grabbed his hand with her own icy hands and is tugging him away down the corridor. But she didn't see what he saw; she doesn't know what she's running from.

'It's not dead.'

Every instinct in Thomas's body screams to run with Maggie, far far away. This isn't a game any more. No ghost hunt, no exciting exploration of a derelict asylum. Terrible things have happened here, and someone dangerous is inside the building with them. There is blood everywhere. If Maggie and Thomas aren't careful, they could be next and it will all be Thomas's fault.

He should have said no, should have stuck to what he believed in and been good and done as he was told. He should be in bed right now, exactly where his mum thinks he is. He clenches his teeth and squeezes his eyes shut, but that's even worse. Behind his eyelids it's still thick blackness, but the images he's just seen are burned on the inside of his eyelids.

He is desperate to run away. Instead, he grabs Maggie's hand and pulls her towards him, whispers in her ear in the dark. 'There's someone in there, tied up. Still alive.'

'Oh my God,' she whispers back. She starts to pull his hand, trying to drag him away down the corridor. 'Let's go. Letsgoletsgo.'

Thomas resists her pull, even though his feet almost follow her. But he knows they can't leave yet. They have to stay here, in the dark with a murderer. They have to stay and help this poor person, this nearly-dead body strapped into a chair.

'We have to help, Maggie.'

She stops pulling for a moment, and then starts again. 'I don't care. We just need to get out of here.'

He doesn't move. 'No. This person needs us.'

Maggie keeps pulling, but a muffled voice cuts through the black like a knife through silk.

'Please.' It's not much louder than a whisper, but it's enough to stop Maggie dead. She doesn't pull any more, letting her hand sit in Thomas's.

'Shit,' she says.

'Yeah,' says Thomas.

'Help me. Please,' says the voice.

Zoe

They're whispering in the corridor. She saw them before they dropped their torch and the light went out again. They were blurred, through the tears pooling in her taped-up eyes, but the outlines she glanced as they stood in the doorway were those of children.

The whispering stops. They're deciding: do they rescue her? Do they save themselves?

Zoe feels like she's having an out-of-body experience right now. She's in so much pain that she's almost numb. Her muscles and tendons scream against the restraints holding her to the chair, the straps digging into her skin, disrupting the flow of blood around the body. Her hands are freezing cold, the fingers prickling like pins and needles. Her bare feet are numb, toes touching the tiled floor.

The silence lengthens.

'Help us,' she whispers again, although quieter this time.

Her desperation has faded and she feels calm, rational. She must be in shock.

She can't stop shaking, her kneecaps twitching.

They might have a chance, these children. If they run now

and run fast, they might get away before the man returns to complete his task. They could call for help. If they can get out, he might never know they were there.

Then there's a footstep. Just one.

And another, the sound of grit under the sole of a shoe.

One of the children is crossing the room towards her.

Then more footsteps: they're both coming to her.

She takes a shaky breath combined with a sob, her lungs expanding to suck in oxygen. *They're going to help us.* The calm restraint dissipates: it was an illusion; she needs to get out of here and she'll do anything, enlist anyone to help.

'My name's Maggie,' a voice whispers in her ear. The girl's breath is warm against her cheek.

'I'm Thomas,' his voice is a little deeper, but still holds the brightness of childhood in the back of his throat. 'We're going to help you.'

She can't see their faces. They smell of outside: wind and rain and leaves. They smell so fresh and alive, not like the dank murky smell of mould and mildew that has filled Zoe's nostrils for what feels like days.

'What's your name?' the boy asks.

One of them touches her hand, fingertips warm against her palm. The reassembled torch flickers on, shines near her face. She flinches away, unable to close her eyes against the sudden light.

'Zoe,' she croaks.

There's a rustling, a whispering between the children. 'The missing one,' she hears one of them hiss. 'The one Mum was talking about.'

She wishes they'd stop talking about her and help.

'You're tied up,' the girl says. 'Your wrists. Anywhere else?'

'Shoulders and ankles,' Zoe manages to mumble.

'It's OK,' she says. 'I have a knife.' The zing of metal is loud as the girl unfolds her knife. 'We'll get you out of here in no time.'

As the blade touches the strap, there's a loud clunk. The sound of footsteps bounces off the concrete walls, travelling towards them along the tunnel.

'Someone's coming,' whispers the boy. His voice wobbles from somewhere deep in his throat. The torchlight dies.

'It's OK, it's the woman,' whispers Zoe. 'She's a prisoner too. She went to find a light so we can escape.' Zoe opens her mouth to call the woman, and she realises she doesn't know her fellow captive's name. 'I've found help,' she calls, turning her head to the right where the woman was before the door opened and closed.

The footsteps move closer.

They're slow. They drag on the ground, as if the person is carrying a heavy weight on their shoulders, struggling to lift each foot from the ground. There's a rustle of fabric, dragging and crunching. Whoever it is, they're looking at her across the room, two coal-black eyes twinkling at her. Her skin prickles with the sensation of being watched.

Zoe opens her lips, unsticking her tongue from the roof of her dry mouth. What's the woman doing? Why isn't she replying? It doesn't make sense.

He must have got to her, returned in the darkness to capture the woman and tied her up just like Zoe. He's probably lurking in the darkness, listening to them talk, knowing it's all futile and he can kill them all at any moment.

The children are in danger too.

She's so afraid, she feels like she's drowning in it. She wants to cling to these two children like they're the only thing keeping her afloat. But she can't. She'll pull them under the water with her.

Her throat rasps as she talks. 'Run. Hide,' she whispers to the children. 'If he finds you, he will kill you.'

***

From the centre of the room, there's the crunch of a cigarette lighter and the flash of sparks, but no flame ignites.

Again: crunch and sparks. No flame.

This time the lighter works, its flame rises to meet the tip of a cigarette held between pursed lips. The fire lights up the face, and Zoe's whole body freezes. She stops shivering as her damaged eyes strain to see the figure for the short moment it's illuminated, before the lighter is extinguished.

She glimpses wild tangled hair, long to the waist. Unbrushed and clumping into dreadlocks. It's not Paul. It's the woman, she's found a light. She looks about fifteen years older than Zoe's mum: maybe late 50s, early 60s. Angry-red fingernail scratches score the woman's cheeks, and dirt fills every pore on her face.

'Oh, thank goodness. You're alright,' she calls in the darkness. 'Do you have a candle?'

The lighter flicks again, illuminating bones jutting at every joint, the skeletal look of a prisoner kept in solitary confinement. Her knuckles are swollen, fingers gnarled like a much older person.

But something has changed. She's not hunched and flinching. Despite her dishevelment and wildness, she has the height, poise and grace of an aging headmistress. Her sunken eyes are not the timid, unsure eyes of a captive. They're steely, focused. The wild eyes of a predator.

Her lips suck at the cigarette, lungs groaning with the strain.

Zoe's skin prickles, every cell jolts with electricity.

'What's happened?' Zoe tries to ask, but all that leaves her mouth is a croak. Can this woman help her? What's she doing, lighting a cigarette in the silence?

She stands still in the centre of the room, looking at Zoe.

It's so dark, Zoe can barely see anything. But something about the woman's stillness tells Zoe that the woman can see her, even with no light.

Zoe's eyes sting, the tape on her eyelids prevents her blinking away the tears. Her eyes water so much, she can't see anything now but the darkness. Not even an outline or a silhouette.

Footsteps advance into the room, still slow. The woman is in no rush. What's going on? The smell is stronger now: it's almost meaty, like raw beef mince.

Zoe tries not to turn away, breathes through her mouth. 'Help me.'

Then, a fierce pain on Zoe's torso, a stinging and burning. The cigarette, shoved into her skin.

'Oh my God,' Zoe whispers, and silent sobs wrack her

body as she realises that no help is coming. Whoever she is, the woman in the room watching her through the darkness, she was never going to help Zoe.

Zoe remembers the woman's words, hours ago in the caravan: *He doesn't work alone. He likes to share.*

She knows why he hasn't raped her, like she initially feared. As if that was the worst thing that can happen. She knows better than that, now.

And why he took her to the caravan and left her there, like it was a waiting room. Because it *was* a waiting room: waiting for something far, far worse than she could imagine. Something was there, all along, lingering on the other side of a flimsy partition wall in that caravan, listening to her wail and struggle and cry. She knows why that man only taped her eyelids, and did not slice them.

The real threat is standing next to her in the darkness, digging the burning end of a cigarette into her ribs.

Then she remembers the woman's other words: the man didn't kidnap Zoe for his own use. Zoe is *an offering.*

The woman's voice pierces the darkness. Gone is the weak whisper of a kidnapped woman:

'My boy brought something for me to play with.'

Retraction: How to get away with murder

By Urban Dark Reporter

Author of fake 'murder advice' article suspected liar!

We have been flooded with emails and comments since last month's publication of '<u>Anonymous: How to get away</u>

with murder'. Although some complained that we would publish something so incriminating and 'evil', many were complimentary about the article's entertainment value, and others were downright creepy. We know you're out there, creeps. Thanks for tuning in.

The interesting letters, however, were those which cast doubt on the veracity of the author's claims. Full disclosure, folks: 'Anon' is unlikely to be a murderer, despite his claims to be a cold-blooded killer / hunter / predator / whatever else he called himself. We're a little bit immoral, but not so immoral that we'd knowingly provide a platform for a serial killer to boast about how great they are. That's a bit much even for Urban Dark Reporter.

As one of our creepier emails stated: 'That writer has never killed anyone. There are small nuances and insights one gathers from taking a life, and the article featured none: no new detail, only repetitive and incorrect information about existing killers and common-sense detail like "clean up after yourself". Anyone with a knowledge of true crime could write this. The writer is a fiction writer with no experience of actual serial killing, just a posturing wannabe trying to prove himself.'

Despite how much ad revenue the viral post has provided, in the interest of reputability we will remove the article and double-check our sources next time. Apologies for any entertainment you might have experienced while reading this site.

Comments:

1488-HH: Thank you. Jesus. If I wanted to read fiction, I'd go to the library.

Rogersmith52: Knew it. All that talk about disposing of bodies, but he never wrote about actual killing. I knew he was full of shit, never murdered anyone in his life.

Combaticus: Glad to hear it. The McVitie stuff was getting interesting, that's the kind of stuff I keep coming back for, not this pseudo-fiction weirdness.

Him

I am important. Fear me. Learn from me.

He strides along the upper landing, aiming his headtorch into each dark corner in search of the source of the noise. Nothing stirs; nothing unusual stands out as the origin of the noise he heard. Everything is as he left it. He's searched throughout the building, just as she expects; if he doesn't find anything on this floor, everything is untouched. Then he can return to the basement and continue his work. Make her proud. Prove himself to her.

I am the pinnacle of power and danger. Hear me. Run from me.

The upper levels of the building feel different to the ground floor, less solid. The floorboards creak and the windows rattle in their frames when the wind blows. He doesn't understand how she stands to live like this, dividing her time between this cold room and the damp caravan in the woods, alone night after night.

I bring death and destruction. Worship me.

He understands her need for solitude – he's similar to her in this way – but not ready for this stark existence with no comfort. She's so self-sufficient, everything she needs is in her head, guiding her like a witch's familiar. She needs nothing else, and one day he will be the same. She eats the food he brings and lights a fire in an old grate to keep warm. He doesn't know if she bathes. She wouldn't appreciate him asking her that.

She taught him everything he knows.

Together, we are the King and the Queen. Nothing rivals our power.

He doesn't pester her with trivial concerns; she's a grown woman who knows what she wants, and he respects that and just helps how he can. She raised him to respect her and care for her as she deserves.

She's lived here for many years, on and off. The doctors moved her here when he was young, her behaviour finally prompting the psychiatrists and lawyers to deem her a danger to herself, her son and others. But that wasn't her first time in the Lune Hospital.

They don't understand a highly evolved brain.

During her final long-term admission, she returned home to him at weekends. Mother and son would play escalating pretend games that she called 'Lessons': pretend it's normal that Mum lives in the asylum; pretend that it's acceptable to observe the world like a predator scanning for prey. Search, assess, pursue, kill. In a few short years, he didn't feel like he was pretending any more: they are predators, a higher class of human than the rest.

Humans are divided into predators and prey. We decide which role to take.

His headtorch illuminates a dusty sign:

DANGER:
ASBESTOS

Smaller text below explains the grave warnings of respiratory damage, cancer and lung disease. He knows what the signs say: he ordered and paid for them years ago after the asylum closed. To protect her from intruders, and protect intruders from her.

This is how we succeed. We are the natural predators.

He climbs over a barrier and passes her room, shining his torch from the doorway, lighting the stark place she calls home. That smell invades his nostrils: the scent which seems to follow her everywhere. Damp, decay and a meaty body odour which oozes from her skin.

The parquet floors, once sanded smooth and carefully varnished, are scratched and dull, dust pooling in the corners. The wallpaper peels off in strips, and there's an area over the bed covered in scribbles where she's scrawled all over it in pencil. She writes obsessively, recording every thought and feeling. When the paper runs out, she moves her scrawls to the next available surface: walls, bedsheets, tables.

Moonlight shines through the window; one of the only windows still fully intact in the whole building, not one pane broken. But the wooden frames are warped and splintered; he estimates just one winter left before they give up and deposit their glass into the room, leaving empty holes through which the wind will invade.

Against the wall is a dressing table and mirror: the only thing in the room which is clean and neat. It's almost exactly the same as its twin in her bedroom at home: rows of bottles and tubes of her lotions and potions, and a well-placed mirror so she can gaze at her reflection for hours.

And a bed: an old hospital bed with rails on either side, musty sheets and a greying blanket.

This is my hunting ground. No one can take this from me.

This was her home, the place where she learned everything she knows. And where he was born, to much scandal and outcry. When the asylum closed, she didn't want to leave. So he worked in darkness for weeks to seal off part of the building just for her, surrounded by barriers and danger signs so no one would dare to enter.

And if they did, they'd be a fly wandering into a spider's web.

He reaches the end of the west wing corridor and turns back, satisfied that there are no intruders. The noise he heard earlier must just have been the creak of a door, or something knocked over by the wind.

Back to the basement. Maybe this time she'll let him do more than just watch.

Nothing can hamper my control.

She taught him everything he knows. He hunts for her, protects her in her lair, and shields her from capture. He lays false trails, covers their tracks, destroys all the evidence. He finds victims for her. He's an expert in the perfect murder, but he's never taken anyone's life. She has never let him.

But this girl is his choice. Not captured to order; she's just for him. Normally they have to look a certain way, live a certain life. They must remind her of her youth – like she's destroying a younger version of herself over and over again, trying to recapture that time by taking it away from someone else.

You're not ready; there's still so much for you to learn, my son.

He's been patient, but he's waited long enough. Now it is his time to kill.

Zoe

'Everyone thinks that killers are men.' By the light of an oil lamp, the woman paces in front of Zoe, spitting and rambling. 'They're paranoid about men, conditioned to believe that the threat is "he", not a "she".'

Her movements are quick and bird-like. She cackles. 'It's why he chose me, selected from all the other patients. I was young then, and so beautiful. "The face of an angel, the mind of the devil", McVitie used to say. He chose me. He loved me.'

Zoe flinches each time the woman comes near. She recognises that name, McVitie. Something Max said in the pub the night she got kidnapped.

'But you have no idea that female killers walk among you just like male ones, and the women don't feature on your paranoid radar. We're undetected, beyond suspicion. Even other women think like this: you, little Zoe, who believes herself so intelligent, insightful and a feminist – the mere fact that I'm female disarmed your primal fear. You didn't think I was a threat. My femaleness deceived you without me even needing to try to persuade you.'

She's holding a knife, waving it around as she paces. Her

tread is slow, almost a limp: one foot is bare, dirt encrusted under the toenails. On her other foot is a little ballet flat. Her legs are bare but unshaved, the skin pale under a fine coating of dark hair.

'They think I'm a man, you know. The police, the press. They call me "Mr X".'

Mr X. Zoe remembers Max in the pub the other night, and how familiar that sounded when he talked about the serial killer who terrorised the city nearly twenty years ago. Suddenly, two parts of her memory slot together like jigsaw pieces. She remembers her parents and their whispered conversations when she was tiny: even though Dad had long moved departments and left the CID, he'd never been able to shake the nagging burden of the criminal he could never catch.

Everyone thought he was dead. Until recently, it's been years since a murder went unsolved in the city; they thought it was over. But Mr X – that spectre of death that dogged her Dad and terrified parents of teenage girls – is standing right in front of her. Holding a knife.

The blade glints gold in the murky light. It's the same one the man waved in front of Zoe's face earlier; desperate to hurt her but holding back for some reason. Now she knows why.

'I thought you might suspect, for a moment. When you talked about your friend Abbie, the one you thought was his accomplice. In that moment, I thought maybe you were different. That you knew women could be just as dangerous; sometimes more so.' Her voice creaks like old floorboards, totally different to the quiet whisper of earlier.

Nausea rises in Zoe's throat. Zoe shakes her head, tries to

tell the woman that she doesn't understand, that there must be a mistake, but the woman continues talking like Zoe isn't even there.

'You're so naive. So ... traditional.' She sneers in disgust. The woman reaches up to her own cheek, running her fingertips across the filthy skin like she's stroking the face of a lover. 'I was always the most beautiful, you know. I've been so hated for it. And I didn't ask for it.'

Zoe focuses on breathing in and out, tries not to think about what horror is yet to come.

The woman pulls a hand mirror from a shelf and gazes into it by the light of the oil lamp. She fluffs her matted hair, pulls her cheeks taut, bites her lips. She pulls her mousy knots back with both hands, twists it to the top of her head and turns sideways to admire her side view with a half-smile. She's holding a new cigarette in one hand, its glowing tip waving close to the matted nest of hair. The skin on the back of her neck is brown with grime.

'My sisters hated me. Even my own mother tried to harm me, tried to destroy this beautiful face. They sent me away, pretended there was something wrong with me. Those liars.' She crosses the room to Zoe, walks right up to push her face into Zoe's. 'And now, girls like you.'

Her breath smells of rotting fruit. Zoe turns her face away.

The woman roars, her voice a screech. 'You don't see my power, but you are jealous. You're threatened by my beauty, just like they were. But you will not damage me; you will not hurt me like they did. I'll cut you first—'

'I haven't done anything to you,' Zoe shouts, but the woman

doesn't hear. It's like this woman is on stage, performing the same show night after night. Zoe's the audience tonight, but the next crowd will hear the same lines, see the same movements.

'He's a good boy. But he gets carried away, and he's not ready yet. I haven't taught him enough; it's not his turn. It takes a long time to learn to kill well. To do it so seamlessly that the authorities don't even know a crime has taken place. They thought I was dead, didn't they? They thought I'd stopped.'

Zoe nods.

'But instead, I was just improving. I got so good it was undetectable. And now I'm passing on my skills, like McVitie did for me.' She nods towards the door. 'Did he tell you his name is Paul? I think that's the one he's on now. He picks a new one every few months, someone quiet and boring to get into trouble.'

Zoe tries again. 'He's a psychopath,' she shouts, as loud as she can. 'You both are.'

The woman stops pacing, freezes in place. 'You do not talk about my son like that.' Her voice is suddenly clearer, the crackle gone now she's talking directly to Zoe.

Zoe's mouth falls open. This crazed, monstrous being is someone's mother. Those hooked claws of hands once held a baby, and presumably nursed it, loved it and cared for it. That wiry, spindly body carried a baby to full term, and raised that child into adulthood. And now, like any mother, she's protecting him, this son she raised.

But the son she raised is insane, just like her. Both of them, roaming this derelict building, night and day.

She doesn't want to provoke this woman, there's no telling what she could do next. But it's the only choice she has, to break out of whatever scripted performance this woman likes to stage, to derail her. 'I'll talk about your son however I like. You're both freaks. And that creep McVitie, whoever he is.' Zoe closes her mouth, a sinking feeling of dread pooling in her stomach.

As soon as Zoe insults McVitie, the woman screeches and runs at her, the knife held in an upraised fist. The woman's eyes are wide open, whites bloodshot and staring. Unable to close her eyes, Zoe rears back, turning her head away from whatever is coming.

She remembers something she read in a magazine once, about rape. 'My name is Zoe. I'm 17 years old.' The article advised girls to say their name to an attacker, to reinforce that they're a human being, not just a target. 'I have a little brother and a little sister. They're three years old.'

The woman starts to laugh, her bubbling cackle wild and untethered. 'I'm Bertha. Delighted to meet you.'

Zoe continues, her voice starting to shake as she remembers Bennie and Lucy, their sticky hands outstretched like little stars. And her mum. Her poor mum. Alone, without Zoe. It can't happen. This can't happen. 'I like reading and going out with my friends. And hiking – walking up the Lune even when it's raining. And there's so much more I want to see and do. I'm going travelling, I want to see the world. You can't take that from me—'

The woman shrieks, a crazed howling laugh bouncing off the tiled walls. 'You will not tell me what I can and can't do. No one gives me instructions. Especially not pretty little teenagers who think the world owes them something.' The woman walks towards Zoe, the knife outstretched once again. 'I was once pretty like you. All the boys wanted me.'

She trails the knife point along Zoe's cheek, tugging at her skin. 'I'm invisible now, but I'm still powerful. McVitie saw something in me. He saw it, he wanted it, and he broke me open.' Still holding the knife to Zoe's face with one hand, she jabs Zoe in the ribs with the fingertips of her other hand, knocking the air from Zoe's lungs with each shove to punctuate her speech. She gestures around the room. 'I was nothing when I arrived in this place. I was no one. I was weak and broken. Barely an adult.'

Zoe tries to breathe between the jabs to her stomach.

The woman's voice gets higher, wilder. 'He tore me apart and put me back together again. I hated him some days. Wanted to destroy him as he was destroying me. Yet I loved him too. It took years, but we had nothing else to do in here.' Her voice softens. 'But even great men must die. The only man who sees me and hears me now is my son. *My* legacy. He loves me so much. He just wants me to be happy. That's what I deserve.'

Zoe watches the point of the knife as it dances in front of her eyes, just millimetres from her face. She freezes. Just one wrong move and that blade is going right into her face, she knows it.

'I'm going to skin you alive. I'm going to flay that pretty little face until you look like a piece of bacon ready to go on the grill.'

Zoe starts to cry, her body racked with enormous sobs. This

creature isn't normal and it's all futile: there's no point saying your name or telling her anything to try and show her that Zoe is a real person with feelings and hopes. She drops her head, her shoulders sag. She pictures her Mum's face, the way her eyes crinkle at the corners when she smiles, curly hair, the smell of her perfume: the smell of home.

'No! This one's mine,' a man's voice interrupts.

The woman stops, backs off. Her face changes, the anger immediately dissipates and her face shifts into a smile. From crazed Medusa to calm, loving mother.

'Baby,' she says. 'You're back. This evil girl was being so cruel, so unkind to me.' She mewls like a kitten, sticking out her bottom lip. 'She insulted McVitie.'

The man puts his hand on the woman's shoulder, comforting her. 'How dare you,' he growls at Zoe.

The old woman stands by his side looking up at her son, her head barely reaching his shoulder. He rests his arm around her birdlike body, as if she needs his protection. There is a familial resemblance; their faces both long and narrow, a slight bump on the bridge of their noses. And a cruel, blank look in their eyes when they regard Zoe as she sits in the chair, restrained in the prison of their making. It almost looks like pride.

'It's time,' she says, and her son's body tenses. He stands taller, squares his chest. It's clear that she's the one with all the power, and he just follows her orders.

Zoe's brain prickles as her understanding of the last twenty-four hours continues to realign. Until a short while ago, she thought this man was the biggest danger she could face. She thought he was the crazed rapist, murderer, kidnapper

– everything. He wielded so much power, and she believed he was the one in charge, following his own motivations and urges. But he's nothing more than a servant, like a cat who hunts for mice to drop at its owner's feet.

This woman seemed so vulnerable, so alone. The faint voice through the caravan wall. Zoe can't believe she fell for it; she would have led this woman to safety. She believed they were both victims.

'Leave us,' the woman demands of her son. 'You're no longer needed.'

The son visibly recoils, a look of intense anger on his face. He balls his hands into fists at his sides.

'No, not this time. This time the girl is mine.'

Thomas

The cupboard is cramped, with Maggie's shoulder pressed into his chest, her hair tickling his nose. She's holding his hand, her whole body trembling with fear.

Through a narrow gap in the wooden door, Thomas can see the mother and son pacing back and forth, like frustrated tigers in a small cage.

'You're not ready for this,' Bertha hisses, and her son slams his hand against the wall. One of the tiles falls and smashes on the floor, scattering shards in all directions across the room.

The inside of the cupboard smells stale, like old cleaning products that have leaked and dried over years and years. An ancient mop leans against the corner, its tendrils crispy and unmoving. There's a roll of paper, which used to be blue but is now a dirty brown colour from whatever leakage it's soaked up while it sat in the cupboard.

Maggie shifts, trying to get high enough to see through the gap too.

'Don't move,' he whispers. 'You'll knock something over and then they'll know we're here.'

'But I can't see.'

'I don't care,' he says, his hands on her shoulders. 'There's nothing to see, and they can't know we're here.'

'They know we're here. She told the woman, remember? Duh.'

He shakes his head.

'She said she'd found help, but that could mean anything. I think we're safe, for now. So, keep still and shut up.'

The son seems really angry, his voice loud and pace fast. 'I've been ready for years. Since we started this.'

'And every time you get a bit more rope, you hang yourself on it. Remember that girl you nearly let get away?'

'I learned from that. I wouldn't make that mistake again.'

'Only because I won't let you.'

'I would never hunt that close to home again. I'm prepared, I'm careful.'

'Not careful enough. Look at this one,' she points at Zoe, who flinches away. 'Her friend can give a dead-on description of you to the police.'

'Her friend was a stupid idiot and I drugged her anyway. She won't remember a thing. And I was wearing our mark's disgusting hat. I introduced myself as him.'

The lady shakes her head. 'Not enough, you know it.'

'I'm well on the road to pinning it all on him.'

'But you pulled the trigger too early. You've always been like this. Too impatient to do something properly. This girl was not part of our plan, I did not request her. But now I have to go and clean up your mess for you again.'

Zoe cries out at this. Thomas flinches.

'I never asked you to. This one was mine, Mother. I worked

hard for this, spent hours at Paul's house laying the groundwork. Pretending to be his friend. Just like you taught me. Taking things, planting things. It was done, ready. I'm not impatient or slapdash, or whatever other names you like to call me.'

'Even if you're right. Even if you know everything, have prepared everything, have learned every lesson that I've taught you, it doesn't matter.'

'What?'

'None of it is relevant when you're a coward.'

There's a huge crash, as the man lifts an old fire extinguisher over his head and heaves it against the wall. The case smashes open, and white dust plumes everywhere. 'I told you, don't call me that.'

Thomas can't see anything except white, like smoke, but it doesn't stop the woman ranting and raving at her son.

'You could have killed this girl at any point in the last twenty-four hours. I know you wanted to. And you had many opportunities. You had the tools, the time, and the victim right there, tied up and waiting for you. So why didn't you do it, eh? Why didn't you slice her eyelids open like you've always dreamed about? Why didn't you cover her airways until she blacked out? Why didn't you press that knifepoint right into her carotid artery and watch the blood drain from her little body?'

The dust clears, and through the gap in the door Thomas sees the man crossing the room, pushing his mother against the wall, holding her shoulders with both hands. His face is bright red, a vein sticking out in the side of his neck as he faces up to her. He looks enormous, puffed up and muscular. The woman looks tiny and bird-like in comparison, but her expression is powerful.

'No, don't answer. I know why you didn't do those things and it's got nothing to do with me holding you back or not *letting you*, as if I'm the problem.' She throws back her head and cackles, her mouth wide. Her teeth are black inside her mouth. 'You can't blame me. The only thing in your way is you, you're a joke. You talk about how we're both predators, and hunters; the self-selected tip of the evolutionary pyramid – but you're no better than your security guard friend Bruce, grooming 15-year-old schoolgirls in front of the space heater in that hut.' Her voice rises to a crescendo as she shouts: 'McVitie would be ashamed of you.'

The man roars so loud that both Maggie and Thomas put their hands over their ears. Thomas sees Zoe, her face screwed up and her head turned away from the fighting pair. The man's hands move to his mother's neck, and he wraps them around her throat.

She's still laughing though. She's enjoying this. Even with his hands squeezing, she keeps going, fuelled by the adrenalin of the destruction caused by her words. 'I am ashamed of you. Give up now. Give up and be normal, live a dull, ordinary life away from here and leave the hunting to me. Leave it to someone who knows how. I've tried for years to lift you to the standard that McVitie taught to me, and you've not got it in you. You'll never reach your father's status.'

His knuckles turn white around her neck and he squeezes hard, screaming with frustration and years of anger that he's never expressed. The woman's laughter stops, and for a moment she looks afraid: she didn't believe he could do it. She didn't believe he *would*, Thomas thinks. The smile slides from her face.

There's a horrible crunch, and silence.

As quickly as it began, the man releases his mother, removing his hands from her neck so fast that it's as if she's burned him. He must have realised what he was doing. She slumps to the floor, and Thomas can't see her any more from where he is peeking through the cupboard door.

The man turns and walks away, out of the room. His footsteps echo through the tunnels as he scuttles away. They listen for a moment. There's no sounds of movement from the woman.

'Let's get Zoe and go,' Maggie whispers, pushing open the door and stepping over the woman's body to get to Zoe, who's still tied to the chair, eyes streaming with tears.

Helen

'Read this,' the text message reads. 'Just published ten mins ago. Gonna make everyone pay attention – we'll find Zoe. Jan x'

Helen clicks to open the article.

Suspected serial killer: Police deny link in missing girl's case

By J. Mitchell

Lancaster police ignore newest evidence in case for active serial killer

A missing teenage girl whose name has not yet been released is locally rumoured to be yet another victim in the case of a suspected serial killer, according to neighbours and friends. Yet local police still deny the existence of this killer, refusing to start the manhunt.

Joining a growing list of local missing teenage girls, sources say the teenager disappeared from a local pub on Thursday evening and has not been heard from since.

Police are known to be searching the area after the teenager was reported missing by her parents. An area in the car park of the Richard the Lionheart pub was cordoned off earlier today, and friends close to the girl have been questioned, but no charges have been filed.

Other victims

She is the sixth individual of this demographic to go missing recently in what Lancaster Police refuse to acknowledge as a potential serial kidnapper and murderer operating in the area.

See also: Is this the work of a "Lancaster Ripper"?

Authorities have been accused of not investigating properly at the time. A source close to the police has said that there's no serial killer: that with no bodies, no suspects and no forensic evidence, there is no case.

Anyone with information about any of the missing women in this article can contact Crimestoppers on 0800 555 111 or email j.mitchell@lancasternews.com.

There is no case.

Helen drops her phone to the bed and looks around the bedroom, blinking back tears and feeling the cold metallic weight of fear. It's so frustrating; she feels like she's the only person screaming and shouting about what a massive situation this is, and no one is listening. No one believes her. They all think Zoe's a typical teenage runaway, and Helen just knows that's not true. Deep in her bones, she knows that Zoe wouldn't leave by choice, that Zoe always comes home.

The riot of colour splashed around the room hurts Helen's tired eyes as she stares at the walls. Zoe's bedroom represents years of devotion to crafting an identity, plastered across every inch of a space which enables self-expression. Looped around the top of the room are white fairy lights, twinkling away and creating the atmosphere of a magical grotto. Against one wall is a single bed, scattered with plump bright-coloured cushions, a doll and a teddy bear.

Helen sits on Zoe's bed and pulls the doll onto her knee, hugging her close as if that might help her connect with Zoe.

There's a noise in the corridor and Zoe's bedroom door nudges. Helen looks up, startled, but it's just Alfie nosing the door open. He flops down on Zoe's rag rug, an explosion of colour that Zoe made herself when she was fifteen.

On the wall next to the door there's a huge collage of photographs of Zoe and her friends, at festivals, concerts, camping trips and parties. They're all blazingly happy, arms thrown around each other's shoulders and huge grins on their faces. Their skin is clear and fresh, like babies. Not a care in the world.

Helen notices a more recent picture: Zoe and Abbie, cheeks pressed together, and Max stood slightly behind, half his face obscured by a pint glass. They're in a local pub – possibly the one they were in last night too, the Richard the Lionheart. She stares at the photograph, combing it for a clue like a detective.

But the background is dark and nothing else is visible except the teenagers and their smiles.

Her phone beeps and she grabs it.

She drops her phone to the floor. Not Zoe.

'*Any more news? Don't forget what I said – do the investigating yourself x*' the text reads. It's Janet again, the journalist from next door. Friends have been checking in all day, bless them, but there's only so many times you can send the same '*No news*' text message before it becomes unbearable.

She starts to text back but pauses with her fingers poised over the touchscreen. Even though there's nothing to tell, she doesn't know whether a journalist is friend or foe. Right now, any help is welcome; but Tony's very wary of Janet based on his past experience with journalists. Helen decides to go for it.

'*Nothing. Police interviewed her boyfriend. Not a suspect but he saw someone who might be. Didn't have much to go on though.*'

She wonders if the police got anything extra out of Dane when they questioned him at the station. She still can't work out whether he has anything to hide.

Alfie whines and pushes his chin onto her knee. She moves the doll out of the way – Alfie has a history of taking custody of Zoe's toys and returning them slightly damp and chewed. She strokes his head, running the tip of her finger along the soft white hair on the bridge of his nose. He whines again.

She looks down at him. 'What is it, Alfie?'

He deposits a toy on her knee and backs off, his tail wagging. He wants her to throw it.

It drops to the floor and Alfie skitters forward, believing the game has already started.

'What have you got there?' She pushes him back gently and reaches down to pick it up. The last thing she wants is anything of Zoe's getting chewed right now.

Helen draws her breath in sharp through her teeth. It's that shoe, the one from the Hospital yesterday. She holds it in both hands and really examines it. Now that it's dry, the stains on it look less and less like mud. It's a size 5, a small ladies' shoe. Why was it there? And why only one? No one loses only one shoe.

She remembers that man, the security guard. Alfie hated him. She's never known him to react like that to anyone before; it was strange. As if he sensed something sinister about the man.

Sure, he was handsome. But his gaze was distant; it made her feel like his actual expression was a covering for something else underneath, like his real face was hiding behind a carefully constructed veil or mask, and the only true indicator was the eyes.

He couldn't get her away fast enough, despite his friendly chat: all the time they were talking, he was escorting her off the premises. He wanted her out immediately.

She looks at Alfie, his head resting on his paws on Zoe's bedroom floor, looking up at her and the shoe in her hands.

She needs to talk to someone, to untangle all these different ideas.

Helen fumbles with her phone to call Tony, but it just rings and rings.

'Your daughter's missing, you idiot, answer your phone.'

She starts to call the police station but stops herself just before hitting the green button. It isn't enough. They won't listen to her. What would she say? 'Alfie didn't like this guy I met once. And I found a shoe'? It's not ... anything. Certainly not sufficient evidence for anyone to do anything, Helen's watched enough TV police procedurals to know that.

She dials Zoe's number again, and her heart sinks anew when it goes straight to voicemail, same as it has been all day. 'Hello, you've reached Zoe's voicemail. Don't leave a message, I never check them. I'll see your missed call and call you back as soon as I can! Bye!' Her cheerful, happy voice makes Helen's eyes fill with tears.

She remembers the conversation they had the day Helen discovered the voicemail greeting, asking Zoe whether she thought that universities and future employers would find that kind of attitude professional, or whether they'd discount her immediately and hire someone else.

Helen shakes her head at herself, disgusted that she tried to change her beautiful Zoe even slightly, ashamed of every time she was short or angry with her. She should have just let her be exactly herself, every single day. No mistake is unfixable, and every experience worth learning from. Why couldn't she just let Zoe be Zoe? Why did she have to nag and whine and try to force her to grow up?

She buries her face in Zoe's cushions and lies back onto the bed, not even moving when Alfie jumps up and snuggles in next to her, sensing her anguish and licking the tears from her face with his big pink tongue.

She's drifting off to sleep as her phone vibrates once more; she doesn't hear the quiet *ping* of a new email in her inbox.

Thomas

Zoe hasn't said a word since they cut her free. They used Maggie's knife to release her from the creepy chair's restraints, and the first thing she did with her free hands was rip the tape from her eyes so she could blink. She's still conscious, barely, but Thomas is grateful for every moment she's still alive, especially as she's moving her feet and holding up some of her own weight. If she faints, he doesn't think they will be able to get her out. Her weight hangs from his shoulder, her arm wrapped around his neck, and Maggie's on her other side.

Thomas winces, and puts his left hand flat on the wall. It feels clammy and rough beneath his fingers as they make their slow progress along the tunnel. He walks carefully, step by step, back towards the stairs which lead to fresh air and freedom.

He's managed to quash his terror for a few minutes; now there are two other people to look after, especially as they're girls. He needs to protect them, get them home safely. And if that's his job, it's the job he'll do, and there's no time to be scared right now. So, he tries to switch off the fear, like a light.

Every sound is magnified in the inky blackness. He can

hear Maggie's breathing near his shoulder, quicker than usual and slightly shaky, and the girl's deep breaths next to him, loud and slow like she's sleeping.

His feet make a gritty crunch on the concrete floor as he steps forward. Maggie's footsteps, next to his. And the dragging of Zoe's feet keeping her upright. Dripping pipes. Creaking from above their heads. The rustling of his jumper sleeves. At every small sound, each crack of branches or gust of wind from outside, he freezes.

They continue forwards, slow step after slow step.

Suddenly, everything tilts with his panic: he's lost. Where are they? Where are the stairs? They have walked too far; they may have passed the entrance to the stairwell. He turns around, trying and failing to peer through the blackness. His chest tightens and it becomes hard to breathe again. Wheeze. Wheeze. He tries to slow down, sucking the air deep into his lungs.

'Maggie,' he whispers. 'Where are the stairs?'

He hears her squeak.

'Have we passed them?'

She makes a small mewling sound, like a kitten. 'I don't know. I don't know. I don't know. I want to go home. Please, Thomas. Please take us home.'

He presses his palm into the wall, as if the rough concrete could tell him which way they need to go. But nothing. Nothing. It is as if part of his brain – the part which remembers where they have been and how far they have walked – has shut down and disappeared, and the more he tries to remember, the further away the memory drifts.

They are lost in the endless tunnels.

He leans against the wall, imagining blood soaking into his clothes from the walls. But it's not true, it's just in his head. All the blood was in that room. And it was dry. Maggie starts to cry; little snuffling, hiccoughing sobs she tries to stifle with her hand.

Then he hears a noise from further down the corridor. The creaking of a door. Footsteps. Thomas bites his lip hard so as not to scream. The man is coming back to clean up his mess. The man thinks he'll find Zoe, and instead there's nothing but her bonds, sliced open. He'll see what Thomas did. He'll see that the girl is gone. And he'll find them. The nasty taste on his tongue tells Thomas that he is on the verge of vomiting with fear. His mouth fills with spit.

He grabs Zoe's arm and hoists her roughly, dragging her along the tunnel, away from the footsteps. Maggie lifts her from the other side, and her feet lift off the ground as they pull her.

His hand finds a doorway, he pushes at it, pushes and pushes but the door won't budge. He shoves them all forward to the next door, clawing with his fingers for a door handle, ignoring the pain as he shreds his fingernails. This door stands half open. He leans against it, but as soon as it starts to move the rusty hinges creak and threaten to give away their position.

He wriggles through the gap, pulling Maggie and Zoe in behind him. He wants to drag the door closed but can't risk the noise.

He has no idea where they are, but it doesn't matter – as long as the man doesn't find them.

The footsteps continue down the tunnel, getting quieter as they reach the far end, and the blood-soaked room where the woman's body lies. Thomas slowly raises his hand and finds Maggie's face, pressing a shaking finger lightly to her lips to tell her to be silent.

Her lips are dry and trembling. He pulls her towards him and holds her in his arms, clinging to her, his nose in her hair, eyes squeezed shut.

There's a shout, a growl of frustration, and a clang of metal as the man discovers what they've done, that they've stolen Zoe from him.

Thomas and Maggie cower together, holding Zoe upright between them, listening through the door as the now-frantic footsteps run back along the tunnel and away.

All is silent as they wait for the right moment to escape.

Alexander

He is the apex predator now.

Lying on the tiled floor, his mother looks like she's sleeping, her face relaxed and youthful like she hasn't looked in years. The two lines between her eyebrows are gone, and her lips are fuller when they're not pulled back in a cruel sneer. She's beautiful, just as she always said. She was right.

Your father. McVitie.

He's always wondered but never known for certain. That celebrated 'genius' she glorified for Alexander's entire life, his predatory accomplishments held up as the ultimate goal. She worshipped at McVitie's shrine as she disciplined Alexander again and again throughout his childhood, attempting to train him to be the next generation's hunter. She was desperate to continue McVitie's legacy and make it even greater, but Alexander always disappointed her when held up against McVitie's greatness.

Yet there's nothing great here; both of his parents were committed lunatics, rutting in their insane asylum, hiding from the nurses while they conducted their twisted affair. The scandal of two patients conceiving a baby got Mother discharged as soon as Alexander was born, and McVitie died soon after. It makes sense, he realises now: she never forgave Alexander for that, as if it was his fault that she was sent away from her mentor.

He feels a deep straining in his chest, between his heart and lungs. His collarbones ache. It's a combination of grief, guilt and anger. He wants to pummel her face until it's a bloody pulp for all the things she said to him, all the inadequacies she made him feel for his entire life. But he also wants to lie on the floor alongside her lifeless body and pull her into his arms, kiss her cheek and somehow bring her back to life to fight another day.

He's not stupid: he knows that the deep love he holds for his mother is as twisted and weird as McVitie's psychosis. And as one-sided: his mother doesn't – didn't – love him. But she loved to control him.

So much one-sided love. He remembers the glassy look in her eyes when she spoke of McVitie; how intelligent he was, how he shouldn't have been in the asylum, caged like a lion at the zoo. Mother loved McVitie, but McVitie didn't love her; he used her as his pawn. She was his way to keep killing after imprisonment, even after death. She was his ticket to immortality, and the plan worked. Until now.

Her skin is still warm under his fingertips. Even the shell of her being, this corpse lying on the tiled floor in the semi-darkness, has more energy to it than any other living human being he has ever met. Her power was immense. All he wanted was to make her proud.

He bends to kiss her forehead, lies a hand on her cheek

to say goodbye, and then stands up, ready to act. He fills his lungs with musty air.

Now it is Alexander's time. He is the lone wolf, the sole predator. Nothing stands between him and greatness.

His shoulders feel wide and strong, like he carried a heavy backpack for miles and someone else just took the burden. No one on this whole earth can tell him what to do now. No one can judge him, hold him back, give him instructions, or tell him 'no'. He is the master of the universe; he can do whatever he wants. No one can stop him and there are no limits.

He has killed now.

He is the hunter, the apex predator. He has taken the mantle from his mother and now wields the power.

He must find the girl, and she can't get far. She's half dead and hasn't eaten in more than twenty-four hours. She's weak, thirsty, injured.

Alexander's first instinct is to chase after her, hunt her down, bring her back here. But he's worked in this labyrinthine asylum long enough to know that she's still in the building, dragging her half-dead carcass through the endless corridors, desperate to find a way out.

The important thing is to keep his cool and think rationally. He needs to destroy evidence of their presence and launch the framing operation. Just as his mother taught him.

When he finds the girl, he'll end it straight away. He'll kill her. He'll stab her in the stomach and rotate the blade, really stir things up in there. He feels a thrill of excitement; his second kill will be easier.

He looks at the body again, his mother's bones sticking

out beneath the thin white nightgown. She used to be taller than him. She looks so small, down there on the ground. He shakes his head. She used to be so powerful. She used to hurt him, until he learned never to disobey her. Just minutes after death, the power is beginning to leave her body. Her skin sags, her eyes bagged and surrounded by creases. Her hair is ratty. She was so magnificent, once. And terrifying. No longer.

She never thanked him. She never said 'well done'. And she never allowed him to make the final cut.

Today's the day. It's Alexander's turn now.

He turns away, runs out into the darkness of the basement tunnels.

He'll slice the girl open. He needs to see the life drain from her open eyes.

Thomas

Thomas has no idea how long they have stood here, Maggie's face buried in his shoulder and their ears straining against the silence.

Zoe has slumped down to the floor, too exhausted to stand any longer, even with their support. She's got a nasty cut on her neck, so Thomas has removed his t-shirt and tied it over the wound. His woolly jumper scratches against his bare skin, but at least she's not bleeding any more.

The man is gone, his running footsteps faded to nothing. He hasn't found them yet, but they haven't got much time before he does. The man was so angry with that scary woman; Thomas has never seen a person so furious in his entire life. He probably could have torn the woman in half if he'd wanted to. Instead he just crushed her neck.

Thomas steps away from Maggie and opens his eyes. A murky light has begun to creep into the room through a tiny window up near the ceiling; too early for dawn, but not pitch black any more. Rusted filing cabinets line the walls of the room in which they stand, some drawers standing open and one cabinet lying on its side in the middle, surrounded by scattered papers and files. Massive pinboards line the walls, pasted with lists of names, dates and unpronounceable drugs. This room must have been some kind of office for the hospital workers.

The girl is curled up on her side, almost asleep, her chest rising and falling rapidly. Her swollen eyelids are closed, face twitching and eyebrows frowning as she dreams with short whimpers. Her dirty cheeks are etched with clear rivers where tears ran their path.

He nudges the door and peers out into the tunnel. Still he can see barely anything, but the tiny amount of light seeping through the few windows helps him regain his bearings and remember where the stairs are. His shoulders release a small amount of tension.

Silence. Maggie and Thomas wake the girl and struggle with her to get her to her feet once more. She keeps her eyes closed. Slowly and painstakingly they pull her into the tunnel, turning right and feeling along the wall for the entrance to the stairs.

Finally, they run out of wall. Thomas pats the air where the corridor turns, using his hand like blind people use canes. They shuffle forward, taking tiny steps until his toes bump against the first step.

He empties his lungs in a huge expulsion of tension and relief. It's the stairs out of the basement. They're on their way out.

At the top of the stairs, Thomas gropes along the door for a handle. Nothing. He pushes hard, but it won't budge. The relief of moments ago dissolves into panic once more. His heart feels like it might leap out of his throat.

'Come on, let's get out,' whispers Maggie. The girl moans, and Thomas winces at the sound, mentally willing her to be silent.

'Come on,' Maggie repeats.

Thomas feels an intense flash of irritation. 'What do you think I'm doing, stupid?' he hisses. He leans against the door with his shoulder, pushing as hard as he can. 'I can't get the door open. It's locked or something.'

Maggie sinks into a sitting position on the stairs, her head in her hands. 'We're trapped.' She begins to sob.

With only one person holding her up, Zoe starts to slump, unable to hold her own weight. Thomas's back aches under the load of a girl at least a foot taller than him, and he nearly tumbles down the stairs, taking the girl with him. He lowers them both to the floor, so all three of them are sitting on the top step, Zoe leaning heavy against him.

Maggie opens her mouth, starting to say something, and Zoe groans again, loudly.

He reaches out and covers both of their mouths as fast as he can. Zoe flinches away as soon as she feels his touch. He presses harder, desperate to show her how important this is. 'Shut up. Shut up. Please. Shut up or he'll hear us and come back.'

Zoe shifts and her voice comes out in a whisper. 'If we can't get out, we need to hide.'

Helen

Helen wakes with a gasp, deeply confused. Blue half-light filters through the curtains, it's not yet dawn but the sun is just below the horizon, ready to flood the world with light. Where has she slept?

She looks around, trying to focus her eyes on the busy walls, flowery scent and bright colours, even in this dusky morning: Zoe's room. It all comes crashing back into her mind: Zoe's gone. Her stomach heaves and she nearly vomits.

She stands up, and quickly slumps down to her knees on the floor – she must have slept at a funny angle, and her legs are full of pins and needles. She digs her fingers into the carpet, desperate for *this* to be the dream she can wake from.

Alfie jumps down from the bed, looking up at her with a guilty expression, waiting to be told off for sleeping on a human's bed. She pats him on the head and his ears rise back up to normal position.

Getting slowly to her feet, Helen tries to sort out her head, remember the facts and there's something ... something niggling at the back of her mind. Before she fell asleep, there was something important she'd hit upon, a tiny kernel of an idea.

She picks up her phone to see an email notification and a missed call from Tony. Her foot nudges against something on the floor; the stained shoe discarded where Alfie dropped it last night.

She calls Tony's mobile again, but he doesn't answer; he's probably getting a little sleep. She tries to marshal her thoughts. Still nothing from Zoe, and her phone is still going straight to voicemail. All the possibilities of where her daughter might be – with a friend, out clubbing, even injured in a hospital – peel away to leave no options behind except a screaming void so terrible that Helen can't think it. It's like a mental flinch if she strays too close to the edge; a stepping-back protection mechanism. But still, that deep void is there, sucking her closer to destruction every hour that they have no news of Zoe.

She needs to act, to do something that might help. Even if it's futile. Her fingers itch to load up a search engine and find more news articles about missing girls, local serial killers, anything that might help, like Janet suggested.

She opens her laptop, and this time Googles 'Lancaster UK serial killer'. The results aren't helpful: the articles are mostly about Buck Ruxton, the doctor who killed his wife and housemaid in the 1930s. She skims over some digitised library copies of newspapers from the late 1980s. Nothing new about the teenage girls case, just Janet's newspaper article, its purple URL indicating a path she's already trodden.

Janet couldn't tell her anything new, really; just what she'd already read online. Some teenage girls are missing but there are no obvious suspicious circumstances, so no one is investigating. One thing Janet had said which gave Helen hope, though, was that it's possible that Zoe's case would 'crack it all open'. Helen hates that her own daughter might become the sledgehammer the police force needs to make progress.

She clicks to her emails, and finds the new one, from Zoe's friend Max. There's no text, just a link in the body of the email.

She clicks the link. It's a grimy, cheap blog-style website with a black background and green font, like old DOS computers in the 80s and 90s. Nothing about this place looks like reputable journalism. The logo at the top shows a cartoon face with a pair of sunglasses and an upturned collar: 'Urban Dark Reporter'. The side menu identifies subcategories like 'urban exploration', 'unsolved crime', 'cold cases' and 'dark web'. She's about to close the tab, when her eye falls on the intro paragraph of a recent article: 'the biggest thorn in the side of Lancaster's police force'.

Investigating Mr X and Family: Lancaster's Heredity of Slaughter

By Urban Dark Reporter

New investigation uncovers multiple generations of murderers never caught: the biggest thorn in the side of Lancaster's police force

The city of Lancaster has been hounded by a series of unsolved murders for almost 100 years, and no one has linked them together, until now!

In the 40s and 50s, a chameleon stalked the UK's city streets, committing crimes under stolen identities and slinking off into the shadows as soon as he might get caught. Leonard McVitie was a prolific serial killer in locations around the country, and even after his capture, his legacy resonates down the generations.

We thought we knew everything about McVitie, and criminal historians marked it 'case closed', but pocket communities on the dark web say that his crimes continued by proxy even after he was imprisoned in Lancaster Lune Asylum in 1959.

How did he do it? With the help of a partner: an equally dangerous and prolific serial killer who has still never been caught. We suspected he had a protégé, but until now we didn't know who that was.

See also: Leonard McVitie's Legacy

My source says: 'After his capture, McVitie was always writing and talking: in the asylum he gave speeches to the inmates and they all hung off his every word. He wanted to teach people what he knew, and the nurses let him get away with it. They didn't have time to monitor every patient, so they just let him do it. I saw it with my own eyes one afternoon: he was teaching the lace-makers how to tie a handcuff knot.'

It's not known how many inmates learned from McVitie, or what he taught them, although his archives are starting to reveal some of his secrets. But it is suspected that one of his pupils was released in the mid-1980s, and continued the monster's legacy.

The rise of Mr X

Still unidentified, Mr X and his multiple murders haunted Lancashire for nearly 10 years—

Helen stops reading and pushes the laptop away from her on the table.

'Mr X,' she whispers.

Her memory whisks back to the early years of her marriage with Tony, the late nights and early starts of his first big case in the Police: the unsolved murders of young women across the county. No matter how many nights he stayed late at the office, chasing leads, interviewing suspects, Mr X remained unidentified and free.

It haunted Tony for years, until eventually he requested a move out of CID and into Special Branch. After Zoe was born, he couldn't bear to be near the parents of murdered daughters. Terrorists – even during the worst of The Troubles – were less disturbing to Tony than his failure to catch a monster and protect the lives of local girls.

She shakes her head, feeling a rush of sympathy and sadness for Tony and the man he used to be. He was so kind, so hopeful, so ambitious. But the Mr X case took that from him, disillusioned him and eventually defeated him into early retirement and a quiet job in security at the University.

But Helen's not finished reading: there's more to this article. She pulls the laptop back towards her:

Many young women went missing during Mr X's reign of terror, with at least three confirmed cases and up to ten suspected.

Constantly in the news throughout the late 80s and early 90s, the murders were also at the forefront of the news due to in-fighting within the Lancashire Constabulary, who failed to charge even one suspect.

The killings continued at a terrifying pace for years, before they mysteriously stopped in the mid- to late-90s. Many now believe that Mr X is dead: a killer that prolific does not just stop their crimes.

Hand-me-down murders?

After the mid-90s, Lancaster enjoyed a brief respite period, with few missing cases and no unsolved murders. But at the time of writing, some circles believe that a recent spate of missing girls (up to six at the time of writing) implies that there's a new serial killer in operation in the local area.

Local police deny the possibility, declaring that no evidence and no bodies means no murders. But commentators and true crime enthusiasts have detected a pattern, and that pattern is an echo back to both Mr X and McVitie:

Helen leans closer to the picture on the screen. It's a grid of girls' faces in two columns, the left column entitled '1990s', the right '2010s'.

'Woah,' she says. 'They're like twins.'

Despite the time difference, the girls look almost identical: all beautiful teenagers with centre partings and long, dark hair.

The article continues:

> As you can see from the image, today's killer has a type, and so did Mr X. The two columns of faces juxtaposed tell a sad, scary tale of a hunter and a pupil, just like McVitie and Mr X – one generation later.
>
> And sure, the police and some members of the public present the argument that there are no bodies, so no recent victims are confirmed dead. The missing girls (including Sadie Duncan, Joanna Bamber, Roberta Clarkson and Anna Keyne) might be in the back alleys of Blackpool as you read this, alive and well. But the demographic, the facial similarities and the very clean MO suggest otherwise.
>
> Urban Dark Reporter believes that there is a serial killer in operation in Lancaster RIGHT NOW. That serial killer learned everything he knows from Mr X, who learned everything he knew from Leonard McVitie.
>
> We need to act now before they activate the fourth generation of monster.

Helen's skin prickles with sweat. Three generations of killers, handing down their knowledge, the police totally unaware. And her poor Zoe possibly caught up in this, the victim of the third generation.

She flattens the palms of her hands to the table on either side of the laptop, focuses her attention on the cold of wooden kitchen table, its surface smooth under her hands.

Her eyes skim the article, looking for a clue to the author's identity. Why did Max send it? Did he write it? And if so, how did he get this information? The only name is 'Urban Dark Reporter'. She clicks on the name and gets taken to the 'About' page.

> *Covering both breaking stories and cold cases,* Urban Dark Reporter *uncovers the crime stories overlooked by local police forces, particularly focussed on the North West of England. We're a team of vigilantes so anonymous that we don't even know who we are; all our reporters write under the 'Urban Dark Reporter' pseudonym and submit articles under false names. Got a scoop? Email urbandarkanonymous@darkreporter.com*

She tries Tony's landline, desperate to speak to anyone.

She waits for their voicemail beep and leaves her message: 'It's me. I found a girl's shoe yesterday. No, not yesterday. The day before, at the old hospital. I think it's Mr X who took Zoe. Anyway, I'm going there, to the hospital in Flagstone Woods. Meet me there if you get thi—'

There's a click as someone lifts the receiver.

'Mr X?' Tony's breathing is ragged, like he ran to the phone. 'What has this got to do with that piece of shit?'

Helen pauses, waiting for Tony to process the rest of her voicemail.

'You found Zoe's shoe?' There we go.

'No, not Zoe's. Someone else's.'

The line crackles as Tony pauses. 'You're not making any sense, Helen.' She can tell he's trying not to snap at her, trying to moderate his tone and not get angry. He always gets frustrated when he doesn't understand something.

Helen closes her eyes. She stops her frantic pacing around Zoe's room, stops and stares at the spines of the books on her daughter's bookshelf. 'I'm going to send you an article. It links together the missing teenagers with Mr X—'

'No. Mr X stopped offending years ago. He's dead. He has to be dead. That's why it stopped.' Tony's probably rubbing his eyes, running his hands through his hair, scratching his stomach through his pyjama t-shirt. She remembers the middle of the night phone calls when they were married, Tony pacing the bedroom as the sun began to peek over the horizon. Tony's voice is frantic. 'Killers like Mr X don't just stop for no reason; they keep slaughtering until they're caught, or they die. They don't go into fucking retirement.'

Helen tries to keep a steady tone. 'I know, but this article says he's passing his knowledge down. And that shoe Alfie found, up at the hospital – that's where McVitie was a patient.'

He groans down the phone. 'McVitie? Who's McVitie?'

'I'll send you the article and you can read it. There's a series of them, on this website. In the meantime, I'll get in the car and go—'

'Don't be stupid. You can't go on a wild goose chase in the middle of the night just because someone lost their shoes in the woods.'

'Yes, I can,' she says, pulling open one of Zoe's drawers and picking up a scarf, burying her nose in the smell of her daughter's skin. Her eyes fill with tears. 'And it's nearly dawn. No one is doing anything to find her, not even you.'

He sucks in his breath at this but doesn't interrupt.

'I just need to be out there, finding her, doing something. I won't sleep any more. I can't sit here waiting and not trying to find her when she's out there somewhere ...' her voice cracks. 'I can at least look for her.'

'Helen, it's four in the morning. There's nothing you can do right now. The police are on it, and they'll be doing everything they can.'

'It's not ENOUGH!' she shouts, and Alfie slinks out of the room, his tail between his legs.

Tony sighs long and hard, air crackling and reverberating along the phone line.

'I know it's not. She's our baby, Helen. Mine as much as yours. And I want her found just as much as you do.'

Helen nods slowly, even though he can't see her. She knows she's grasping for options, desperate to do something. Even if it makes no sense.

'The press have reported on it. On Zoe. Janet Mitchell says her case looks like the others. The ... the other missing girls.'

'Mitchell is a hack, Hel. You can't trust a journalist. They'll say anything to get information for a story. She's using you.' Tony doesn't sound as sure as he did last time. 'But it can't be Mr X again. It just can't be. Send me that article too, I'll have a look.'

Helen sighs with relief. 'Thank you. I'll send the links.'

'Do you want to come over here?' he asks quietly.

She stops pacing and frowns. 'Now?'

'Yes, now. Why not? You said it yourself: neither of us will get any more sleep tonight, and there's no need for you to be on your own, rifling through Zoe's stuff and torturing yourself remembering every argument you ever had with her.'

Helen lets out a short, dry 'Ha,' and covers her eyes with her hand as they sting with tears. 'You know me so well.'

'Come over here, love. Be with the rest of your family right now.'

She starts to cry again, wildly relieved at the idea of being with other people, people to talk to and who can absorb some of her ranging thoughts, instead of them bouncing around her head getting bigger and scarier in the echo chamber of her mind.

'Thank you. I would really like that.'

'Bring Alfie too. He shouldn't be on his own and then you won't have to worry about him needing to go outside.'

'What about the kids' allergies? And Melanie?' Melanie has never allowed a pet in the house.

'The kids can take an antihistamine if they get snuffly. And Melanie can deal, it's just for one day. She loves Zoe too; she won't make a fuss on a day like today.'

Helen nods. 'I'll be over in ten minutes. Thanks, Tony.'

'Bring some biscuits to soak up all the tea we'll be drinking.' He starts to say goodbye but interrupts himself. 'Mr X,' he mumbles, almost to himself. 'I can't frigging believe it. I won't believe it.'

DAY THREE

Thomas

In the bluest, scariest part of the dawn when the creeping light makes the shadows move, they find a hiding place in what looks like an old staff room: two ripped sofas, rusted lockers and most importantly, a lock on the door to secure them inside.

'Anything?' Maggie whispers, opening and closing lockers as slowly as she can so they don't squeak.

He shakes his head, trying to find something, anything that might help them escape. The lockers contain nothing but old papers, mouldy clothes, some chipped mugs and an ancient tin can with no label. He pulls some papers from a locker and drops them on the floor.

The sun has started to rise, illuminating the winding corridors of the asylum's basement. The twists and turns, dead ends and locked doors are both a panic and a relief to Thomas: a panic because they're lost and have no idea of how to get out, and a relief because if they can't find their way out then maybe the murderer can't find them either. Their only goal is to hide from the bad guy.

Zoe lies on one of the sofas, her face still. He's not sure

whether she's sleeping or unconscious. Her breathing tells him that she's probably asleep, so he wills himself to stop worrying about her maybe dying and decides she's okay for a bit. Now he's got more brain power for thinking about escape.

Maggie drags a wooden chair across the room, its legs making scraping noises on the floor.

'Stop!' Thomas hisses, running across to her and snatching the chair. 'Don't do that, are you trying to get us killed?'

Maggie bites her lip.

'What are you doing?'

She points at one of the windows. It's around seven feet up, about as wide as Thomas's shoulders and pretty narrow, but maybe big enough for them to climb through if they can get up there and prise it open.

He sets the chair under the window and Maggie climbs onto it, but she's still too short to reach it properly; she certainly can't climb high enough to push it open.

'Here, let me try.' He climbs up on the chair beside Maggie. He's about five inches taller than her but it's still too high to grip the handle and open it. 'Okay, get down,' he says, and they both jump to the floor.

He turns the chair around so the back of it is against the wall, and climbs up again, stepping carefully onto the top of the chair back, which he leans against the wall so it doesn't topple. His head is now level with the window, and he can see that there's a metal bolt which locks the window from the inside.

'Yessssss,' he whispers.

'What?' asks Maggie.

'I think we can get out,' he says, grabbing at the bolt. But the bolt won't move. It's rusted shut.

'Shit,' he says, enjoying the feeling of swearing like a proper grown-up for the second time. 'It's stuck.'

'Shit,' says Maggie.

'Pass me the knife?' He reaches down and Maggie places it in his hand. The wooden handle is smooth against his palm and it's shaped perfectly to fit in his fist. It feels nice. He unfolds the blade and wiggles it behind the bolt, trying to loosen some of the rust so he can slide the lock. He does this all along the bolt, and it feels like it's working because soon he can jiggle the handle.

'Here, let me have a go,' says Maggie, and climbs up on the chair while he's still standing on the back.

'No, it's not strong enough, get down,' he says, but it's too late. There's a splintering noise as the back of the chair breaks and they both tumble to the ground, a sharp pain in Thomas's hand as he lands.

All the air escapes from his lungs and he lies on the floor for a second, thinking about how close they'd come to escape.

'Oh, God, Tom, your hand,' says Maggie.

He sits up and looks at his right hand. It's covered in blood. It's dripping everywhere and there's a pool of it underneath him too. His vision goes fuzzy, like an old television tuned to a non-existent channel with black and white static. He takes a big breath, and another. It doesn't hurt yet, but the knife must have sliced his palm as he fell.

Maggie runs to one of the lockers and grabs one of the

old t-shirts. She pulls his arm over his head and ties his hand up tightly.

'Keep your hand in the air and don't move it,' Maggie orders, and looks around the room for the next escape solution.

He lifts up the old t-shirt and stares at the gash, wide and open like a mouth, laughing at him.

'What's this?' Maggie pokes at the papers with her toe, the ones Thomas pulled from the lockers earlier.

Thomas glances at it and shrugs, looking down at his injured hand. 'Nothing useful.'

But Maggie's not listening. She crouches down to peer at the papers. A lot of them are torn and crumpled, but a few are intact. 'This one's a newspaper article, about this hospital.'

Across the room, Thomas feels a flash of frustration. 'I don't care, Maggie. I'm trying to get us out of here. I don't care about a stupid old newspaper.' He tries to keep his voice quiet, but it comes out with such force that it's almost a hiss.

She picks up the papers.

Thomas grumbles. 'Come on, Maggie.'

'Shut up for a second and look at this.' She holds out the papers towards him, dust cascading from them and floating around in a shaft of morning light oozing through the dirty window.

He snatches the papers from her hands, frowning. 'Whatever this is, I'm sure it's less important than getting out of—' he stops talking. 'Woah.'

He pulls the papers close to his nose. It's an old newspaper, stained brown with age. He can tell it's old without even looking at the date, because there are so many words and stories crammed onto each page; newspapers now look a lot different. He checks: it's a *Lancaster Guardian* from July 1984. She stands next to him, looking at it over his shoulder. 'Right?' she says, a touch of glee in her voice. She jabs at the photograph with her fingertip, crumpling the page.

The headline reads 'Lune's the Daddy?'

'What does that mean?'

Maggie shrugs.

'Move your finger,' he whispers. There's a picture of the Lancaster Lune Hospital, with a group of people smiling on a lawn in front of the building. The lawn doesn't exist any more, swallowed by trees and weeds. The caption reads 'Staff and patients ready for a day out at Morecambe Beach, June 1984. Unnamed patient circled.'

Maggie places her finger back on the page, over one of the faces, the one with a circle around it. It's a girl in her mid-twenties standing next to a woman in a nurse uniform, both of them smiling like everyone else.

'She looks like Zoe,' Maggie whispers.

Thomas doesn't agree, but she's definitely familiar. Even in black and white, the nose and the hair ... His stomach churns, acidic and burning. He shakes his head. 'We know who that is, but it's not Zoe.'

Maggie's eyes widen as she stares at the picture. Thomas can't take his eyes off it: she does resemble Zoe, but even in black and white, he knows who that is.

'It's the old woman,' Thomas hisses.

Underneath 'Lune's the Daddy?' the subtitle reads 'Scandal as asylum patient pregnant'. And below that, in smaller letters:

'Questions raised about supervision levels as pregnant female patient discharged early'.

'Look at this.' She slides her finger down the picture, towards the girl's wrist.

The girl's right hand is restrained, shackled to the nurse. Her left hand is resting on her pregnant stomach.

Helen

Helen drives across town in the blue-grey dawn, feeling a strange kinship with the other drivers on the roads and those out walking the streets, wondering why they're out so early – are they going home or setting off somewhere? Have some of them had as much upheaval as her today?

It's possible that others have had a life-changing, eviscerating twenty-four hours too. That jogger might have lost someone, or might get hit by a car on his morning run. The driver in front might have been sitting by someone's bedside in A&E, wondering if their loved one would survive the night. Or maybe they caused an accident, but were away from the scene before they even knew the devastation behind them.

Everyone's got something going on, something big, life-changing, and none of them know what's going on for Helen; that she's driving to her ex-husband's house to sit vigil waiting for news about their missing daughter. Her car passes by them and they won't see it and think 'that poor woman'. They'll just think she's like everyone else: heading to work, or home, or school like a normal day.

There'll never be another normal day again, not for Helen.

Tony answers the door in his pyjamas and holds a finger to his lips to show that Melanie and the twins are still sleeping upstairs. The sight of him gives her a striking pang of nostalgia: in his tartan pyjamas, his hair ruffled and his face showing two-day stubble ... he looks like home. All they need is Zoe.

She steps into his arms and they hug tightly, in a way they haven't hugged in many years. She feels her heartbeat start to slow a little.

'Hey,' she whispers.

'Hey you,' he whispers back. 'Hey Alfie,' he nods down at the dog, whose tail beats against the wall as it wags in response.

'I've just put some coffee on,' he says as he leads Helen to the kitchen. It's not as pristine and immaculate as Melanie usually keeps it. Two matching high chairs are at the table, their trays smeared with orange-coloured crumbs. There are a couple of bowls and a mug on the table. Any other day, Helen would feel a glimmer of satisfaction that Melanie isn't as perfect as she tries to pretend.

Helen sits on the leather sofa in their kitchen, and watches as Tony shuffles around in his slippers pulling together coffee and toast. He looks much more comfortable than he ever did in their old kitchen; the master of his domain in a way he never was with Helen. 'I read those articles,' he says, as the kettle roars to life.

Helen looks up sharply, but Tony won't make eye contact. 'And?' Alfie jumps up on the sofa next to Helen and snuggles in next to her. 'No, Alfie – get down,' she points at the floor, but Alfie looks at her with a defiant expression.

Tony shrugs. 'Don't worry about it. We'll make an exception for today.' He smiles and walks over to pat Alfie on the head. 'But don't tell Melanie,' he says to the dog. 'So. A speculative article from a freelance wannabe journalist trying to make her name by poking holes in the local police force. That's not new; it's rare that those types uncover anything genuinely new. And the other is a conspiracy theory website designed to tap into the fears of other conspiracy theorists. And neither of them have any tangible evidence for their claims.'

Helen's face gets hot, her muscles tense. 'But, we have noth—' Tony winces. She stops herself. Her voice is high-pitched and loud, and from experience she knows that he won't listen if she's like this. And what she needs more than anything is for Tony to listen. She tries again, willing her voice to be even and low, almost a whisper. 'We have nothing to lose from looking into this. I understand what you're saying, about the conspiracy theorists and stuff ... but ...'

Tony brings her a coffee. 'Mr X nearly ended my career.'

She nods. 'I know, I was there.'

He looks irritated. 'I know you were. What I mean is that we found everything there was to find about that case. And there wasn't much. This new article that links the three criminals together ... it's thin, at best. There's not much to go on. We don't even have any proof that the contemporary one has actually killed anyone. I mean, what does the article say links them together, in the end?'

Helen opens her mouth, closes it again. She pulls up the article on her phone. 'Clean MO ... the girls look the same.'

He shakes his head. 'Clean MO literally just means that

there's not enough evidence left behind to conclude anything. And the girls looking the same, that could just be coincidence.'

Helen swallows hard. She really thought there was a way forward here, something to cling to.

'Have you heard anything from Dane?' Tony asks.

'Not since last night,' she says with a grimace.

Tony nods. 'Not the sharpest tool in the shed, is he?'

'I don't trust anyone any more. It was Max that sent me the article on that seedy website.'

Tony rears back with a frown. 'Max, as in that friend of hers, boyfriend of the little shit who got Zoe into this in the first place?'

Helen nods.

He folds his arms. 'Something stinks about this.'

'Who stinks?' says a chirpy voice, and Helen's heart sinks. Tony on his own was a relaxing, familiar presence but the whole dynamic changes when Melanie enters the room, with her arched eyebrows and spiky tones.

Melanie's carrying Lucy on her hip, and Lucy's got her thumb in her mouth and her head resting on Melanie's shoulder, her eyelids half-closed.

Tony crosses the kitchen and kisses his wife on the cheek. Helen looks away and strokes Alfie, who is resting his head on his paws looking like he's trying to blend into the sofa.

Melanie looks at Tony, then at Alfie on the sofa and her best Le Creuset cafetière sitting in a puddle of water on the counter. Helen can almost see the cogs whirring in Melanie's brain as she works out whether it's worth making a comment, and then thinks better of it, considering the circumstances.

'Just popped down to say hi,' says Melanie. 'Any news?'

Helen and Tony shake their heads.

'Glad you're here, Helen. Family's got to stick together at times like this.'

Helen feels a brief moment of genuine warmth towards Melanie, even though the only thing they have in common is having been married to the same man. She takes a sip of coffee, which is so strong it makes her heart beat faster immediately.

'Helen, do you know Zoe's email password?' Melanie pours herself a cup of coffee and leans against the counter.

For once, Lucy's quiet, patting Alfie on the sofa.

Helen frowns. 'Maybe. I mean, I might. Why?'

Tony's eyebrows pull down in a puzzled look. She meets his eyes and he forces a smile at his wife.

'She has an iPhone, doesn't she?' asks Melanie, pulling open a laptop and typing something.

Tony's eyebrows raise as he realises what Melanie's driving at.

Helen doesn't understand. 'Why? What are we talking about here?' Helen's never had an iPhone and isn't very good with technology at the best of times.

Tony grins at his wife. 'Genius,' he says, and Melanie grins back at him. She swivels the laptop around to Helen. It's open to a login screen, requesting username and password. The page title reads 'Find my iPhone'.

'If you can get into Zoe's account, it'll tell us where her phone is.' Melanie folds her arms, a wide smile still on her face. She looks so proud of herself.

Helen's throat constricts. 'There's a way to locate her phone?'

Melanie nods, her smile wide.

Helen's skin burns and prickles. She clenches her fist, holds it with her other hand. 'Melanie, you're telling me that my daughter has been missing for more than twenty-four hours and this is the first I've heard of it? You didn't think that it might be a good idea to mention that there's a frigging website that'll show me where she is? Jesus, Melanie.' She wants to slap Melanie's face until that smirk disappears. She stands up. She sits down again. She pounds her fist into her free hand, into her thighs.

'I didn't think—' Melanie reaches out, tries to touch Helen's shoulder but Helen wrenches herself away. Helen can't stand the idea of that woman touching her.

'And the police; don't they have access to this software? And they didn't say a word about this. How dare they? No one is doing their job.' Helen growls. They had a way of finding Zoe immediately and did nothing with it until it was too late. 'What time is it?' She stands up. 'I'll drive to the station as soon as it opens and scream at the first person I can find. Why does it take desperate amateurs in the middle of the night to think of this approach?' She starts pulling on her coat, ignoring Tony's attempts to calm her.

The police did nothing with it until it was too late. As suddenly as it began, her fury dissipates. She drops her head into her hands and shakes her head. 'Don't even bother, Melanie. It's not going to work,' she says.

Melanie frowns. 'Why not? It's worth a try, surely?'

Helen rubs her hair, pulling her strands taut with her

fingers. 'Her phone is off. I've been trying to call her since yesterday morning, and it's gone through to voicemail every time. It must be out of battery or something.'

Tony stands up. 'Give it a go, Hel. It'll show the last known location. Where the phone was when the battery died.'

'If that setting was switched on, anyway,' Melanie says, sounding less sure of herself now.

Helen shrugs and pulls the laptop towards her. She types in Zoe's email address: zsummertonz@gmail.com

She pauses, her fingers hovering over the keys. What would her password be? Helen thinks back to helping Zoe set up her first email account, years ago.

She types 'Alfie1234' and presses Enter.

Incorrect password. You have 3 more attempts before your account is locked.

'Shit.' Helen puts her head in her hands, trying to think.

'Wait,' says Tony. 'Zoe used this laptop the other day, right?' he asks Melanie.

Melanie nods.

Tony smiles and pulls the laptop towards him. 'Keep your fingers crossed.'

He opens up the settings and navigates to the saved passwords. 'I just hope she's silly enough to ... yep. There it is.'

Tony's got tears in his eyes as he turns the laptop back to face Helen and Melanie. 'She's such a good kid.'

In the list of saved passwords, there's Zoe's email address and her password:

AlfieLucyBen

'Yesss!' says Melanie, grinning.

The screen goes blue, and then a compass spins over a map of the world while the page loads.

All three of them crowd around the computer screen, watching the compass spin. After what feels like minutes, the map materialises over Lancaster and zooms towards a grey circle in a patch of green, far away from houses and streets.

'What?' asks Tony, squinting at the map. 'The middle of nowhere?'

'Next to the M6,' says Melanie, pointing at the nearest landmark: the motorway.

Helen squints at the map. She reaches for the mouse and clicks on the grey circle.

> *Device name: Zoe's iPhone5*
> *Last known location: 26XJ+R3 Lancaster*
> *Last time device seen: 28 hours ago.*

'Twenty-eight hours ago,' mumbles Melanie. 'She could be anywhere by now.'

'Oh my God,' says Helen. 'Tony, put your coat on.'

Tony frowns. 'What? Where is that?'

Helen pulls on her shoes. Alfie leaps off the sofa and wags his tail at her, looking expectant.

'It's the Lune Hospital.'

'The old asylum?' asks Melanie. 'Isn't that apartments now?'

Helen ignores her and grabs her coat. 'Tony. Coat.'

Tony holds his hand out in a 'stop' motion. 'I think before we do anything we should call the police station and tell them our hunch. They can send someone over with us if needed.

It's just best to have backup, or at least stuff on record. Just in case.'

She waves him away. 'It'll be patronising bullshit about not jumping to conclusions and having enough evidence, but it was in the article. McVitie lived there, the first killer. And I was there the other day. I know what I saw, Tony.'

'What? What did you see?' asks Melanie.

Helen shakes her head. 'It wasn't enough without this, but now that we can see where Zoe's phone was ... it's something. That shoe I found. And here's something funny going on with a guy who works there, and it matches what Dane said about the guy in the bar. It all links together.'

Helen feels like her brain is fizzling with new connections as she outlines it all to Melanie, whose eyes get wider with every word: the serial killer sentenced to the insane asylum in the 1960s, his pupil Mr X operating throughout the 1980s and 90s, and now the missing girls who look just the same as Mr X's victims. Almost a century of murders with no sign of stopping.

'I understand McVitie's link with the old hospital; he was a patient there. But what about the other two? Mr X and this new guy? What links them all together?'

'Sounds like you have an idea?' Melanie asks.

'It's the old asylum. It's like the centre of a spider's web.'

Melanie gathers Lucy from the sofa next to Tony. 'You two get going. I'll call the police station and catch them up. No time to waste.'

***

In the car, Helen clips in her seatbelt. She looks at the side of Tony's head, examines the rough stubble on his jawline as he checks the rear-view mirror and turns on the ignition.

'Look.' He turns in his seat to look out of the back window as he reverses out of their drive. 'I know you want to find Zoe, I do too. But one thing I do know from my police days is that we're going to have to be very careful, especially if this hunch is right.'

'Careful how?'

He checks both ways as he pulls out from a junction. 'Now, I'm not saying that these articles are reputable journalism in any way. But if they are right, there's someone incredibly dangerous out there. If we encounter him, we can't provoke him. Even if we think he's the new Mr X or whatever the internet's calling him, we can't show that to him. We have to pretend that we suspect nothing, and we walk away. We're just out to look for Zoe.'

Helen glances at the clock. 'At six in the morning.' She peers out of the windscreen as the Lancaster Lune Hospital emerges out of the dawn light in the distance, its turrets poking over the surrounding trees.

Tony chuckles. 'Yep. At six in the morning. That's all.'

'Got it. Pretend we know nothing, otherwise we're dead.'

Alexander

He's been prowling around the building for nearly two hours and there's no sign of the girl. Not even footprints. Back into the grounds. She can't get far. It's not possible after what she's been through.

He is the ultimate apex predator now. The only one. He imagines he is a panther: black, sleek and muscular. He stalks through the undergrowth, thigh muscles stretching and flexing, stretching and flexing. Twigs brush his face, scratch his skin. He barely notices; his concentration is absolute. Powerful and strong, he crouches low to the ground, his eyes glowing through the dawn. His steps barely make a sound.

His world is divided into predators and prey. And he's going to hunt down his prey and end its life.

Every rustle of leaves in the morning wind, every bird cawing into the night; his ears prick at each tiny noise. He can smell the dirt ingrained under his fingernails where he has been pawing, scraping at the ground. He can smell the bark of the trees, the dog piss, the rotting vegetation and the decay. Nasty, putrid and damp; even in the dawn light his senses tell him exactly where he is.

He pushes through the bushes and into the open, listening, smelling the air. The whole building seems to shiver, as if it's alive.

A crunch from deeper in the woods, crackling of leaves and snapping of twigs. He stares through the darkness; his eyes open wide. Something moves.

He plunges into the trees, following the sound, running as fast as his strong legs will push him.

This is his territory. It is his duty to guard, protect and destroy. That's how he was raised.

Is that a flash of colour ahead, through the trees? Is there a faint scent in the air? Chocolate. Chocolate and skin. She's not far away, he can sense it.

He feels a quick shiver of excitement prickle over his flesh.

He edges past branches and twigs, taking care not to make a sound. He's just like his cat Petra, pressing his paws gently into the forest floor, testing his weight on every step before he commits.

The woodland has stilled and the wind has died. Nothing moves.

He halts behind a large tree and listens to the quiet forest. He's going to find her, and when he finds her he will destroy her so that it will be as if she never existed.

But there's nothing: no movement, no sound, no girl.

***

He enters the security office, a pokey room in what used to be the gatehouse of the Lune Asylum. Back when the mental hospital was in operation, the gatekeeper would sit in here and ensure that only the sane ones left through the gates.

The damp seems to rise through the floors. The security company provides a pitiful electric two-bar heater and a kettle, but nothing can prevent the oozing chill of the old stone building.

He scans the CCTV feeds, eyes flicking from screen to screen. There are three monitors, with twenty-one cameras covering the perimeter of the building, a couple covering the grounds and one inside the entrance hall above the main door, showing the large staircase. Most of the perimeter cameras overlap in their coverage, so if she's outside the building he should be able to spot her quickly enough. The only place not covered is the security office itself, but he can hear anything that happens just outside the door.

He clicks through each feed looking for the girl throughout the building and the grounds. There's no movement on any of the screens, their fuzzy grey flickering taunting him with blankness. His hunting instincts failed him, and now technology too. He's one moment away from punching his fist through one of the monitors. But that won't help. Keep your cool, Alexander.

He clicks through the feeds a couple more times, examining every flicker of a pixel. For a second, he thinks he sees something at the edge of the wood, but it turns out just to be a crow hopping around, pecking at twigs.

'Where are you, you little fucker?' he whispers. 'I'm going to get you.'

There's a knock at the door and Alexander jolts with sudden

energy, his heart pounding. The computer mouse crashes to the floor, its case bursts open and the battery rolls out and under the desk.

'Shit.' He kicks the rest of the mouse under the desk and rushes to the door. It's only 6am, long before Paul would arrive for his nine o'clock shift. Who the fuck is knocking on the office door at this time in the morning? It's not exactly going to be the girl, is it?

He unlocks the door and pulls it open slowly. Two people stand outside in the dawn light, a man and a woman. The woman looks vaguely familiar, her thick grey-blonde hair tucked into a purple paisley headscarf, curls escaping out at the sides. Her eyes are tired, her skin pale and cheeks hollow. Why does she look familiar?

'Hello,' says Alexander. 'Can I help you?'

The man steps forward and holds out his hand for Alexander to shake. 'Tony. Retired Detective for the Lancashire Police.'

Alexander takes his hand and releases it as quickly as he can. 'I'm Paul Herbert,' he says quietly. 'And you?' he looks at the woman.

'Helen.'

As she speaks, Alexander realises why she's so familiar: this is the one who was prowling around the asylum a few days ago. The one he saw on the CCTV monitors and followed as she trespassed inside the building. She's often here as the sun rises, striding through the long grass in her wellingtons and bright red jacket.

Her wavy hair and button nose are the same as the girl he's been playing with for the past few hours. This is the mother.

The one whose daughter was tied up in the basement until a short while ago.

A growl rumbles through the air. Ah yes. The one with the dog.

She's holding a lead, and the animal is straining against its bonds, trying to get at Alexander, but every time the dog gets closer and catches his scent, it gets scared and backs behind the woman's legs again. The dog must catch a whiff of the girl on Alexander's clothes and can't decide between its revulsion of Alexander or the scent of its owner. Ridiculous creature.

'We met the other day.'

The woman opens her mouth to speak again but the man cuts her off.

'Can we come in?' says Tony, gesturing into the office. 'It's a bit nippy this morning.'

Alexander grips the doorframe so tightly it could splinter in his hands. He digs his nails into the wood, trying to control his frustration. 'I'm afraid now isn't the best time. Lots to get done before the end of my shift – perimeter checks, patrols, you know. If you come back around ten, though, you might want to talk to my colleague Pau—' he stops. Slow it down, Alexander. You're in danger of making a grave mistake.

But the girl – where is she? She's either lost in the tunnels or she got out of the basement somehow and is in the main building or the grounds. She can't have gone far. She's not on any camera feeds, so she's either in the woods or downstairs inside the building, somewhere deep in the maze of corridors and tiny rooms. He's got three hours until Paul arrives to start his shift. Three hours to find her and dispose of her and all evidence she ever existed. Three precious hours that these two people are now wasting.

She taught him not to transport more than once. That kind of precaution reduces the likelihood of DNA transfer, and witnesses; but today's little unravelling triggers a shift in protocol. Mum had her chance, and she didn't take it. He just needs to get the girl off the property and then he can destroy her.

Even if there's evidence left behind, he's done enough to direct attention away from him and towards Paul Herbert. For a while, at least. And, like always, he's ready and willing to pick up everything and start again somewhere else.

The man coughs, a forced bark startling Alexander back into the moment. What do these people want? How could they possibly have traced him here?

'I'm afraid we can't wait until ten,' says the woman, and Alexander grits his teeth. 'This is an emergency.' She steps forward as if to push her way into the office. He's moments away from lashing out, caving their skulls in and having four bodies and a dead dog to dispose of in the ever-diminishing time remaining before Paul shows up.

'Fine,' he says, and steps aside to let them into the room. 'Make yourselves at home, I suppose.'

Helen sits on the battered armchair in the corner and Tony takes the desk chair, swivelling it around so he sits with his back to the monitors, their grey glow lighting him up from behind and casting his face in shadow. Alexander wonders if he's chosen that seat specifically to gain an upper hand, like a power stance. Maybe they taught that in the police back in this guy's police training days. It's a good tactic.

This leaves Alexander with the rickety folding chair that ordinarily rests against the wall behind the door. He unfolds it and sits down, blocking the door and positioned directly across from Tony so he can watch the screens over Tony's shoulder. Two can play the power game.

'Well, let's get right to it, as I don't have much time.' He speaks quickly to get this over with as soon as possible and get back out there. 'What brings you here at 6am? Can I help with something?'

He knows what they're here for, but he needs to know *why*. How have they traced her here? It's not GPS; he threw her handbag and dead phone in a ditch near Heysham, Paul's home town.

'Our daughter is missing.'

He looks at them, from one to the other, his face blank of any expression. The woman is hunched over, leaning forward. Her head tilts towards the floor but her eyes look directly at Alexander under a frown. She definitely doesn't trust him. She looks at him just like her dog does. Thankfully, she left the creature tied to a post outside.

Next, he raises his eyebrows high on his forehead to look surprised and concerned. 'Your daughter? Sorry to hear that. How awful. How long has she been gone?'

'Nearly forty-eight hours,' says Tony.

Actually, Alexander knows it's closer to thirty-one. He nods. 'Forty-eight hours. You must be beside yourselves.'

Helen looks up at him carefully.

He wants to have a little fun. 'She could be anywhere by now. With anyone.'

Tony stands up, his large frame blocking the screens and reducing what little light shines into the room from their grey flicker. 'The police are working very hard to find her.'

'I'm sure they are.'

Helen reaches into her coat pocket and pulls out a photograph. Alexander takes the photo and pretends to examine it. It's from a couple of years ago; the girl's face is rounder here, skin clearer – her cheeks smooth and plump. She's grown up since this photograph was taken, her childish cheeks hollowing out and her whole face elongating. He resists the temptation to tell the woman that she should have picked a better picture, something more recent.

'This is Zoe. She's only seventeen years old. Have you seen her?'

He shakes his head. 'She looks like you,' he says to Helen.

'Have you seen her?' Tony asks again.

Alexander looks up at him. Over his shoulder, the screens cycle through their feeds. Alexander shifts in his seat to see a sliver of their flickering displays: the main entrance, the driveway, the edge of the forest, the back kitchen doors. Nothing. No movement.

'I haven't seen that girl before,' he looks Tony right in the eye as he speaks, daring him not to believe his words. 'What makes you think someone here at the asylum would have seen her?' he asks, sitting up straighter to scan the feeds behind Tony's shoulder.

Tony coughs and looks out of the window, but Helen shifts forward in her seat.

'The location of th—'

Tony cuts her off. 'We're exploring a lot of lines of enquiry at this time.'

Helen closes her mouth.

A movement on one of the CCTV screens catches Alexander's eye. He glares at the screen, but the feed circulates to the next camera before he can focus on what was happening. Is it the girl?

He stands up out of his chair. He needs these fools to leave immediately.

'I'm sorry, I still don't understand why you're here?' he asks, taking a step towards the screen. But he stops; if he looks too intently, they'll follow his gaze to the screens too and they might see their daughter, and it'll all be over. He must keep their gaze on him. 'You said you've called the police? If there's something to find, they'll find it, surely? I hear Lancashire is a particularly strong force.' He nods at Tony and the man almost swells with pride.

'It is,' he agrees, nodding. 'It's won a number of—'

Helen cuts him off with a raise of her hand. 'We have called the police about this. They're conducting enquiries and I'm sure this is on their list to get to later today.' Her gaze flicks to Tony and then back to Alexander. 'But we were anxious to start work. If we can find anything, we want to try.'

He nods. 'I understand. I wish I could help.' He makes his face look serious and focused, instead of mirroring the frantic flutterings inside his brain.

The feed flips around to the next camera. Another thirty seconds and it'll be back on the feed where he saw the movement. What was it?

'But unfortunately, I don't think there's anyone here who will know anything. I've been here all night and it's been very quiet. There's just me and two other colleagues, both normal, friendly guys with nothing to hide. In the main. I mean, I'm sure they have their pasts,' he pauses here and makes eye contact with Tony. 'But nothing relevant to this kind of investigation. I'll say the same to the police if they come around later. I'll give all the details I can, of course.'

He gestures to the door and strides across the room to open it. 'I'm afraid I have to get on with things, so you'll forgive me if I usher you out.'

Twenty seconds until the feed flips. She's out there somewhere. Alexander must find her. Before they do.

Helen remains seated. Alexander nods at her, trying to encourage her to move. 'I'm sure the police will be here later today; I will get contact addresses for my colleagues, pass them onto the investigators. That's best, right? Communicate with the appropriate channels?'

Fifteen seconds.

'Oh yes, that's best,' says Tony, clearly a slave to process and convention.

'Again, I'm sorry I couldn't offer more hope. If I see anything which might be even slightly important I'll be sure to report it.'

Helen finally stands up and Alexander tries not to sigh with relief. They walk slowly to the door and he closes it behind them as quickly as he can without hitting them in the back.

Five seconds to go. He scrambles to collect the wireless mouse and its lost battery under the desk, and rights himself to standing just as the feed switches around. As he's watching, his eyes scanning the blurred and grey, pixelated image to discern any detail, he shoves the battery back into the mouse and clicks to lock the display onto that feed so it won't cycle again.

It's one of the cameras trained on the perimeter of the asylum building, at the corner of the west wing. There's a movement near the ground. A head emerges from underneath the building. Head, hands, shoulders, arms. A child. A boy. The boy wriggles out and turns back to the window, reaching his head and shoulders back through.

Alexander stands up, gripping the sides of the monitor. 'What the fuck?' he growls.

There's another one coming out, a girl this time. He's pulling her out by the arms.

When she's out of the hole, Alexander realises what he's seeing. They've been in the basement. Alexander's basement. They're climbing out from one of the windows.

They lean back down, reach into the basement again and there she is: the girl. The black and white, grainy CCTV feed shows the stains on her clothes of sweat and other bodily fluids. She can barely move, but the two kids are dragging her out of the hole like a sack of potatoes.

His skin tingles. His forehead beads with sweat. They've been in the basement. It's all he can think, over and over. They were in the basement all the time. Those children know what he is. How long have they been down there?

He's caught.

Okay. Cold, calculated, rational. He can deal with this, just like he dealt with Zoe missing from the tiled room. He's got a plan; it just needs executing.

He bursts out of the office, plunging into the forest, pushing through the undergrowth, branches scratching at his arms and face. They've been in the basement.

He runs, runs, runs, thigh muscles stretching and flexing, lungs full bursting heaving. Out of the trees, into the open, heading straight for the west wing.

Zoe

Zoe's blind.

Her eyes have swollen shut, some kind of reaction to the tape, and it's a relief not to open them; she doesn't need to see, she just wants to keep her stinging eyes closed and drift off to sleep.

Her lungs are bursting and everything hurts in her whole body. Her limbs won't carry her much further. She managed to muster the strength to climb up the filing cabinets the kids moved to the window and out into the fresh air, but now she's done. She just wants to lie down on the ground and go to sleep, she's so tired.

Her mouth is so dry and her nose is blocked. Her lips are chapped and all she wants is a big drink of water and a warm bed. A while ago she was scared, but she's not any more; she's just so, so tired.

The little kids won't let her lie down, whenever she tries to sit on the ground they pick her up again, shake her awake, and once the little girl even slapped her around the face. The boy shouted at her for that, but the girl – Maggie – was adamant that's what you do in films when someone's falling unconscious. But Zoe doesn't feel like she's losing consciousness, she just feels like she wants to sleep.

They've hoisted her up again, wrapped her arms around their shoulders and are pulling her through grass and trees. She's not wearing any shoes; no idea where they went, so she can feel the grass, twigs and soil under her feet as they move.

'Come on, we've got to go faster.' Thomas sounds really worried.

Are we being chased? She wonders, but her mouth is too dry to speak. She tries to move her legs, to help.

'He's not following us,' says Maggie.

'He will be. He's not going to let us get away with her. And Zoe saw him kill that old woman; she's a witness.'

Maggie lets out a sob.

Zoe will never, ever forget the horrific crunch when the man dug his thumbs into his own mother's neck, crushing her windpipe. It's playing on repeat in her brain. He'll never let them get away. They're still trapped, even though it feels like they've escaped. They've just moved into a different part of his territory.

She listens like an observer, like it's all happening to someone else. She just keeps moving her feet, stumbling over branches and trying to stay upright, waiting for a moment when they stop so she can lie down on the soft forest floor and fall into a deep sleep.

She does a mental appraisal of her body from the ground up. Her feet are one of the only parts of her which don't hurt, but the way these kids are dragging her through the woods, they probably will soon. She nearly got caught in a tree root earlier when they stopped paying attention to her while they argued about which direction they should turn.

Her legs are shaky and weak, like she's walked miles and tired them out. But that's not the case, she's barely walked anywhere in what must be days. She's just been tied up, waiting, hurting. Her thighs sting, the skin tender from dried urine, and despite everything her cheeks burn with shame knowing why her skin is sticky and why she smells.

Her stomach aches because it's so empty, and she knows there's a cut on her neck but strangely that doesn't hurt too much. The man did that one almost for fun, he didn't mean for it to hurt her or even kill her, she thinks. But the blood dried on her t-shirt and she knows she must look like someone out of a horror film.

She *is* in a horror film, but it's real life. It's like *Texas Chainsaw Massacre* or something. Did the main characters survive in that one? She can't remember. They usually all die at the end, though, right? Or just one of them survives, so they can pass on the story.

These kids are cute, but if it comes to it, Zoe hopes she's that one, the one who survives. Just as she thinks this, her foot catches in a tree root and she smashes face first into the forest floor.

Helen

'We can't go yet. We need to stay longer, have a look around,' she says, turning to gaze up at the hospital, its stones damp and mossy.

Tony pulls open the driver's door and throws himself into the seat. 'Just get in.'

'But we could go into the main build—'

'Helen.' Tony talks through gritted teeth. 'Get in the car. I'll explain in a minute.'

She stays where she is. 'Tony, why do you have to be so obstructive? We've come all the way here, now why—'

'For God's sake, Helen,' Tony says, his voice barely louder than a whisper but very forceful. 'Trust me on this one. It's just like we talked about. Get in the car.'

There's something about the look in Tony's eyes: desperation and panic combined with complete certainty. She climbs in the car and slams the door behind her.

Alfie is panting in the back seat, his front paws on the central console and his hot doggy breath brushing against her cheek. She reaches back and pushes him down. 'Get down,' she pats his head to apologise for her roughness.

Tony starts the engine and pulls away from the hospital, tyres crunching on the old tarmac.

'Watch the mirrors,' he says.

'There's something about him, right?' she asks, gazing at the hospital in the rear-view mirror, willing Tony to agree with her.

He doesn't reply. The only noise is the car's engine and Alfie's panting. They're driving slowly down the long, narrow driveway, with trees growing thick on either side, so big and leafy that they join at the top to create a green tunnel. It must be almost sunrise, but the dawn light is grey.

'We've got to look like we're leaving,' Tony says. 'There's something off about that guy, and he can't know we're still here. A normal human would be sympathetic when two parents arrive, searching for their missing daughter. They'd ask if we're okay, make a cup of tea, ask her name. I was in the police for decades, Helen, I know what typical reactions look like, what innocent looks like, and guilty. That man is not normal. His reactions were cold, defensive.'

Helen nods. 'So we're leaving? I don't understand.'

'Suspects like him ... we need to give him space to act. He'll incriminate himself if he thinks we're not looking. But as long as he thinks we're sniffing around, he'll behave like the model citizen.'

As Tony slows to mount a speed bump, Helen glances behind them at the hospital peeping through the trees. A dark shape streaks across the driveway.

She shrieks. 'Stop the car!'

Tony slams on the brakes and Alfie catapults forward, his claws catching on Helen's arm and rending a deep, red welt along her skin. 'Shit!' She pushes him into the back seat.

'What?' shouts Tony, looking around frantically, trying to see the danger that caused Helen to shout.

'Sorry sorry sorry, I know you said we had to leave and everything. But I saw something,' she says.

'Saw what? What is it?'

Helen gets out of the car and Alfie scrambles across the passenger seat after her. She slams the car door and starts running back up to the building, Alfie close behind her holding his tail high like a flag.

'What, Helen? We can't just leave the car here. And you can't just shout like that and not tell me what's going on. I thought I'd hit something. Now tell me what you saw. Jesus.'

She jogs ahead, back up the hill. She darts into the trees, away from the path so they can't be seen returning. Tony stumbles after her, rustling the undergrowth like a bear running through a forest. Her heart is pumping and her breath coming in short gasps. 'The guy – Paul. I saw him running, across the top of the drive.'

'Which way did he go?'

Helen picks up her pace and shouts over her shoulder. 'He was *really* running. Like he was chasing something.'

Tony starts a slow jog, just as a huge group of rooks burst out of the forest to their left, up by the main building. The rooks caw and call to almost deafening levels, a deep shriek through the trees.

'Come on,' she shouts, 'let's go this way,' and sprints up the hill towards the hospital.

***

The hill up to the hospital is steeper than it seemed while they were in the car, and the woods much more overgrown. The drive looked almost flat when they were driving up and down it.

Helen's not used to running, and the burning in her lungs reminds her of an abandoned new year's resolution to join a gym and stick with it. Even so, she's doing better than Tony, who keeps stopping, pretending he needs to cough even though Helen's pretty sure that's a ruse.

'We should have just turned the car around,' gasps Tony.

She lets her breath dictate the rhythm of her feet as they pound through the bracken and twigs, chanting a mantra in her head with every in breath and out breath: *Find Zoe. Find Zoe.*

She reaches the top of the hill, where the trees thin out into open space in front of the Hospital's main entrance. She stands with her hands on her hips, breathing heavily through her nose. Alfie skips around her, excited for the sudden burst of activity and scanning the ground for a stick or a ball she might throw. He has no idea.

She shakes her head at him. 'Not now.'

The sky is tinted orange towards the horizon as the sun begins to emerge over the landscape, but in the opposite direction over the hospital, the sky is still almost night.

Tony's footsteps and gasps get louder as he climbs the last few metres of the hill to join her, and in the distance the occasional caw of crows from inside the trees. Everything else is silent.

'Well, which direction did he go?' Tony asks, his hands on his knees as he bends over to gather his energy.

She points into the trees that surround the hospital building, but now she's not sure. The grounds are massive: nearly forty acres. She knows that from the plans. And this security guard knows every inch of them, better than anyone.

'Let's go back to the security office ...' Helen strides towards the old gatehouse. 'We'll be able to see the CCTV,' she calls back over her shoulder.

The door to the security office stands open, swinging in the slight breeze. The lights are off, but the room is lit by the strange grey light of the three monitors, which flick through different views at regular intervals.

Helen steps into the room, which smells of stale men: sweat, feet and the hamstery odour of unwashed laundry. Now that she's here without that creepy security guard, she looks around in more detail, noticing the mess and the dirt ingrained on every surface, clearly not cleaned for years. It's grim in here.

There's a metal sink in the corner, unwashed bowls and mugs floating in grey water. Above the sink, an electric water heater drips steadily onto the draining board. On the wall behind the door there's a 'Nuts' calendar from a couple of years ago, open to October. Someone has drawn a moustache on the topless model in the picture. 'Nice,' she mumbles.

Alfie whines from the doorway and steps from foot to foot. He won't come in the office, standing with his front paws just inside the door and the rest of his body outside. He sniffs the air, his tail low.

'Find anything?' asks Tony, nudging Alfie out of the way to get inside. He crosses the room to the screens, watching the feeds cycle through their displays.

'I don't know. There's crap everywhere,' says Helen, using two fingers to pick up an old sock from the armchair. She wrinkles her nose and drops it to the floor.

Tony lowers himself into the same chair he sat in earlier, when they were in here with that security guard. But this time he swivels around to face the screens. 'Nothing's happening,' he says, after a minute or two of watching the camera feeds cycle through their various views around the asylum. 'The guy's either inside the building or in the woods.'

Helen pokes around the office, opening the cupboards to find empty food packets and cereal boxes and stacks of smutty magazines. She picks up a black backpack and opens the zip to glance inside: an old lunch box containing an orange peel and sandwich crust, a wallet, a pair of leather gloves and a piece of rope. She holds up the piece of rope and raises her eyebrows at Tony. It's about a metre of blue rope, the type that leaves splinters embedded in your skin.

Tony shrugs. 'Could be anything,' he says, and turns back to the CCTV feeds. Frowning, he reaches down the side of the armchair and pulls a crumpled tie from the crevice, pinched between finger and thumb. It's maroon with green stripes, a uniform tie from the local secondary school.

Gooseflesh prickles Helen's cheeks and arms. 'That is too creepy. I can't even think about why that's here.' She opens the wallet, but this is even weirder: it's almost empty, with no drivers' licence, about £70 in cash, and an unsigned debit card belonging to 'Bertha Caul'.

Her phone buzzes against her leg.

'Some credit card fraud going on here, I think. I can't

imagine anyone who works in this room being called Bertha.' Helen drops the bag behind the armchair and reaches into her pocket for her phone. There's very little signal, but the little envelope blinks at the top of the screen: a text. She clicks.

'Oh my God.' Her heart's thumping hard. 'This is crazy.'

Tony looks up. 'Everything OK?'

She shakes her head. 'It's Janet, the journalist next door. Her son's missing, and his cousin too. She went to wake them for school and their beds are stuffed with pillows.' Tears prick at her eyes; she knows exactly the panic that Janet must feel, her own feelings of fear magnified even more knowing that someone else is going through the same thing.

Tony glances to the CCTV screens, and then back to Helen. 'Sounds like two kids messing around to me. The classic pillow trick.'

Helen tries to text back, but the message won't send. Her phone signal has dropped to zero. 'Poor Janet. This is such a nightmare.'

'Unlikely to be connected, they're not the demographic,' Tony mumbles a reply, his gaze fixed on the feeds. 'I think I see something,' he says.

Helen crouches in front of the monitors, her face so close that the image is almost unintelligible.

'There's some movement,' says Tony, squinting. 'I didn't bring my glasses.'

She leans back. There's a shape streaking across the driveway, towards the woods.

'What is that?' she asks.

The faint noise of a dog bark floats through the open door.

Helen turns quickly; Alfie is no longer in the doorway. She jumps to her feet and runs to the door.

'It's Alfie,' she shouts, bringing both hands to her mouth to whistle as loud as she can. But she can tell from how fast she saw him running on the CCTV that he's not coming back. No way. He's on a mission.

'He's gone into the trees,' says Tony, his gaze still on the televisions.

'Come on. We've got to get him back. There must be something in the woods.'

Thomas

His hand is bleeding again. It pulsates with pain every time his heart beats, and blood oozes from the now sodden cloth Maggie tied around it.

Zoe's steps are slow; her weight pulls heavy on Thomas's shoulder. There's a thin trail of blood from her left nostril, a nosebleed from landing face first after tripping on a tree root.

Maggie sounds out of breath. They're pushing through trees in a thicker part of the wood, and although the sun has almost risen it's too dark to see far through the forest.

'How much further to the caravan?' he pants, asking Maggie.

Maggie just shakes her head, too exhausted to speak.

'Maggie?' he asks.

'Don't know. A couple of minutes maybe,' she manages to whisper.

Zoe groans, her head lolling about like a puppet's on a string.

'I want to stop for a rest,' says Maggie.

Thomas's throat clenches. 'He's probably right behind us.'

But Maggie's already started slowing down, and starts to lift Zoe's arm from around her shoulders.

'No, Maggie, please don't let go. She'll fall again and I can't carry her on my own.' Tears prickle his eyes. Their footsteps have slowed and they're almost stopped.

'He's not even chasing us,' she says. 'He's probably given up by now.' She starts lowering Zoe to the ground.

Thomas braces his legs and struggles to keep Zoe upright on her feet. 'No, Maggie, don't—'

A bird caws from the trees above their heads, and a gust of wind roars through the treetops, bare branches screeching as they grind together. Tears threaten to spill from Thomas's eyes.

As the wind dies down, he hears a rustling back from where they came, the sound of someone pushing through the undergrowth. He turns his head in the direction of the noise, and his glasses slide from his sweaty face, into the grass and leaves of the forest floor.

Maggie bends to try to pick them up while still propping up Zoe, but Thomas stops her with a hand on her shoulder. The rustling gets louder.

'Leave my glasses. Come on Maggie, let's go,' he hisses, and finding a reserve of strength he didn't know he had, he almost lifts Zoe's full weight on his shoulder and starts to half-run through the wood, with Maggie right alongside taking her share of the weight.

Zoe also seems to have dredged up an extra store of strength, because although she doesn't open her eyes, she moves her feet and takes a bit of weight back onto her legs, helping to propel them forward. The rustling behind them fades beneath the sound of their own frantic footsteps, and soon they emerge into the clearing and there's the caravan, its door standing open, waiting to take them inside and protect them.

That caravan looked so sinister when they first visited, a lopsided lair containing who-knows-what. But compared with the danger of a psycho killer man chasing them through the woods, Thomas's relief is huge at seeing the haven of the caravan. A tear rolls down his cheek. He tries to gather one more push of energy now that he can see their goal.

They run as fast as they can into the caravan, and Maggie rushes towards the sofa to sit Zoe in it. They lay Zoe carefully on the sofa.

'Here, Mag. We need to block the door.'

There's a lock on the inside of the caravan, but it's not strong enough to keep the man out for long. They heave the rusted oven in front of the door, scraping long grooves into the lino. Thomas's hand throbs with every tug, but he grits his teeth and pulls. They're just in time: as soon as they slump their weight against the oven, a huge thump comes from outside as the man throws himself against the door with all his weight.

Maggie shrieks. Zoe whimpers, curling herself into a ball.

Thomas resists the urge to cover his ears and close his eyes to make everything go away. He knows that won't work. He presses his whole weight against the oven, holding the door closed to keep the man out. Maggie follows his lead and leans alongside him, her eyes screwed up in fear.

He makes his hand into a fist, trying to stop it from bleeding. The cloth is soaked through, his whole hand is hot. But he will push against this door for as long as it takes; they must protect themselves from the monster outside. He has to protect Maggie and Zoe and they'll wait here until help comes.

'But no one knows we're here,' he whispers to himself and fists away more tears from his face.

No one knows the caravan exists.

No one is coming to rescue them.

Alexander

He's found them, tracked them through the forest like a true predator. At one point he thought he'd lost them but a small pair of glasses and a streak of fresh blood on the grass confirmed he was headed in the right direction.

They're even more stupid than he thought, and he didn't have high hopes for their intellect before. All this open space, places to hide, trees behind which to cower, and they've trapped themselves in the very place where he started all this: in *his* caravan. His holding pen. A patch of woods he knows like the back of his hand, and a flimsy, plastic box he can break into at any moment, smashing through the thin door like it is made of paper.

It's like he planned it this way.

At least they locked the door. Shows *some* drive for survival, even if they're the lowest of the food chain, they're not quite lemmings doing a mythical cliff-jump. Yet.

He grabs the handle and shoulder-charges the door. It splinters and bows but doesn't open. Inside the caravan there's squeaking and a sob, and then the noises muffle again.

'There's no need to be quiet,' he says. 'I know you're in there.'

'Leave us alone!' a girl's voice says.

He laughs, impressed with her. 'Nice try. Not very persuasive though, kid.' He shoves his shoulder against the door, and once again it buckles but doesn't open. They must have barricaded themselves in; he could have broken the weak lock by now with just his shoulder.

Truly, it's not necessary to get in and finish them, not really. It's two kids and a girl who's half-dead who thinks he's called Paul Herbert. Everything is in place. He could just leave, abandon this life and move on without a trace, as his mother taught him.

But then he remembers his mother's crumpled body lying on the floor of that room, in the dark. She raised him, guided him, taught him to fight, to love, to hate, to capture, torture and kill. Everything he is, he owes to her. But she never allowed him to fulfil his potential.

So yes, he could leave right now. He could abandon this building, this life and his mother's body. He's lucky: there's no official record of him anywhere, the product of a relationship between two patients in a lunatic asylum. The hospital administrators were very happy to pretend that didn't happen.

He could run away, start somewhere new all alone. Free to take control of his own future, capture and kill whoever he likes instead of to someone else's order.

Or he could burst through the door, and tear apart these children with his bare hands, finally take what is rightfully his: his turn to continue the legacy of destruction.

And right now, this is almost sport, like shooting pheasants or hunting foxes. There's a reason why the hunted creatures are called 'game'. He's having fun. When he stops having fun, he'll stop hunting.

He crawls under the caravan and thumps his fists up into the base, listening with glee as they skitter around inside the caravan trying to get away from his advances. The ground under here is bare and damp, with woodlice crawling through the soil. It hasn't seen sun in years. He thumps again, but this is purely a scare tactic; he can't get enough force behind his arm from this angle.

He shuffles out and gets to his feet, throwing his whole weight against the door once more. It cracks and he feels a buckling that suggests he's nearly in. Another: and this time the plastic cracks beneath his force.

There's a squeal of horror from within the caravan, and Alexander grins to himself. He creates the fear.

Zoe

This is it. She gets to seventeen years old and no further. For a while, earlier, she really thought she might get away from this terrible, dark place where so many people once lived troubled lives. For some moments she had hope and could see a future ahead of her. She thought they were on their way home.

Even when they were running through the forest and she could hear his footsteps behind them, there was a chance. But now, to her utter despair, they're back in the caravan, the place where all of this started, the place where she woke up yesterday morning with her hands bound behind her back and the door locked. Even the smell of the place is the same, making her feel sick with dread and fear.

Only this time, the monster is outside and they're locked in, just waiting for him to break down the door at any moment. That's all they can do.

Her eyes fill with tears and they roll down the sides of her head and into her ears. She's always hated crying when she lies on her back, only before this the crying was different. Before this, she cried over tiny things like boys who didn't fancy her and losing her favourite necklace. But this crying is real and brutal and her heart feels like it's on fire with how fucking unfair this all is.

She's hardly started anything; she can't be finished yet. There's so much more to do, to live. She's still a VIRGIN for God's sake. She can't die a fucking virgin. How pathetic is that?!

'This can't be how I die,' she whispers to herself.

'She's saying something,' says Maggie from the door, where she's still holding herself against it alongside Thomas. 'Zoe's speaking, Thomas. Can you hear what she's saying?'

'I can't die like this,' she says louder.

'I heard her that time,' says Thomas to Maggie.

Zoe sits up slowly, rubbing her eyes to try and open them. They're sore and swollen, sticky with residue from the duct tape, but she manages to pry her eyelids apart. Everything is blurry and her eyes only open a small sliver. Her eyeballs sting like she's opened them under salty water.

It's daylight now, and the two kids are pressed against the door, pushing against the old oven they dragged over there. Their faces are streaked with dust, dirt and tears, their eyes wide with fear. The girl's dark blonde hair is everywhere, a twig sticking out of the top. The boy looks familiar, but she can't place him.

'She's sitting up,' whispers Maggie, just as there's another ear-splitting BOOM against the door as the psycho throws himself against it. The crack in the plastic expands; they can almost see through to the outside now. Only another minute or two and he'll be in here.

'Give me your knife,' Zoe says to Maggie.

Maggie looks at her for a moment, as if she's considering refusing.

Zoe stands up slowly, her body aching with every movement. She holds out her hand.

'It's my brother's—' Maggie starts.

'Do you want to die?' Zoe hisses at her. 'I don't care if it belongs to the Queen, give it to me.'

Maggie reaches into her back pocket and pulls out the knife, handing it to Zoe. Zoe unfolds the blade and looks at it. Her eyes struggle to focus.

It's engraved with curling cursive script, and in the half light of the caravan she can just make out the words: 'D – Use this knife only for good. Love, Grandpa.' She nods.

With a huge crack, the door finally splinters, sending Thomas and Maggie sprawling across the caravan floor in a tangle of arms and legs and the oven. Daylight floods the caravan, exposing them to him.

He's there, silhouetted in the doorway. The morning light behind him obscures the details of his features. All she can see are his white teeth, bared like a wolf about to attack.

Zoe steps forward, the knife in her right hand.

There's a loud growl and a snarl as if he really is a wolf. She flinches away from the noise, terrified and shocked that a human can sound so much like a wild animal.

But as she flinches at the snarl, the psycho also moves. He turns away from her, switching his attention to something outside the caravan.

A black creature bursts from the trees and launches itself at the man. It wasn't the man who made that growling noise, it was a real animal, a dog.

The dog snarls and growls, its jaws locked around the man's hand, shaking his arm from left to right like a tug of war, only this is no game to the dog. Its hackles are up and there's bloody drool pouring from its mouth onto the grass as it rips and pulls and tears at the psycho's flesh.

He tries to kick the dog, but the dog moves fast, it's too lithe and pulls too hard; the man can't get his balance.

As the dog turns, Zoe sees a familiar white stripe down the dog's nose. It's Alfie, growling and snarling and biting. For her. Her beloved, beautiful childhood pet who sleeps on her bed every night.

Her eyes fill with tears. 'Alfie!' she shouts.

As soon as the shout leaves her lips, she realises her mistake and clamps her hand over her mouth. She can't distract him. He's fighting for her, fighting against this man alongside Zoe and the children.

But it's too late, and Alfie drops the man's hand and turns to Zoe, believing he's been naughty. His tail moves from side to side in a tentative wag.

As soon as Alfie's attention is broken, the psycho kicks out, his foot smashing into Alfie's jaw. The noise is horrifying: Alfie's teeth clack together with the force of the kick, and he yelps over and over and over until it fades to a small whimper. He retreats to the bushes, his tail between his legs.

'NO!' Zoe screams. It's not a shout, it's a screech of rage

and pain and frustration and sorrow for poor Alfie. Her own pain is forgotten, replaced with pure fury.

The man cradles his hand for a brief moment, then turns again to the caravan door, advancing on Zoe once more. The injury is nothing in comparison to his focus on her and the children. He glares at her, his eyes dark with hatred and anger. He's fixated on his targets like a robot, the Terminator in real life. His face is covered in sweat, his skin pale with a streak of blood on his cheek.

As he's about to step into the caravan, he looks up at Zoe, an inhuman grin on his face. He's all teeth and a blank-eyed, soulless stare. Zoe stares, her eyes not leaving his. His movements are swift, but Zoe's adrenaline is pumping hard and she's ready for him.

He raises his foot to enter, and from her height advantage in the caravan's doorway, Zoe raises the knife and plunges it down as hard and straight as she can.

At exactly the same moment, the man steps up into the caravan. She drives the blade into his eye socket as his whole body moves upwards, into the knife.

She feels the 'pop' as the knife's point punctures his eyeball. Against all of her instincts, she keeps pushing. Her arm shakes with the force.

For a moment, the man doesn't seem to realise what's happening. He keeps advancing on her. He reaches out and grabs her shoulders, ready to throw her to the ground.

She braces her feet, gathering her last store of energy for a final fight. This is her last chance to save herself. She's ready to do whatever it takes, and whatever is needed to stop this man getting to Thomas and Maggie too. She'll fight for her own life, she'll never give it up, and she'll fight three times harder for all of them.

Alfie's outside, ready to pounce; barking and snarling like a wild animal. Over the top of everything, Zoe can hear her own sharp gasps and the sobs of Thomas and Maggie, huddled together behind her in a corner.

She wrenches back the knife, pulling it out of his eye socket with a twist of her wrist. Blood drips from the blade, slapping onto her bare toes.

As soon as he realises what has happened, the man doubles over and screams, raising a bloody hand to his destroyed eye.

She stares through her blurred vision, trying to predict his next action. The knife handle is firm in her hand; she's ready for the next strike.

Blood seeps through the man's trembling fingers as he holds them away from his face, his one remaining eye trying to see the blood and mess of his chewed up hands.

Zoe raises the knife, point first, ready to stab again.

Without looking back at her, the man leaps from the caravan, runs past snapping Alfie and stumbles into the trees, leaving a trail of blood behind him on the bracken.

Zoe stumbles down the caravan steps and sinks to her knees in the grass, her arms around Alfie's neck and her nose buried in his fur. She closes her eyes.

The sound of Alexander's wails and screams fades as he stumbles further and further away.

Helen

'We don't even know what we're chasing, Helen. For all we know, that stupid dog is after a pheasant again.' Tony is falling behind, out of puff and red in the face.

They follow Alfie's trail through the trees, pushing through frosty bracken and fallen leaves.

She can no longer hear Alfie's progress. She follows the thin path hoping it will lead to her dog, but she's not certain. She's not certain of anything any more. It could be a path made by a fox, a deer or some other woodland animal. Her jeans catch on thorns, scratching at her legs even through the fabric.

Where's Zoe? Where's Alfie? Just two days ago her life was perfect and she had no idea. Her biggest worries were her bathwater going cold before she finished a chapter of her novel, and the cord on her phone charger being too short to reach her bed. It all seems ridiculous now.

And poor Zoe, wherever she is. It's been two nights now, with no coat. Has she been eating? Sleeping? What if she's thirsty? Injured? Helen can't bear it. She can't breathe.

She pauses, gesturing at Tony. 'Run faster,' she says, and turns back to the forest. The trees are a mixture of evergreen and oaks, thick trunks showing the phenomenal age of the woodland. 'Come on, let's go.'

She puts her hand on a moss-covered trunk as she pushes forward, feeling the ridges of the bark rough against her palm. But Tony isn't following her. She turns around again, opening her mouth to deliver a loud yell at him to hurry up, but he's bending down, his hands on his knees. She can only see the top of his head, almost obscured by a fern. His shoulders heave.

'Tony, what are you doing? Are you okay?' She runs back to him, mentally calculating how long it would take for paramedics to get here, deep in the forest, if he's having a heart attack or something. He's never looked after his health or fitness; she's dreaded this for years.

'Helen,' he wheezes.

Her heart beats faster with panic. Not Tony, too. 'What? What happened?'

She puts her hand on his bent back, feeling the sweat which has soaked through his t-shirt and jumper. The warmth of his back on her hand. He's so solid, so strong. She can't live without him. He's her family: him and Zoe. And Melanie, Lucy and Ben.

He straightens up, his hand outstretched, his face red and sweaty.

She empties her lungs in a huge whoosh of air. Tony holds out his palm, a pair of smashed glasses resting on his hand.

'These are children's glasses,' he says quietly, his breath slowing to a light wheeze. He's right: the light blue frame is too narrow for an adult's face. 'A boy's, probably.'

'Why would they be here, in the woods?' She looks

around, but sees nothing but trees and shrubs. Janet's boy, Thomas, wears glasses like those. The boy who's also missing. She clenches her fists, praying he's not wandering these woods.

Tony shrugs, slipping the glasses into his pocket.

A breath-taking snarl pierces the morning silence. 'Oh my God,' whispers Helen. 'That's Alfie.' Now there's barking and growling, out of sight through the trees.

'Come on.' Tony strides forward and takes her hand.

They sprint towards the sound, lifting their knees high to avoid catching their feet on roots and plants. They emerge into a clearing, where a sagging caravan hunches in the shadows.

There's no time to look around. Their daughter lies on the ground in front of the caravan surrounded by blood, coating every blade of grass and twig. Lovely Zoe, crumpled in a heap. Alfie stands guard by their side, whimpering. His tail thumps once at their approach.

'Zoe!' Helen shouts, and runs across the clearing, Tony right by her side. They crouch down, knees in the grass.

'Call an ambulance, Tony.'

Zoe lifts her head at the sound of her mother's voice, but she doesn't smile. Her face is dirty and bruised, her hair stuck to her head with grease and sweat. Her eyes are puffed up and red, swollen almost closed. There's a nasty cut on her neck and blood under her nose.

It hurts Helen's heart to look at her, but at the same time she can't take her eyes off her. 'My baby,' she whispers, and gathers Zoe into her arms on the forest floor. 'My poor baby. What did he do to you? Are you hurt? Where are you bleeding?' She buries her nose into Zoe's hair, trying to inhale her daughter's scent, reconnect with her. But she doesn't smell like Zoe.

Zoe doesn't hug her back. She turns her head first left, then right, her eyebrows pulled low with fear. 'Where did he go?' she asks.

Tony gets to his feet, wiping tears from his cheeks with his fingertips.

There's a noise from inside the caravan and Tony braces, ready to fight.

But in the darkened doorway crouches a little boy, and behind him a little girl. They look almost as grubby as Zoe, less battered but just as terrified.

'Thomas?' asks Helen.

The boy nods, and points into the woods, where there's a trail of blood leading out of the clearing. 'He went that way,' he whispers. 'I don't think he'll come back. He got stabbed.'

The little girl starts to cry, big sobs wracking her whole body. Both the children jump out of the caravan and crouch next to Zoe.

The boy looks up at Helen. 'Is she going to be alright?'

Helen holds her daughter closer, Zoe's body limp like a doll. 'I don't know,' she says, and kisses Zoe's hair, even though it smells of damp and mould.

Thomas

Maggie's being really annoying, strutting around like she was really brave through the whole thing and wasn't a blubbing cry-baby moaner while Thomas had to lead them all to safety. Mum won't stop crying and ruffling his hair, and holding Maggie's hand. Thomas is the proper hero, but Maggie's taking all the credit. Even though she was the one who got them into the whole mess in the first place. She's definitely not allowed to play with the iPad tonight.

'What happened?' Thomas asks. He needs to know what happened to the guy. He could be still out there.

'I had no idea where you were,' says Mum, sniffing and wiping her eyes on a tissue. 'I woke up this morning and... oh my God, I nearly had a heart attack.' She squeezes Thomas's hand and he winces because that's the one the needle is in, giving him fluids because they said he's dehydrated. He doesn't feel that thirsty though because the nurses keep giving him orange squash. His other hand has three stitches in the palm, where he got cut with the knife trying to open the window. He's never had stitches before. They're pretty cool.

'Never do that again, okay?' Mum asks, looking hard at him

in his eyes. Her hair is messy and she's still in her pyjamas, with smudged mascara under her eyes.

'We won't, I promise,' says Maggie, even though it was all her idea in the first place.

'Shut up, Maggie,' says Thomas, wriggling his hand out of his mum's grasp and folding his arms. 'Did the police come? Did they get the bad guy?'

Mum shakes her head, as if she doesn't hear him. She strokes the back of his hand. 'When I woke up and found you gone, I ran around the house phoning the police and everyone we know. Then as soon as the police found out where you were, I came right to the hospital without even getting dressed,' Mum says, pointing at her pyjamas, trying to make it funny.

'Mum,' he says loudly.

She looks up, frowning, and puts a finger to her lips. 'Shh, Thomas. There are sick people in this ward. We need to let them rest.'

He pulls his hand away again. 'I *said*, did they arrest the bad guy?'

Mum flinches. She doesn't want to talk about it.

Thomas doesn't care. 'We saw it all, Mum. We were there. You need to tell us.'

Mum closes her eyes, her face very still. She opens them again, and smiles at Thomas. 'The nurse says you're both going to have to talk to a psychologist to make sure your minds recover from the bad things you saw and heard. And that psychologist will make sure you're happy and not scared.'

Thomas thinks that sounds nice. He can't think about all the things that happened to him last night, it's too scary and he's too tired. He just needs to know that they're safe, that the bad guy won't come for them.

'Mum, tell me.'

Mum looks over at Maggie, who's humming to herself in the next bed. He wants to shut the curtain between their beds so he can't see her.

Mum makes her voice quiet. 'They're still looking, but they said they're confident they'll find him – he can't get far.'

Thomas's heart pounds. He raises his knees to his chest, looks around the ward towards the door, working out how fast he can run to get away if he comes looking for them.

Mum reaches out, strokes his hair, makes shushing noises to calm him down. 'There are police looking everywhere, baby. They're even here in the hospital, asking lots of questions.'

Thomas lets himself relax a bit, sinks back into his pillows. He suddenly feels so, so tired that he can barely keep his eyes open. Mum's hand strokes his forehead, her fingers running through his hair.

'Who was he?' he asks.

Mum shrugs. 'A very very bad man.'

'A bad man,' says Maggie. 'He said he was going to skin Zoe alive.'

Thomas wants to cover his ears. He never wants to think about that again, everything he saw and heard in that room.

Mum shivers and swallows, like she's trying not to be sick. She turns to Maggie. 'Your mum's on a plane, Mags. She went straight to the airport to come home as soon as she heard you were missing.'

'Am I in trouble?' Maggie asks in a small voice. She looks

down at the blue woolly blanket on the bed and fiddles with the edge, pulling at a loose thread.

'You're not in trouble.'

'Am *I* in trouble?' asks Thomas.

She shakes her head, her mouth a thin line but turned up at the corners, like when people are sad but pretending not to be. 'Neither of you are in trouble. But I need to know that you've learned your lesson about sneaking out of the house.' She looks at them both, a serious expression on her face. She reaches out for Thomas's hand again, and he lets her hold it. Her eyes fill with tears. 'Never, ever go anywhere at night without a grown-up, okay?'

They both nod. He can tell by Maggie's frown that she really means it.

'And you saved two people.' She looks at Thomas, and then nods to Maggie. He did save two people; Maggie definitely needed saving.

Mum carries on: 'Especially getting Zoe out of that place. Two little heroes, Thomas and Maggie.'

Maggie shakes her head. 'But we didn'—'

'I don't want to be,' Thomas says, sticking his face into the pillow. Thomas feels tears coming and turns on his side, facing the wall.

Mum reaches out and strokes his back. 'What's up, baby?'

'You keep saying that, that I'm the hero and the man of the house and need to be a grown-up. But I don't want to be the man of the house, it's not my job.' He's annoyed because tears run down his cheeks and saliva is getting in the way of his words coming out. 'I don't want to look after people and save people, it's scary and I'm tired. I want Dad to come back. It's his job, not mine. Can you ask him to come back now?'

Mum's quiet and Thomas wonders if he's upset her. Sometimes she goes a bit weird when he asks about Dad, quiet and pinched in the face.

Maggie leans forward in her bed. 'That's it. You have to tell him.'

Thomas looks between Maggie and Mum. Mum's face is red around the edges, with white patches on her cheeks. She's sucked her lips inwards even more and is glaring at Maggie.

'Tell me what?' He frowns, feeling a sharp pain in his forehead. 'What does Maggie know that I don't? Where's Dad?' He's furious with both of them, no matter what secret they've been keeping from him all this time. 'Why does Maggie know?' He's angrier than he's ever been, and jumps out of bed even though it tugs at the IV tube sticking out of the back of his hand.

Maggie shrieks and covers her face with her hands. 'Thomas! Watch out!'

Mum stands up and straightens the IV stand, bending down so her face is level with his, her hands on his shoulders.

'It wasn't a secret we've been keeping from you; Maggie shouldn't have found out, but her brothers told her. I asked her not to talk about it with you until I'd found a way to tell you properly, *at the right time*.' Mum says the last bit through gritted teeth with a glance at Maggie.

Maggie sits on her hospital bed, her face still dirty, her hair a wild mess. He hates her. 'A way to tell me what?' He balls his hands into fists.

Mum opens her mouth, but Maggie interrupts her. 'Uncle Tom's in prison.'

Thomas freezes. 'Dad's in prison?'

Mum hangs her head and seems to shrink. 'I didn't want you to find out this way, I'm sorry, TomTom. It's a short sentence; we're hoping he'll be out by Christmas.'

'What did he do?' Thomas asks, his brain filling with the awful images of the last twenty-four hours. He's seen such badness, such evil; his kind, clever Dad can't be like that.

Mum runs her hands through her hair, pulling it back into a ponytail. She looks out of the window and flinches a little bit. 'He took some things that didn't belong to him. Pieces of copper from old buildings, nothing of value to anyone; and then he sold them. He thought no one wanted them and he could make some money to buy you nicer presents.'

Thomas's cheeks feel hot. 'You knew,' he hisses at Maggie. 'You knew all along and you pretended you didn't. You little ... you little ...' he can barely form words.

Maggie kneels up on her bed. 'I didn't – I'm not – I was trying to give you clues, TomTom. So you could work it out.'

'You're a snake.'

'I'm not! I was *hinting*. I thought if you guessed, then I wouldn't break my promise.'

'You're a liar and a pig.'

'That's enough, Thomas.' Mum's voice is sharp but her face is sad, eyebrows knotted together in the middle.

He looks away from Mum, over her shoulder and out of the ward into the corridor. There's a bottle of hand sanitiser stuck to the wall by the door, visitors and nurses walking past, their shoes squeaking on the lino.

He grabs his IV stand and steps away from the bed.

'Where are you going?' Mum asks.

'For a walk. To get away from you two liars. I'll come back in a few minutes.' He wheels his stand away from the bed, unable to stay near Mum and Maggie for a second longer.

Helen

The doctors and nurses at Royal Lancaster Infirmary have been amazing, with one nurse even lending Helen a phone charger so she can let people know that Zoe has been found.

Zoe's in a private room, and the doctors have given her medication to keep her calm while her body recovers from the physical trauma. She's on a drip to replenish her fluids, and she keeps dropping off to sleep; Helen doesn't know whether that's the calming medication, the painkillers, or the effects of the last three days.

For now, Zoe's asleep in the hospital bed, machines beeping and whirring alongside her. Helen wants to hold her hand, but there's a pulse meter on her finger measuring her heart beats, and a cannula in the vein on the back of her hand.

Helen watches her chest rise and fall. Her face is so pale, the cuts and bruises a stark red against the white of her skin. They've taped up the wound on her neck and it's covered with gauze.

'Oh, Tony. Her poor eyes. Our poor baby.'

Zoe's eyes are red and swollen, the doctors don't know if

there'll be any lasting vision problems. They won't know until the swelling reduces and they can examine her eyes properly.

Tony sits on the other side of the bed, occasionally reaching out to touch Zoe's arm, running his finger along her skin and then pulling his hand back as if he's worried she might break under his touch.

He keeps reaching up to brush tears from his cheeks. Helen pretends not to notice. She stands up, stretches and stands looking out of the window. It's a great view of the city's landscape, with trees and hills stretching into the distance.

'Helen, look,' Tony calls.

Zoe's pulling herself up in bed, reaching for the bandage at her neck.

Helen rushes towards the bed, but Tony is there faster. He reaches for Zoe's arm and stops her from pulling at the bandage, placing her hand gently back on the white sheets. Rope burns wrap around each wrist.

'Hey, Zo,' says Tony.

'Don't try and open your eyes,' says Helen. 'The doctors say you need to rest them.'

Zoe nods.

'How are you feeling?'

She shakes her head. 'Bad,' she whispers, and asks for water.

Helen holds out a plastic cup and lifts a straw to Zoe's lips. She drinks for a long time, until she's breathless.

'That's better,' Zoe says, her voice a little stronger.

'Dane wanted us to say hi,' says Helen. 'He'll come to see you when you're ready.'

'No rush though,' says Tony in a quiet voice. 'But he's a

good guy. Came over while you were missing and helped the police.'

Zoe gives a small smile.

Helen places the plastic cup back on the side table. 'And I think – now that Max knows you're okay – he's desperate to interview you for an article on his true crime site.'

Zoe laughs and then winces from the pain of the sudden movement.

'Only when you feel up to it, of course. And Abbie's mum called too, to apologise.' Helen tries to keep the resentment from her voice. Zoe flinches a bit at the mention of Abbie's name. 'Apparently, Abbie's been acting strangely for a while.'

'Oh?' Tony sits forward in his seat. 'You didn't mention this.' He frowns at Helen.

Zoe's face pales even more than before.

Helen puts a hand on Zoe's arm. 'She's been having a relationship with an older man. Much older. Secretly, of course. It's why she was being so evasive with questions; she didn't want Max to find out, or her parents.'

Tony exhales, his cheeks puffing out. 'And she nearly compromised an investigation for that? I think she can wait a while before we let her in this room. Maybe about twenty years, if she ever learns some responsibility for herself.'

'And her friends,' adds Helen. 'I'll never trust her again.'

Tony blusters, 'It's not like she was involved, I suppose. She's just a stupid teenager, that's all.'

'Her mum says she'll be grounded for a very long time.'

Zoe opens her mouth to reply.

'Knock knock,' says a man's voice from the doorway.

Zoe flinches.

Helen turns, and it's the police officer who visited them the night before.

'Detective Constable …?' Tony stands.

'Healey,' he finishes. 'And DC Parks. We're sorry to disturb you. We need to ask Zoe some questions, if she's up to it.'

Zoe turns her head towards the door. 'Have you found him?'

The police officer hesitates, and takes a step into the room, followed by his partner officer. 'That's a complicated question. Can we chat?'

Helen frowns. 'I don't know if she's feeling up to—'

Zoe holds out a hand. 'I want to help.'

Helen and Tony stand up and move to the end of the bed, relinquishing their chairs to the police officers.

'Can we ask you a couple of questions, Zoe? The nurse said you're feeling okay, but if you're not up to it then, just say the word.' His tone is gentle, and Helen is grateful. These are the people who will find that scumbag and bring him to justice.

Helen borrows a couple of chairs from a nearby empty room for her and Tony. She pulls them to the end of Zoe's bed; their legs squeak on the lino floor.

Zoe sits up in her bed, a slight wince as she moves. 'Have you found him?'

DC Healey shakes his head once. 'We're scouring the area. We're undergoing forensic testing on the whole area to see if we can get an ID from anyone on the system. An item found in the pub car park links someone with your kidnap, Zoe. And some other items hidden in a house in Heysham.'

Parks gives Healey a look. He's given them more information than he should, Helen suspects.

Zoe nods. 'Who's house?'

'We're questioning a man named Paul Herbert. Does that name sound familiar?'

Zoe sinks back into her pillows. 'Thank God. I thought he was going to come and find me to finish what he started. Especially after I stabbed him.'

The police officers exchange a glance.

'What?' asks Zoe. 'Why are you so quiet?' She moves her head between each officer, still not able to open her eyes to look at them.

'It was a very intense few hours for you, Zoe. So we understand that you might have got some things mixed up or confused.'

'I haven't got anything confused. What are you on about?'

'There's a few things that don't quite fit,' says Parks. She lifts her hat and scratches her scalp through her plaited hair. 'Your Mum said that you stabbed your attacker in the eye, but Paul Herbert isn't injured. There's not a mark on him.'

Tony coughs. 'Sounds like you've got the wrong guy.'

'I've never seen a case like this before,' says Parks. 'Everything points to a particular suspect, but doesn't at the same time. Is it possible that you thought you stabbed him but actually missed, or hit a tree or the caravan or something? I mean, with your eyes ... so sore ...'

Zoe shakes her head like she's trying to rid her brain of unwanted thoughts. She speaks slowly, taking her time over every word. 'No, that's really not right. I remember it so clearly, and—' she pauses. 'Sorry, Mum, this is going to be gross. I remember the weird *pop* the blade made when it punctured his eyeball. And he bled a lot. There was so much blood.'

'We are testing the blood we found at the scene. It's possible that there's an additional suspect we haven't found yet, or some kind of ring. It's not a clear-cut case at the moment.'

Zoe's face turns even paler. Her eyes fill with tears, and Helen stands up. 'Maybe we should leave it for today?' she asks.

Zoe turns to the wall, hiding her tears from the officers.

DC Healey nods. 'We don't want to push you too much, Zoe. You look after yourself.'

They stand to leave, shaking Helen's hand. DC Parks pats Zoe's shoulder and she flinches slightly at the touch. 'We'll be back to speak to you when you're feeling a bit better, love.'

'He's still out there,' whispers Zoe as they leave the ward. 'He got away. He said he would.'

Helen shivers. 'He won't get far. They'll get him.'

'I did stab him, Mum. Dad, you guys believe me?' Zoe reaches out for a hand. Tony and Helen take the seats near the bed and grab a hand each, Helen reaching up to stroke Zoe's cheek.

'You can't have imagined it, Zo. I saw the blood on the grass. I believe you.'

'We'll find the bastard who did this,' growls Tony.

The nurse knocks on the door. 'Just to let you know that hospital visiting hours are ending.'

Helen and Tony gather their coats and kiss Zoe goodbye.

'Do you want to grab a cup of tea before we go home?' she asks Tony.

He gives her a tearful nod. His nose is red. He's looking older, bags under his eyes and eyebrows bushy with streaks of grey. He's always had a full head of thick black hair, but now under the harsh lights of the hospital Helen can see a thinning on top, and the occasional grey amongst the black.

She stops at the doorway to squirt sanitising gel onto her hands from the dispenser on the wall.

The nurse enters Zoe's room and Helen hears her singsongy voice to Zoe: 'There's another patient wants to pop by and see you for a couple of minutes, if you're up to it.'

Helen smiles at the nurse, and catches up with Tony, who's looking at a noticeboard further down the corridor. 'Sounds like one of the kids is coming to visit Zoe, isn't that nice?'

Thomas

There's a play area at the end of the ward, and a boy in a Batman mask is moving toy cars around a rug. It looks like there might be a PS4, and other toys that are fun. It doesn't matter to Thomas though, he's not in the mood to play with toys.

He crosses to a small red armchair and picks up an *Alex Rider* book to read, but he's so angry that his eyes won't take in any of the words. He skims the lines without reading them, thinking about what a traitor Maggie is and how his mum is such a liar. Lying is something she has specifically told Thomas is wrong and that he shouldn't do.

Two nurses are drinking coffee just outside the door, leaning against the reception desk. Their clothes look comfortable, a bit like pyjamas. And they're wearing crocs on their feet. He likes crocs.

Thomas stares at the page, the words blurring and running together like snakes. The nurses whisper to each other, and he catches the occasional word. 'And the two kiddies on this ward.'

Dad in prison. Thomas tries to imagine Dad in a pair of

orange overalls, like in films, eating his dinner off a compartmentalised tray with a section for each part of the meal. Caught stealing; something else his parents have always told Thomas is bad. He squeezes the book in his hands until his bandaged hand aches.

'The derelict asylum?' one of the nurses says, and takes a sip of tea. Thomas looks up from his book; they're talking about him and Maggie, that little traitor. And Zoe.

'And one of them had been in there for years. His captive, like Elizabeth Fritzl or something. Apparently, she's very emaciated.'

Thomas frowns. Who are they talking about now?

'Yeah, hair all matted, really dirty looking. I caught a look as I went down for my break. She's pretty wild. They've got her in her own room; she's in a bad state. Ranting and raving, apparently.'

Thomas scrambles up, his IV stand crashing to the ground. *Alex Rider* slaps to the lino. His vision goes dark and fuzzy for a moment, and he stops to wait for it to clear. 'Hey. Be careful,' says the boy in the Batman mask, picking up his toy car and moving it to safety.

'And the teenager, too?' A nurse whispers. 'Poor love.'

Spit rushes into his mouth like he's about to vomit.

'Yeah. Both victims are on the third floor, adjoining rooms.'

Anonymous: Make a clean getaway

By Urban Dark Reporter

*Anonymous contributor claims to advise readers on the best techniques for changing your identity and starting again after committing a crime**

* Editor's note: This article is a work of creative non-fiction, for entertainment purposes only; *Urban Dark Reporter* accepts no responsibility for any harm caused by following the directions outlined below.

Stay off grid

Operate only in cash: work cash-in-hand, pay rent to inattentive landlords. Avoid leaving an electronic trail.

Relinquish all glory

You cannot take credit for your crime. Fade into the shadows, relinquish all ownership and allow someone else to gain the title of 'killer' on your behalf.

Steal an identity

Adopt the identity of someone recently dead and don't report their death. Use their bank cards, income, benefits, vehicle etc. Just make sure their body is never found.

Destroy your old identity

Eliminate your previous existence. Stage a fire, plant a body that could be mistaken for yours, phone a local newspaper to post an obituary of yourself. Leave everything behind, no matter how difficult that is. And do not say goodbye.

Adopt a new appearance
Change what you look like. Get glasses if you don't wear them, switch to contacts if you do. Buy a wig, develop a penchant for hats, change your body weight or size – whatever you need to do to look like a different person, do it.

Blend into a crowd
Go to a busy city where you know no one and no one will notice you. Local police will be overworked. Populations shift regularly in university towns and students don't take notice of anyone outside of their own demographic.

Find your new mark
Identify your next mark to frame for your future crimes. Start this process before you commit any new crimes.

Prepare to leave everything behind at any moment and accept that no one will know you ever existed. But you did exist, and you will continue. We are hunters; superior human predators who adapt and hone our skills for this evolutionary arms race, and we will continue to kill despite the limitations of this inferior society and its laws.

Don't forget, in the words of the Zodiac Killer: 'Man is the most dangerous animal of all.'

Comments are closed.

THE END

If you enjoyed *Secrets of a Serial Killer*, be sure to follow Rosie Walker on Twitter @ciderwithrosie, on Facebook @rosiewalkerauthor, and check out their website at www.rosiejanewalker.com for all the updates on their latest work.

You can also find us at @0neMoreChapter_ on Twitter and @0neMoreChapter on Facebook where we'll be shouting about all our new releases.

Acknowledgements

To you, the readers of my debut novel: thank you for taking a chance on this book. I hope you enjoyed reading it. If you did, please recommend it to a friend, talk about it on social media, or post a review somewhere like GoodReads or Amazon. It's astounding how much difference word of mouth can make to an author at the start of their career. Thank you!

A novel isn't written by just one person. There is a whole crowd of kind, interesting and imaginative people behind *Secrets of a Serial Killer*, and I'd like to try and thank some of them, as the novel wouldn't be the same without them.

I am so lucky to have a collection of fantastic writer friends, many of whom were kind enough to read multiple drafts and talk over ideas throughout the writing of this novel.

A huge "thank you" goes to Suzy Pope, my first reader, trash-TV-and gin-friend, and fantastic fellow writer. She read this novel almost as many times as I did and never once complained, providing so much useful advice, helpful points and enthusiasm. I couldn't have got here without Suzy, and have learned so much from her.

My friend Colm Boyd has been invaluable throughout the entire writing process: always at the end of the phone to offer his thoughts on every little snag and niggle. He also provided some amazing suggestions for what the dregs of the internet might say in a comments thread.

Massive thanks also to Laura Gavin, Lauren Humphries-Brooks, Anna Eberts, Chanoch Wiggers and Dave Shedden who all read this novel and offered their thoughts on its various phases and stages. And thank you to Louis Kitchen, a really talented photographer who cheerfully wandered around Edinburgh one winter afternoon with a camera trying to capture my good side.

As a student on the University of Edinburgh's Creative Writing MSc in 2010/2011, I met many of the writer friends that I still call on for their advice and expertise. That remains one of the most enjoyable years of my life, yet I am surprised I can remember any of it due to the amount of alcohol we consumed. Nevertheless, the people, the course, and its workshops made me the writer I am today. Thank you to all of my fellow students from that course, and the fantastic tutors we were lucky to learn from: Robert Alan Jamieson, Dilys Rose, Allyson Stack, Lesley Glaister and Alan Warner.

So many people answered questions, explained concepts and pointed me in the right direction while researching. For their patience and assistance with factual matters, I'd like to thank Fraser Neasham for his expertise on property development, Jamie Bartlett for his insight into the dark web, Naomi Parsons at Lancaster City Museum for pointing me towards so many fantastic historical resources, and the members of the

Lancaster Moor Hospital and Royal Albert Facebook groups, who share so many memories of their time working there when it was in operation. Any factual errors or purposeful adjustments are my own.

I'd also like to thank the security guard who was on patrol the day I tried to sneak through a gap in the perimeter fence at the derelict Lancaster Moor Hospital site in 2008. I still don't know how he materialised from nowhere and how he found us so quickly, but I admire his professionalism and determination in not allowing us one step inside the grounds, despite my very persuasive lie that I was a photography student who wanted to take photographs of the building. Without him, this novel would not exist. Thanks also to Chris Steedman and Dave Steedman, who have been by my side for almost every moment of mild misbehaviour since 2003.

From this whole writing process, I have learned that the writing and publishing industry is packed full of really, truly nice people. Even rejection letters are kindly written. I'd like to thank the amazing people who took my manuscript and made it into a book:

My literary agent Charlotte Robertson at Robertson Murray, who saw promise in the early manuscript and pushed hard for it to be a thousand times better than it was when I first submitted it. I've learned so much working with Charlotte and am a better writer because of her.

I'm delighted to be part of the Harper Collins / One More Chapter family, who have been so great to work with over the last few months, in particular the amazing editors Hannah Todd, Bethan Morgan, Laura McCallen and Paul Sellars. I'm

so lucky to work with such a talented team, and I can't wait to see what happens next.

And it's very important to thank the people who literally made me who I am: my Mum, Dad and sister: Hilary, Alan and Emily Walker. As a toddler I stalked them around the house with a book in my hand demanding that someone read to me. They fostered my interest in stories and writing, and (mostly) said yes to my book-related demands.

Finally, Kevin: I am so grateful for his unwavering support and patience while I tore my hair out over this novel. I am very lucky to have a husband who not only lets me throw myself into many ridiculous whims and challenges, but also cheers me on while I'm doing it and picks me up off the ground if I fall flat on my face. He's a keeper.